BEHIND CLOSED DOORS

USA TODAY BESTSELLING AUTHOR

J.L. BERG

Copyright © 2016 by J.L. Berg

All rights reserved.

Editors: Jovana Shirley, Unforeseen Editing, www.unforeseenediting.com, Ami Waters, Book Glam

No part of this book may be reproduced or transmitted in any form or by any means, electronic or mechanical, including photocopying, recording, or by any information storage and retrieval system without the written permission of the author, except for the use of brief quotations in a book review.

This book is a work of fiction. Names, characters, places, and incidents either are products of the author's imagination or are used fictitiously. Any resemblance to actual persons, living or dead, events, or locales is entirely coincidental.

Visit my website at www.jlberg.com

ISBN-13: 979-8-9914109-7-7

ALSO BY J.L. BERG

THE READY SERIES

When You're Ready

Never Been Ready

Ready to Wed

Ready for You

Ready or Not

The Ready Series Box Set

When You're Ready - 10th Anniversary Edition

THE WALLS SERIES

Within These Walls

Beyond These Walls

Behind Closed Doors

The Cavenaugh Brothers - A Box Set

THE LOST & FOUND SERIES

Forgetting August

Remembering Everly

BY THE BAY SERIES

The Choices I've Made

The Scars I Bare

The Lies I've Told

The Mistakes I've Made

The Secrets We Keep

The Bridges I've Burned

STANDALONES

Fraud

The Tattered Gloves

The Affair

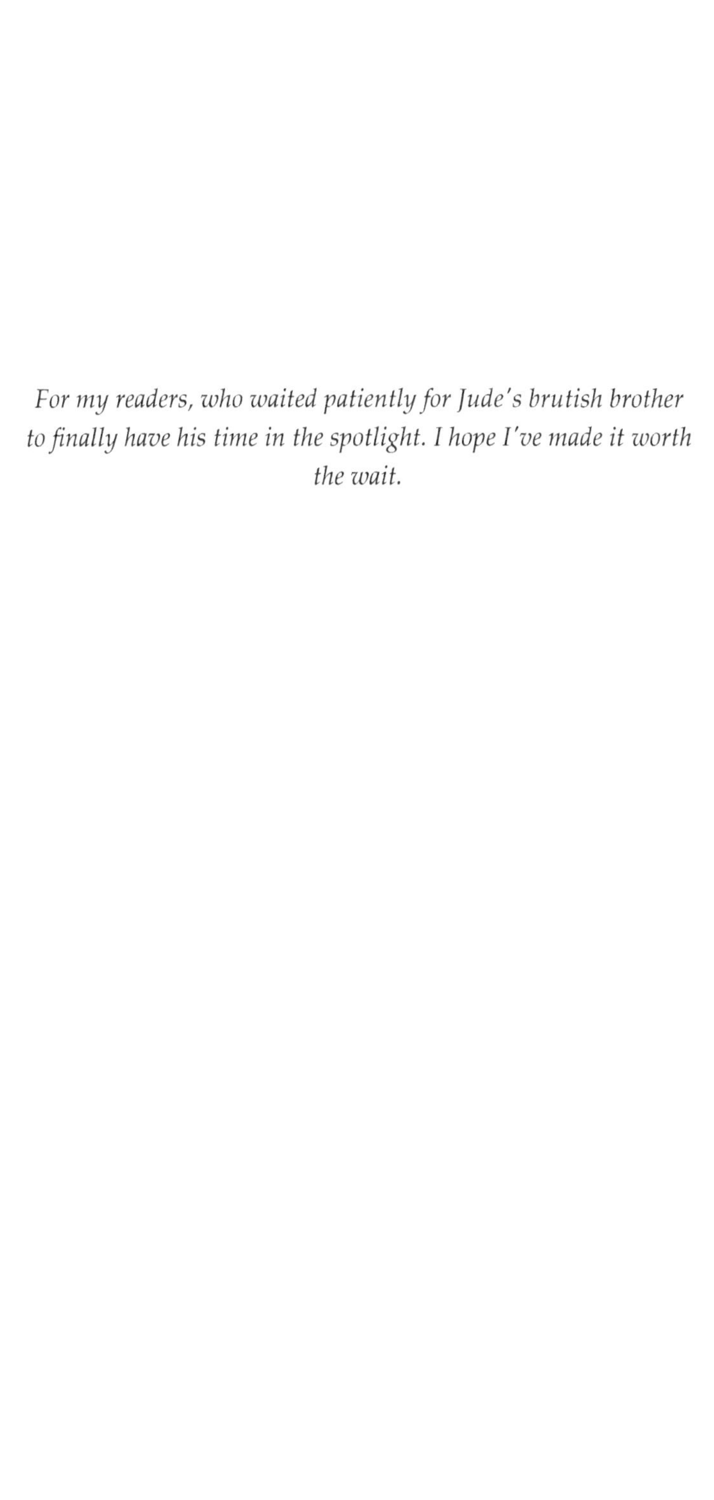

For my readers, who waited patiently for Jude's brutish brother to finally have his time in the spotlight. I hope I've made it worth the wait.

PROLOGUE

ROMAN

"**A**re you excited Roman?" my mother asked, straightening my tie, as I peered at myself in the mirror.

Nodding with enthusiasm, I stared at my reflection with a mixture of pride and bewilderment. It wasn't the first time I'd been in a suit or fancy clothes. Growing up as a Cavenaugh, even one as young as me, had its duties.

I laughed internally at the way my hair molded to my head. Mom always had the hardest time with it. She called it her biggest challenge yet as a mother because, no matter how she had it cut or styled, she could never get the crazy strands to bend to her will.

It didn't help that I was constantly messing it up, running my hands through it before a big test or when Molly Adams smiled at me during art class.

"Well, your brother is just finishing up, so get your shoes on, and I'll meet you at the front door," she instructed, giving me a warm smile, before leaving the room.

I did as I was told, double-knotting each loop to make sure I wouldn't trip.

He might be my father, but I still wanted to make a good impression.

I'd never been invited to his work before. Mom had said it was a big deal.

My future.

I didn't quite understand what all that meant, but I wanted to make my father proud. So, on a Monday morning, when most kids my age were still in their pajamas, reveling in the teacher workday we had off from school, I was making my way downtown to a high-rise that had my name written on the side.

Jude, my annoying little brother, was bouncing in the backseat, rattling off facts about Dad and his work. I couldn't understand half of what he said—constantly rattling off things most high schoolers would scratch their heads at. Jude was some sort of prodigy with numbers, and my parents were already tutoring him to hone that talent.

It just made him all the more irritating.

My mother had stayed behind at home, stating that this was a day for the men of the family, leaving us in the trusted care of our longtime driver, Ed.

We pulled up to the curb of Cavenaugh Investments. I had to admit, I was a little disappointed not to find my father waiting for us, but I guessed he was a busy guy. Ed walked us in through the glass doors, and I took a brief glance around.

I'd been in the lobby dozens of times. I'd just never made it much further than that.

Today though, I would be taking the private elevator all the way to the top.

I felt like a superstar.

My father's assistant fetched us from the lobby, thanking Ed for delivering us.

"Did you know, only three people in the entire building know this code?" Jude said proudly as we entered the elevator. "It goes directly to Daddy's office. The rest of the executive offices are on that floor, but they have to use the regular elevator and can only access Daddy's office by appointment or permission."

"Shut up, Jude," I said. I smiled awkwardly at the pretty woman.

"He's right, you know," she said with a quick wink.

"Yeah, I know," I sighed.

He was always right.

The elevator zoomed to the top, and before I knew it, the doors were opening, and we were standing in the waiting area outside my father's office. His assistant's desk was to the right, and a large seating area was to the left. I took a step toward the large wooden door that led to my father but was stopped.

"It looks like your father is stuck in a meeting. How about I show you around the executive floor? Maybe take you to the fancy break room for some snacks?" She waggled her eyebrows at us, making Jude jump up and down.

I was so not impressed.

I wanted to see my dad, not sit around eating snacks—I could do that at home. But I followed the perky young woman anyway, looking back at my father's office. It didn't take long for us to make it to the break room, but unfortunately for our host, all the doughnuts had been devoured.

"Well, let's see..." she said. Clearly panicking, she started going through cupboards and drawers.

I used her moment of distraction to my advantage, and

I grabbed her keys off the counter and slipped out the door. I'd come here to learn… to impress my father. And that was what I was going to do.

Walking back, I easily let myself into my father's office, thanks to the keys the dopey woman had left unattended, and I was once again standing at the large door.

His meeting must have just ended because the door was slightly open. I lifted my hands to the door to push it open and stopped.

"They should be here any minute," he said, clearly talking to someone on the phone.

He laughed, and I heard the squeak of a chair. I took a step back.

"Thank God for Jude. That poor boy, Roman, doesn't have a lick of sense in him. He's a sweet kid — and he definitely got my good looks," he chuckled, briefly before continuing. "He's cute, but dumb. If it wasn't for Jude, I'd be worried sick for the future of this place. Roman would run it into the ground."

My heart plummeted as he laughed again.

"Listen, I've got to go. I'll talk to you later. Bye."

Taking another step backward, I kept going until I felt the cold touch of the elevator at my back.

"Cute, but dumb."

My father thought I was an idiot.

My hands clenched tightly to the keys, still in my hands as anger grew in my heart.

And it never stopped.

CHAPTER ONE

"**W**hat the hell is all that noise?" I snapped, my voice booming through the thin walls of my spacious office.

No one answered, and the commotion outside my door continued as my hands moved to the sides of my head where a headache was quickly forming.

Ever since I'd officially taken over our family business, Cavenaugh Investments—for the East Coast division anyway—I'd been working in this oversize office that I'd inherited from my brother, which had originally been passed down from my father. Sitting here, where Jude and my father had once sat, was both terrifying and exhilarating.

Of course, all those feelings were dashed and tossed aside because of the incessant racket happening outside my door. Calming silence usually filled my afternoons, but it had been replaced with animated feminine screams, excited laughter, and squeals of glee.

Fucking hell.

I really should have listened to my inner monologue when I'd contemplated the idea of soundproofing this place or hiring a virtual assistant.

I needed silence. Dead silence. All the time.

It was how I operated and what I demanded in order to do what I did for this company, which was basically everything. My employees, although they might find it strange, knew this, yet here they were, causing a shitstorm right outside the boss's door.

Who even allowed them in to the office?

Slowly massaging my achy temples, I sat stoically, hoping whatever pandemonium was happening outside would eventually die down. When it failed to dissipate five minutes later, I groaned, knowing I'd have to intervene.

Here comes the asshole.

I was already known in the company as the Dickhead of the East, never speaking to anyone unless absolutely necessary and barely acknowledging a single person's presence. Now, I was going to have to yell.

Again.

Rising from the expensive leather chair, I brushed the front of my jacket, tightened my tie, and straightened my back, feeling my bones strain from being hunched over my computer for far too long.

Walking toward the door, I caught a glimpse of myself in the mirrored wall of the old bar my father had put in ages ago, back when handing your business partner a glass of liquor was as common as lighting up a cigarette indoors. Although the practice might have gone out of style, neither Jude nor I could part with it. Business deals might be made over conference tables more than bottles of gin, but I still loved the look of it.

It had a special place in my memories as well. Sitting

atop the sleek brown mahogany shelves were irreplaceable crystal decanters that my father had had imported from Ireland. This place, the office I'd inherited from him always reminded me of my father—the good, the bad, and everything in between.

Raising a hand to my dirty blond hair, I tried to straighten out the indentations I'd made over the many hours. Seeing the dark circles and tired green eyes staring back at me, it was a wonder I was even awake at all.

When was the last time I slept?

When was the last time I was home?

I couldn't remember.

Since Jude and his family had gone, that left me here. Alone.

He was in charge of our new West Coast division, and of course, he was making strides and handling it all like a pro, and he probably wasn't even losing sleep over any of it.

Nothing ever seemed to challenge him.

Me on the other hand? I would be up at all hours, just trying to keep afloat. Of course, I'd never tell him that.

Or anyone else, for that matter.

To the rest of the world, I was just the asshole, the guy who didn't give two fucks about anyone. And, mostly, they were right. I didn't.

But this company? Well, that, I did care about. It was the legacy that had been passed down through three generations of our family, and like hell would I let it slip through the gutter on my watch. When the next generation of Cavenaughs took over, they would find this place solid and thriving.

Because of me.

This business was my family, my lover, and my only friend.

I'd made my fair share of mistakes, and now, nothing else mattered.

Nothing else would ever matter.

THERE HAD BEEN A BRIEF TIME IN MY LIFE WHEN THE IDEA OF walking into a room filled with happy, exuberant women was a welcome task. The old carefree Roman would have put on a charming, wolfish grin, immediately zeroed in to pick his target, and gone in for the kill.

But, unfortunately for me and the women I used to take home with me, those days were long gone.

My father had once called it my rebellious period. It was a period in my life when I'd thrown caution to the wind and abandoned every responsibility I had in a vain attempt to be someone else for a time.

See, the thing with growing up and knowing your inevitable outcome in life was that there was no guessing and no spontaneity. Everything, every tiny detail, was already hashed out into a nice, neat, orderly package for you, and you'd find yourself powerless to stop it.

As I'd watched my life slowly unfold while my brother and I were groomed from a young age to take over a life we'd had no choice in having, I'd decided to take another path, becoming the stereotypical rebel of the family. My parents believed Jude was the saving grace of our generation. With his gifted ability and talent for numbers, he was a shoo-in for the coveted top spot after my father retired. Why should I have sat around and waited for inevitable? It had been my chance to step out and discover who I really was — or at least have fun trying.

My father, of course, being the man he was, had spun my shenanigans into something more wholesome for the media, making me more of a modern-day spokesperson for the family and the company we were known for… but we'd all known what I was doing.

I had been turning away from my family.

Or, at least, I had attempted to.

My brother though? Like always, he succeeded where I failed.

When he'd all but dropped off the face of the earth after the death of his fiancée, I had known my carefree existence was over. When our father's health had begun to decline, there was no one but me to take over the family business.

Me—the cute but dumb one.

I would have laughed in the old man's face at the irony of it all—his dim-witted son taking over while his favorite wasted away his talent in a hospital, doing janitorial duties. But instead, I proved him wrong.

I'd been walking the line ever since.

Every day felt like a slow crawl into hell.

The outside world had faded away as family and what few friends I'd had ceased to exist. Nothing mattered, except for what happened within these walls.

I'd become a robot of sorts, a drone to the establishment.

I wasn't a complete ass though. Everything I did, every hour I spent, was to keep this company afloat, to ensure the job and security of every employee who walked through those doors. Even if I did end up being the enemy in the end, at least every single one of them could pay their rent, send their kids to daycare, and afford to keep their coffee habits going for another month.

Thanks to me—the Dickhead of the East.

And now it was time to be an ass once again. Turning

the handle of the heavy wooden door, I pulled it open and stepped into a giant clusterfuck of female frenzy.

Pink and blue balloons were floating around the ceiling, their tiny ribbons creating a curtain of colors as I tried to make my way through the mayhem. Nearly every woman on the floor was gathered around my assistant's desk with beaming bright eyes as they each waited their turn to hug and congratulate her for some marked accomplishment.

Did I miss something?

Glancing down with obvious curiosity, I instantly noticed her protruding belly and inwardly sighed. I'd missed a *big* something.

Bethany's eyes caught mine as several women continued to ogle her pregnant belly. Surprise, followed by what appeared to be fear, swept across her features, and she suddenly cleared her throat, alerting the others of my arrival.

"Mr. Cavenaugh, I'm so sorry. Did we disturb you?" she said, barely able to meet my gaze.

"Why do you think I'm out here at"—I glanced down at my watch, sighing at the time—"three o'clock in the afternoon?"

"We apologize, Mr. Cavenaugh," one of the ladies said, stepping up.

I recognized her from accounting. She proudly held her chin up, her eyes never wavering from mine. It was an odd reaction to receive from one of my employees. *Was she new?* Usually, it didn't take long for the beware-of-the-boss speech to make its way to the newbies, furthering the healthy dose of fear from one staff member to the next. It kept things simple, clean, and easy. If they feared me, they wouldn't bother me.

I wouldn't win any Boss of the Year awards this way,

but it helped me get things done, and in turn, everyone could keep their jobs.

"We were just surprising Bethany with a sweet baby shower that we'd been planning for weeks. We just wanted to give her a few things before this little bundle of joy arrived! We'll move down to the break room momentarily. Won't you join us?" she asked.

The way she'd said it made it feel like a dare, like I'd just stepped back into middle school and the dreaded Coke bottle had landed on me.

Truth or dare, Roman?

As if the attention hadn't already been focused on me, it doubled in that moment. Everyone waited in hushed anticipation for my answer. My fingers dug into my disheveled hair as I tried to hide the nervousness in my demeanor.

How had I missed my assistant being pregnant? Shouldn't that have been something I noticed?

Had she told me, and I'd forgotten?

Fuck.

I looked back at the group of women standing in awkward silence, waiting for my answer. The leader of the group—the blonde from accounting—smiled smugly, as if she already knew my answer. Her hand rested at the curve of her hip as it jutted out, accentuating her long, lean legs and pert round ass.

How I'd love to wipe that pompous grin off her face with a few lashings of my tongue. My dick twitched at the mere thought.

"No, I don't think I'll be able to make it. Sorry," I replied swiftly, pulling my gaze away from the daring blonde with the chocolate-brown eyes. "And, Bethany? Don't take too long. You have a job to do," I added bluntly, turning quickly toward the door that led back to my office.

That led back to hell.

But, for now, at least it felt like my salvation.

Every bone in my body seemed to moan with exhaustion as I rose from the plush leather chair, cracking my neck to ease the tension that had slowly been building throughout the day. Flexing my fingers, I looked out to the panoramic skyline, noticing the brilliant orange sunset I'd seen hours earlier replaced with thousands of twinkling bright lights dotting the skyline.

What time is it?

Glancing at my watch, I groaned, realizing I'd been here far longer than planned.

Again.

My stomach audibly rumbled in protest to the lack of concern for my well-being, and I began gathering my things for home.

Home.

What an odd word. There were so many quotes, songs, and poems about the simple four-letter word. It empowered people, ignited wars, and gave hope to those who were lost.

But, as I walked through the halls of the darkened building, on my way to the place I called home, there was nothing remotely close to hope. The large apartment I rented in a sought-after Manhattan high-rise was more than most people would ever have in their entire lives, yet when I entered, I felt hollow.

There was only ever one place in my life that truly felt worthy of the word *home.*

Our family's country estate.

Tucked far away from the city, it was like stepping back

in time. Long forgotten was the hustle and bustle of the metropolis, replaced with long, winding paths through the rose garden with our mother and evenings on the porch, searching for fireflies.

It was where I felt most at ease, like a child rather than a walking, talking insurance plan for the future of our family. But just like my short-lived childhood, the beautiful house lay barren, like a ghost town, covered in white sheets and layers of dust.

Much like my memories of the place.

Stepping into the elevator, I pressed the button for the lobby and watched the doors shut. The lights slowly blinked, showing my descent. I rocked back on my heels, willing myself to stay awake for just a bit longer.

The familiar sound of the doors opening slightly startled me but spurred me into action. I now felt the emptiness in my stomach, reminding me it had been far too long since my last meal.

Time for food.

And maybe a hefty dose of vodka to effectively shut off my brain for the night.

Leftovers and drinking alone.

What an amazing life I'd made for myself.

When there had been two of us here to run things, I could fit in my extracurricular activities with ease, stepping out for the evening at a decent hour without a twinge of guilt. Granted, those activities had mostly been limited to the four walls of my bedroom, but it had been a good life.

No strings. No responsibilities after leaving the office.

But now that Jude had started business on the West Coast, basically doubling our workload, I felt like I was paddling up a river, going the wrong way.

With only one oar and maybe a broken arm.

If I told him this though, he'd be here in two seconds, ready to help and lead where I had failed. He'd uproot his family, tearing them away from the life they'd built in Southern California, just to be here for me because I'd asked, even after everything I'd put him through.

He was a better man than me, and because of that, I'd never ask. Otherwise, my father would win. His belief that I'd eventually fail and the entire company would crumble at my feet?

Yeah, I don't think so.

I was so lost in my thoughts and possibly consumed with ravenous hunger that I nearly missed the leggy blonde sitting on the upholstered bench near the exit. Her familiar Cheshire Cat smile though caught my attention.

"You keep long hours, Mr. Cavenaugh," she said, lifting one beautiful, long leg over the other.

I watched in fascination, wondering what those legs would look like wrapped around my neck. Remembering her brazen attitude with me earlier, I took a step back.

This was exactly the type of female I liked—strong with a no-bullshit attitude and a body that could keep me entertained all night long.

"Are you keeping tabs on me?" I asked casually.

"Maybe."

My fists clenched at my sides. Suddenly, food was the last thing I hungered for, but I would not cave to her bold attempts. This wasn't the first time I'd been hit on by a member of my staff. I might be known as an asshole, but that hadn't deterred a brave few.

All of whom, I had easily turned down.

This one though...

I took another glance as her eyes followed me. I could see the smirk forming at the corner of her pouty red lips. Lips I knew would feel goddamn perfect around cock.

Fuck.

I wasn't above one-night stands. Hell, they were my definition of a normal, healthy relationship, but none of them ever involved an employee. I'd learned early on to keep my dick out of business, and unfortunately, that rule still remained firmly intact.

"Well, I appreciate the sentiment, but I really do have to be going," I announced firmly, sidestepping her, as she rose from her spot on the bench to stop me.

"I knew you'd say no to the baby shower," she said, the smirk on her face growing to a full-out grin.

"Then, why did you bother asking?" I asked curtly.

"I guess I was hoping you'd surprise me."

"And now?" I asked.

"I guess I was hoping for the same," she simply stated, taking a step closer. I could feel the heat from her body radiating off her smooth tan skin. "I was hoping for a surprise."

As my jaw twitched in restraint, I purposely stepped back. Taking a full breath, I tried to ignore the soft jasmine scent that encompassed her.

"Keep waiting," I answered, finally walking away.

The doors swung behind me as I exited the building. Fresh, cool air hit my face, clearing my senses and reaffirming my decision to leave her behind.

No good could come from falling in bed with an employee.

CHAPTER TWO

"**W**hy do I feel like the new kid, getting ready for her first day at a new school?" I called out to my boyfriend of eight years as I stood in front of the tiny bathroom mirror, fidgeting with my hair for the tenth time.

"Are you sick to your stomach, nervous yet a bit excited at the same time?" Tyler asked, peeking his head out of the shower.

Tiny water droplets dripped down his face and his chin as he grinned mischievously. Our New York apartment was the size of a shoebox for a toddler, and his nose nearly touched my shoulder in the confined space.

"Yes," I answered, a cheesy smile plastered across my porcelain face, as I stared back at my reflection.

I'd already done my makeup, opting for the less-is-more strategy. A few swipes of the mascara brush and a little blush—that was all I needed. Being blessed with clear skin since I was a baby, there was no reason to hide it.

My hair though? I was definitely considering wearing a

paper bag. So far that morning, I'd braided my long chestnut-brown hair to the side and then thrown it up into a sleek ponytail, and now, I'd done some sort of half-up, half-down thing with a twist.

I hated it all.

"Well, there's your answer," he offered as his hand reached out to grab a towel off the hanging bar.

I sighed in frustration. "Were you this nervous when you started your new job a few weeks ago?" I questioned. I pursed my lips together as I made the final decision to leave my hair down and let it hang naturally around my face. At least then, I wouldn't be worried about it getting messed up on the subway.

Subway.

Just thinking about it made my stomach flip. No matter what I did to my hair, it wouldn't hide the fact that I was clearly the brand-new, extremely naive fish in a scary large pond.

New York was everything I'd expected it to be, yet it was so much more. When I was younger, sitting in my cozy Midwestern bedroom, watching reruns of *Friends* on one of the few channels our family got, I'd always known I'd eventually come here.

I'd just never expected to live here at the ripe age of twenty-two.

Now, everything just seemed big, intimidating, and completely overwhelming. *Where were Ross and Phoebe when I needed them?*

"A little, I guess," Tyler said, answering my question, as he cuddled up close behind me.

I could smell the woodsy aroma of his soap as his hands slid around my waist.

"But I knew what I was walking into," he explained. "Interning there during my last semester definitely helped."

"I know," I answered in a pout. "But it still has to be different, right? A four-month internship can't be the same as a full-time position."

"No." He grinned back at me through the mirror. "But I wasn't going into someplace completely blind. Now, if you asked me how I felt the first day of my internship at the accounting firm, well, that was a different story. I nearly ran back to my dorm and crawled under my covers like a scared little girl."

I cleared my throat, eyeing him.

"I mean, a dog, like a scared little puppy. Because girls —females are strong and totally capable of everything, including fancy new jobs."

He saw me crack a smile as I was enchanted by the never-ending bucket of charm that he always seemed to have on hand. It was one of the reasons I had fallen for him in high school. While so many of the boys had been goofy or just downright mean, Tyler was always sweet and caring.

Even back then, he had known what he wanted to do with his life. During our senior year, as we'd sat under a maple tree outside the school, he'd go on and on about moving to the Big Apple and finding his niche in the world. Some young boys would dream of racing cars or fighting fires when they grew up. Tyler had always wanted to be an accountant.

When I'd first met him our freshman year, I'd thought he was kind of an oddball, despite the obvious charm that came with him. Who dreamed of becoming an accountant? For a history lover like me, it sounded like a lifetime sentence of boredom.

For Tyler though, it was all about the numbers. He had a natural ability and keen insight to finding answers. He'd begun studying tax laws well before college applications were even due, which was why he'd so easily earned a major scholarship at NYU in their honors program. Since then, he'd interned for several major firms in the city, finally settling on working at a top Fortune 500 company to begin his career.

Me? I'd done exactly what my parents wanted and attended a state college, living close to home, while Tyler had been discovering a city I'd only seen on television.

"Stop messing with your hair and come have breakfast with me," Tyler suggested as he scooted around me, attempting to finish his morning ritual.

"You just want me to cook for you." I snickered, catching his eye, as he grabbed a bottle of hair gel.

It was still so strange to see him every time I opened my eyes in the morning. He'd changed, losing that Midwestern roughness, now replaced with expensive hair gel and sleek suits.

"Do you blame me?" he asked as he stepped out of the bathroom and into our bedroom.

The apartment was a disaster from my arrival. Boxes and clothes were strewed everywhere. I'd been rushing around, trying to find a job as quickly as possible so that I wouldn't have to cut into my savings, that I'd barely had time to unpack in the few weeks I'd been here.

"I thought you'd grown fond of the New York life? Bagels every morning, dinners out. Isn't that what you said to me?"

He turned, the towel from his shower wrapped around his lean frame. "Yes, but now, I have you. And I am still a Midwestern boy. Who can say no to home cooking?"

He smiled when he noticed my attention had waned as I followed a tiny drop of water making a long path down his chest.

"On second thought"—he grinned, taking several steps until the gap between us vanished—"I think we might just skip breakfast this morning."

Tyler's hands wrapped around my waist just as the alarm clock on my phone began to go off, reminding me of the time. His eyebrow rose as my expression changed to something close to panic.

"That's the alarm I set, so I'd know when it was almost time to leave," I said, my voice becoming higher with each word. "I'd be late."

The fear so clearly written all over my face didn't seem to faze him in the slightest.

"First lesson of becoming a New Yorker, everyone is late. Just blame it on the subway or a crazy cab driver."

I pulled away from him, searching for my shoes in one of the many boxes all over the room. "Did you know the subway used to accept coins as payment, and when they switched over to passes, there was a surplus of over sixty thousand coins? Where do you think they all went?"

"In these boxes?" he joked, stopping me once again.

I turned toward him, and another droplet of water fell down his chest.

Who needed breakfast when I had him?

I was a New Yorker now.

What were a few minutes now that I had everything I wanted?

"You're late," the polished young woman at the front desk announced sternly after I'd politely told her my name. She tapped her perfectly manicured nail on the desk, looking up at me, as she waited for a reply.

"Um, yes, well… the subway, and the, uh…" I stammered, trying to find any decent excuse, anything at all, but all I could come up with was a mishmash of words that made my cheeks flare to life as I remembered the real reason I was late.

I am going to kill Tyler.

Miss Perfect leaned over the counter, wrapping her fingers with the impeccable red nails around the crisp glass edge, and smiled. "Just moved here?" she asked.

I tried not to let my attention wander.

It was the first time I'd been to Cavenaugh Investments, landing the job based on my résumé alone. Going through a temp agency had been a last-ditch effort on my part, but it was the only one that had actually paid off. Had I not received a call from their Human Resources department last week, asking me to fill in for the CEO's administrative assistant who was out on mandatory bed rest, I probably would be searching for waitressing jobs, like the rest of New York.

Nodding, I answered her question without a sound, and I watched her grin grow wider.

"Well, let me give you a bit of advice, sweetheart, okay?"

As her ruby-red lips turned cold, I opened my mouth to respond, but she quickly cut me off, "Don't be late. Ever. Mr. Cavenaugh likes his assistants to be punctual, and he doesn't give second chances."

My heart raced as her words hit home.

First day on the job, and I was already being scolded.

Awesome.

"Yes, of course," I responded. I took a deep breath in an attempt to keep the tears threatening to break free at bay.

"Great. Now that we have that taken care of, I'll have someone show you where you'll be working. Why don't you have a seat?"

Feeling like I'd been waved off like a disobedient child, I turned and took a seat near the elevator, hoping I'd melt into the walls.

Do not cry, Cara. Do not cry, I chanted silently in my head.

Needing a distraction, I pulled out my phone and quickly sent a text to Tyler, letting him know the late policy was apparently vastly different in his accounting world. He immediately sent a text back with a frowny face and admitted to perhaps stretching the truth in an effort to get me in bed.

"Figures," I huffed under my breath, shaking my head, as I slid the phone back into the five-dollar purse I'd found at Goodwill last semester.

Looking around, I felt completely out of place. Everything, even down to the bitchy receptionist, was modern and sophisticated. Clean lines and polished silver adorned the waiting room while I sat in an uncomfortable boxy chair, wearing items I'd picked up secondhand to save money in an attempt to make early payments on my school loans.

This wasn't the first time I'd second-guessed my decision to leave Nebraska. Things were simpler back home. Life moved slower. People moved slower. It was a pace I'd grown accustomed to, and I wasn't sure how quickly I could adapt.

Here, everyone was on the go—from the moment they awoke to the time they fell asleep. Nothing ever stopped, and I constantly felt like I was being dragged down by the complexity of it all.

My parents had warned me that I'd miss home, but I'd just assumed they were having trouble with letting me go. Empty nest syndrome or whatever it was called. I guessed they weren't the only ones. Could that empty nest thing work in reverse? Long gone were the endless cornfields and clean air. Friday night Dairy Queen runs and picnic lunches by the pond, replaced with fancy coffee and never-ending traffic.

But, despite everything, I knew I was here for the right reasons. This was what Tyler and I had worked for, planned for, and now, it was finally a reality.

"Miss Hamilton?"

I turned to see a petite redhead in mile-high heels and a tight black pencil skirt. Her beautiful sapphire-blue blouse looked like it cost more than my monthly share of the rent.

Straightening my already wrinkled dress as I rose, I grabbed the ratty purse at my side and quickly walked toward her. Rather than staring me down while mentally ticking off all the reasons I was obviously going to be eaten alive in a place like this, she offered me her hand, welcoming me to the building.

"Thank you so much for coming on such short notice," she smiled, turning toward a long hallway.

I sped along behind her, trying to keep up.

"We thought we would have loads of time to find Mr. Cavenaugh a temporary assistant, but I guess pregnancy can never be counted on for following schedules," she said with enthusiasm.

I nodded but realized immediately that she couldn't see my response. Before I could offer up anything vocal, she came to a halt in front of a shiny glass elevator.

"This is the elevator that leads to the executive wing," she explained as I stepped beside her.

"And—oh dear, I forgot to introduce myself. Forgive me, I talk too much, and I've already had about a gallon of coffee this morning, so I'm running a little faster than usual. I'm Gretchen from Human Resources. We spoke on the phone earlier this week."

"Yes," I answered, nodding my head in agreement, "I remember."

"Good." She smiled warmly and we entered. "Now, what was I going to say? Oh, right. Make sure you take this elevator. It's the only one that goes to Mr. Cavenaugh's office directly. You can get there by other means, but believe me—this is a lot easier. He's on the top floor with all the other executives. You'll need a code for the elevator," she explained, handing me a small piece of paper with a four-digit code.

Since she hadn't entered it, I figured this was my first job duty, and I quickly punched in the numbers.

When the elevator began slowly crawling to the top, she nodded her head and said, "Good."

I slightly felt like a small puppy being rewarded for performing a neat trick, but the praise was much more pleasant than the grim atmosphere I'd left behind in the lobby.

"That code will also work to get you into his office after you've ventured out."

"Ventured out?" I asked in confusion.

She nodded. "When you visit other departments, you'll need this to get back to your desk."

I nodded and continued to stare at the polished glass, feeling intimidated by the access code and the VIP elevator. I started to wonder why the owner of a major company would go to such drastic measures to sequester himself from everyone else.

Was he Quasimodo hiding in his bell tower?

Before I had a chance to ask any questions about my new boss, Gretchen intervened. "Where are you from?" she asked, finally breaking the awkwardness between us.

"Um, Nebraska," I answered softly, somewhat embarrassed that she'd already noticed I somehow didn't belong. Was it the shoes? The funky purse? Or me altogether?

As if sensing my trepidation, she responded with a warm smile on her face, "I noticed the accent. I'm originally from South Dakota, so hearing you speak is like taking a trip back home."

I have an accent?

Something to ponder later.

"You're not from here?" I asked, slightly shocked.

I would have pegged her as a New York native. I took another glance at her, and not a hair of hers was out of place. She carried herself like she owned the entire damn city.

"No," she answered. "You'll find, many of us are transplants hiding in plain sight. Don't worry; you'll join our ranks soon enough."

I somehow found it hard to believe that I'd ever be mistaken for a New Yorker rather than the corn-and-potatoes-fed Midwestern girl I'd always been.

Remembering my manners, I quickly nodded, my nerves rising with each floor.

Why had I taken this job? I wasn't capable of handling someone like Mr. Cavenaugh –a multimillionaire of a major corporation. The most experience I had was some light office work as a work-study student, something I'd seriously embellished on my résumé. *Alphabetizing files and answering phone calls? Sure, count me in.* But managing the life of one of America's richest men? Surely I was doomed.

The elevator dinged, announcing our floor.

Gretchen turned toward me once again. Her megawatt smile still in place, she announced, "We're here!"

Looking around as I stepped out, I took one last gulp and smiled back with force.

Here goes nothing.

THE ELEVATOR SUDDENLY FELT MILES AWAY RATHER THAN FEET, like I'd fallen through a black hole, when I stumbled upon Bethany's—Mr. Cavenaugh's pregnant permanent assistant—pristine, clutter-free desk.

Okay, maybe I was exaggerating… and slightly rambling.

But, as I listened to Gretchen briefly explain my job duties, pointing here and there at the neatly organized desk that would be my home between the hours of eight and five for the next three months, I suddenly felt extremely small and insignificant.

I was sure Bethany the Great had tons of experience under her belt before she'd left to become Mommy of the Year, and sure, her bed rest was a bit of an inconvenience to everyone, but glancing down at her desk, she'd obviously started planning for such an occasion. There were sticky notes and printed out directions for her worthy successor, who'd somehow turned out to be me.

Perhaps I'd fudged a little too much on my résumé, exaggerating my duties as assistant to the university president over the four years I'd been a student. Fetching coffee and alphabetizing files just didn't look that exciting when I'd typed it out, so I'd embellished.

A lot.

And now, here I was. Administrative assistant to one of the most prestigious businessmen in all of New York.

Holy mother of God, am I sweating?

As I casually glanced down to do a quick pit check, I noticed Gretchen staring at me.

"I'm sorry, what?" I said, heat burning my cheeks, as my stomach rolled with nervousness.

"Is there anything else you might need?"

"Oh, um… no?" I answered, insecurity woven in each hesitant word.

"Okay, well, I will leave you to get settled, and I'll check back with you after lunch. I still have a few documents for you to complete, so I'll bring those with me then."

"Right."

"Good luck," she said, her eyes going soft.

It was the same expression I would give my mom before she went to the dreaded dentist.

Good Lord, what had I gotten myself into?

In a daze, I watched her walk away. Before her slender frame disappeared behind the adjacent door, using the keycode we'd discussed, she stopped and turned abruptly.

"Cara?" she said, her voice reminding me of the tone my mother had used when I was younger.

"Yes?" I answered, looking up at her from the leather chair I'd somehow fallen into.

"Breathe. You'll do just fine."

Nodding, I did as she'd suggested and hoped like hell she was right.

***

When I was the ripe old age of nine, I had gone to my parents and explained that I thought I was old enough to start earning a living. Being the understanding and nurturing parents they were, my mother and father had agreed and actually helped me find my first job.

Hamster caretaker.

Our neighbors had planned a trip to Worlds of Fun in Kansas City and sadly couldn't bring their pet hamster, Pringles. For the total of five dollars, I had been employed to care for Pringles for that long week. I had been so excited –my very first job!

I'd quickly found out that having a job wasn't nearly as exciting as I'd thought. Pringles had done little to nothing all day, and the most thrilling aspect of my job had been cleaning poop.

I'd retired after a week, and my career as a hamster caretaker had quickly ended.

This job though—working for Mr. Cavenaugh—was just as boring. Minus the poop, thankfully.

I spent the first hour reorganizing an already perfectly organized desk.

Total waste of my time.

I then proceeded to set up my email, or attempt to. It had already been done for me and I had one email waiting for me—a welcome message from Gretchen. After reading it several times, I moved on to staring at the door.

The one that had been closed since I arrived.

The one that led to him—the mysterious man I worked for.

So far, it had been hours, and he hadn't made a sound, not even a peep.

I quietly ate my sack lunch at my desk in fear that, if I left, I might miss his grand arrival.

As the assistant to one of the most powerful men in the city, I'd thought I would be busier. I'd envisioned a lot of running around, yelling at people, asking for favors, staying late and taking notes, or whatever else it was that assistants did. Kind of like *The Devil Wears Prada*—minus the fashion and Meryl Streep.

But, instead, I was sitting here, in silence, staring at a door.

Would he ever come out?

Did he actually exist?

I let out a small giggle as the scene from *The Wizard of Oz* with the infamous man behind the curtain came to mind.

Maybe this great and powerful man really wasn't who everyone thought he was after all?

Maybe he was someone else entirely?

Suddenly, I really wanted to know.

Considering my high level of curiosity when it came to the unknown and my knack for research, it was strange that I hadn't looked up my new boss before now. But I had been a little off my game with the move and the boxes and whatnot.

Pulling up Google, I typed in the name *Roman Cavenaugh* and waited to see what would come up. Turned out, it was a lot actually. My boss was quite popular on the Internet.

There goes my man-behind-the-curtain theory.

Clicking on a recent article, the title read, *Former Troublemaker of the Cavenaugh Empire Officially at the Helm.*

I barely made it two words into the article when I caught sight of the photos. Several had been inserted along with the text, and I immediately became fixated on the man staring back at me. Broad shoulders, dark blond hair, and eyes the color of jade.

He was handsome and frighteningly beautiful at the same time. Power effortlessly clung to him as he posed for the camera. I was so captivated by him that I hardly noticed the creak of the door beside me as it swung open for the first time since I'd arrived. Looking up, I found those same hypnotizing eyes I'd been gawking at on the screen glaring down at me from the now wide open office door.

I gulped audibly and quickly closed the Internet

browser, thankful that my computer screen faced the wall, away from prying eyes.

Or an angry, intimidating boss.

"Can I help you, sir?" I managed to squeak out in record time.

"Who the hell are you?" a deep voice answered.

No introduction. No warm smile or polite handshake. Just like his picture, Mr. Cavenaugh was pure business and power.

It frightened me to no end.

"I'm Cara Hamilton, your new assistant," I replied with as much confidence as I could muster. When my words failed to rouse any reaction at all, I continued, "Your permanent assistant, Bethany, was put on bed rest due to complications with her pregnancy… high blood pressure or something." My hands were now involved in this lengthy explanation waving around in front of me like mad. "So, HR brought me on as a temp."

Bringing my crazy hands back to my sides, I waited for him to respond. To show a shred of something. A blink, a casual nod… anything but this rigid, hostile persona he seemed to be exuding.

Instead, he said nothing. He turned back toward his office and left nearly as quickly as he'd come.

The door slammed, making the thin walls shake and quiver. I sat at my lonely desk, looking around at the various Post-it notes, wondering where exactly Bethany had stashed the one about his lack of personality.

Because, clearly, my new hot boss was an asshole.

CHAPTER THREE

ROMAN

My blood pressure was going through the roof as I stormed back into my office.

I was in charge around here, wasn't I? Why hadn't I been made aware of this change? It had taken months to train Bethany to my specific needs and demands.

And, now, she was just gone?

Bed rest? Was that a normal thing with pregnancy? Hell if I knew.

What I did know was it put one hell of a kink in my life. And how HR expected that wide-eyed, pretty young thing outside my door to keep up was beyond me.

Damn it all to hell.

I had resorted to pacing now. I didn't know how many times I'd watched my father do this same thing—pace this exact path through this office as he'd work through problems and solve crisis after crisis.

This was small compared to some of the issues he'd

hashed out within these walls. But I was tired, restless, and irritable. I'd already worked a full week, and it was barely half over.

I needed a break. Otherwise, I was going to snap.

Yes, a break…

Grabbing my coat and a few miscellaneous things, I felt more and more confident in my decision to leave with each step I made. As my hand closed over the door, the normal feeling of guilt that would fall upon me when I exited for the day was instead replaced with exhilaration and excitement.

It was the same feeling I'd felt years ago before this building and everything it represented had completely taken over my life.

Carefree Roman was back, if only for a night.

I guess I'd better make the best of it.

Normally, I had an assistant to schedule all of my events, both in and out of the office, even though my social calendar had been sorely lacking as of late. But, if it was a part of my life, then Bethany knew about it.

This new girl though, I didn't trust her.

I couldn't even remember her name. *Had she told me?* I thought I'd blocked the whole event out of my memory. Blowing through the reception area of my office, like a man on a mission, I didn't even bother with saying good-bye to the woman.

I just left.

Let her figure out what to do for the rest of the day. Consider it her on-the-job training.

As the glass elevator whisked me away from my worries, I sighed, knowing sooner or later, I'd have to train her. It wasn't like I could pull Bethany and her ever-growing belly from bed rest and demand that she work. I'd probably be sued.

And then I'd really deserve all those nicknames I was known for.

What was really bothering me was, I hated change. And I'd been knee-deep in it for years now—first, with my brother leaving and then with my father getting sick and eventually passing away.

When Jude had returned, everything had seemed to level out, but I had known it wouldn't last. It never did. Ultimately, something or someone would come in and mess everything up, and my life would be uprooted again.

Training a new assistant was a minor change in the grand scheme of things, but it was one I didn't have time for. With the board of trustees meeting quickly approaching in a matter of months, I needed all the time I could find to make sure we would be ready.

Because I knew they would all be looking for a reason to replace me.

Hell, I would.

I didn't exactly have the best track record, and God knew they had a mile-long list of those who could do a far better job—with one hand tied behind their back, no less. But I wouldn't allow this company to fall into the hands of someone other than me. It said *Cavenaugh* on the side of this building for a reason. My family had built this company from the ground up. We would always be in control.

But, to do this, I would need a clear mind. I'd been banging my head against a brick wall for far too long, working endless hours on a half-empty tank.

I was in desperate need of a refill.

And there was only one kind of pick-me-up that worked on my engine.

Not bothering to wait for my typical car service, I took a cab back to my apartment, in need of food and a long, hot shower. It had been days since I'd taken the time to eat a complete meal and spend more than minutes in the shower. Both felt like a luxury, which was humorous, standing in the million-dollar penthouse I'd bought back in my easygoing days.

With a full belly and a fresh outlook thanks to a few gallons of hot water, I made a few calls and went to my closet, feeling more exhilarated than I had in months. I took my time, letting the sun set and the evening settle. I had nothing but time tonight. Deciding to dress down, I went with a pair of designer jeans and a green button-down. Feeling confident and eager for the first time in a long while, I finished tying my shoes, slid on my father's vintage Rolex, and headed out the door, ready for anything.

I HAD THE DRIVER DROP ME OFF A FEW BLOCKS DOWN FROM the club, deciding I needed some air. I didn't know how long it had been since I'd just walked without purpose or a desperate need to get from one place to another. With the speed of a ninety-year-old turtle, I strolled the streets of my city, letting the smell of cheap pizza and gasoline fill my nostrils.

It wasn't everyone's ideal notion of a hometown, but it was mine. The smog, millions of people, and traffic, all of it made New York home, and although I dreamed of someday living somewhere simpler, right now, I was just happy to be outside.

Away from endless meetings and detailed business models.

Yes, this was exactly what I needed.

The pumping bass from the club grew as I closed in on the block. About twenty or so people stood in line, dressed in their finest, waiting for the bouncer to grant them entrance. This was one of the hottest clubs at the moment, and everyone was dying to get a golden ticket inside, hoping to rub elbows with the rich and famous.

The reason I came?

The women.

Where the celebrities mingled, so did the hot women. And if I was allowing myself only one day out of my cage, then it was going to be a night to remember. I barely had to nod in the direction of the beefy bouncer, Tony, a guy I'd known for years. He'd been doing this gig at more than a couple of local hot spots, and he and I always had an understanding.

Roman Cavenaugh didn't do lines.

A few groans and curse words were tossed my way as the rope was lifted, and I made my way inside with nothing more than a friendly handshake with Tony. Colossal chandeliers hung from the ceiling. Velvet curtains were sectioned-off intimate seating areas for more elite guests. With the lights off, it would have reminded me of the entrance to a grand palace or an opera house. But with the DJ spinning chart-topping music and hundreds of flashing lights moving in every direction, it was like watching the elegance of the old world colliding with the chaotic new planet we'd created.

During our quick handshake, Tony had mentioned that he'd saved a spot for me in the VIP section, due to one of the calls I'd made after my long shower and dinner. I was one of the richest men in the city, but even I wouldn't just show up here, demanding shit. I could be polite… if the situation called for it.

Not wanting to disappear into the VIP section quite yet, I headed toward the bar, hoping to spend some quality time checking out the scenery. As I approached, I found myself grinning from ear to ear. Women in short skirts and high heels for miles waited, some leaning over the bar for drinks and others dancing to the pulsating beat of the music, and I felt nearly intoxicated. It was paradise, and I was in dire need of a vacation.

The bar was circular and had eight men tending it.

Great, I'd never get a drink.

It was general knowledge that male bartenders earned more tips from women than they did from men, so being a guy at a bar filled with women meant I was practically invisible. I could head over to the VIP section and have a cold drink in my hands in a matter of minutes, no doubt delivered by a gorgeous female, but the whole point to VIP was privacy, and I wasn't quite ready for that.

I needed someone, or a few someones, to enjoy that privacy with.

Otherwise, it would be just like the rest of my life, only with better drinks and louder music.

"Hey there, need a hand?"

I turned to my left to find a beautiful redhead watching me with captivating brown eyes. I took a moment to blatantly check her out. She wasn't dressed like some high-class hooker, like most of the women here, but she wasn't trying for modestly either. The fabric of her black dress flowed seamlessly, barely covering her ass. It gave me a nice view of her more than ample cleavage, too, thanks to two thin straps and a plunging neckline that showcased all of her assets well.

Yes, she'll do nicely.

"What do you have in mind?" I asked, stepping close to talk over the bass.

A slight smirk developed at the corner of her enticing mouth before she responded, "Seems like you're in need of a drink."

"And how might you be of service? Are you going to climb over the bar and make me one?" I said as my eyes briefly caressed her bare skin.

"As enticing as that sounds, I wouldn't want to break a nail," she quipped, her smile growing. "I was thinking of something a bit more conventional. How about I flirt with that bartender?" she said, pointing to the one nearest us.

He was good-looking, young. Probably an actor, working his way toward his big break.

Weren't they all?

"He's had his eye on me all night. I think it's time to cash in."

"And what do you get out of this deal, besides the obvious—a drink and a few compliments from the bartender?" I inquired, quirking my eyebrow in curiosity.

"Well," she began, "the compliments are always nice to hear, but you've got me. I do have nefarious plans. You see, I noticed you when you walked in. And I happened to see you shake hands with the bouncer. Now, I come here a few times a month, and I've noticed a pattern. A hand-shake from Tony means a spot in VIP. Am I wrong?"

I took a long look at her one last time, wondering what angle she might have.

Money? Just sex? Money and sex?

Suddenly, I didn't care anymore.

"So, how about that drink?" the redhead with no name asked.

"I'll have a whiskey sour."

"Done."

THE SEXY REDHEAD, WHOSE NAME I'D LEARNED WAS MORGAN, had kept good on her word, and we'd both had drinks in our hands within minutes. She'd even scored a phone number from the young bartender, who was—as I'd guessed—paying his dues in an off-Broadway play until he made it big.

Him and half of New York.

The longer I lived in this city, the less and less I actually came in contact with true New Yorkers. Everyone was from some small city in some unknown state, looking to make it big. Some, like our bartender, wanted to act while others had loftier goals and wanted to make it to Wall Street.

Whatever it was, the people in this town were hungry for it.

It was why I couldn't let my guard down or fall behind in business. There were half a dozen guys just like me waiting to take my place, either by buying us out or stomping us out as the competition.

That was why I always beat them to it.

There were no friends in business—at least, not here.

"So, what do you do during the day?" Morgan asked, lounging back in the plush velvet sofa in the VIP area.

After grabbing our drinks and dancing for a bit, we'd headed back to the secluded area, so we could get to know each other better.

I hadn't actually planned on talking.

"Investments," I answered. I casually sipped my drink.

I hadn't given her my real name, assuming she hadn't given me hers. To her, I was John, the mysterious investment banker, and that was all the information she would get out of me for the evening.

"You don't like to talk much," she said as a statement. Her ruby-red lips curved into a knowing smile as she watched my eyes run down the length of her body.

"Only when it's necessary," I answered.

"And you don't find it necessary now?"

"Not really. You made your intentions at the bar perfectly clear. I liked what you had to offer and took you up on it. Is there anything else to discuss? From the brief knowledge I have of you and the vast knowledge I have of myself, I don't think we'll be seeing each other past this evening, so in reality, unnecessary words are just prolonging the inevitable."

Her eyes were calculating as she replied, "And just what does this foregone conclusion entail?"

"A hell of a lot more fun than we're having now," I said with a wolfish grin.

"Well…" she said casually. She took time to finish her drink. She set the glass down on the table next to us and rose slowly, letting me appreciate every curvy inch of her. A few steps had her reaching for the privacy curtain, and she pulled the dark velvety fabric tightly behind her. "I guess we should just shut up then."

THERE WAS A REASON MEN IN PROMINENT POSITIONS IN THE world were always caught cheating. Sure, one could argue it had to do with power corrupting their brain and what-not. But when you became a world-class athlete, a senator, or an actor all the paparazzi kept following, there was one thing that was sure to follow.

Stress.

Over the years, women had found endless ways to deal with stress. Yoga, bath salts, and God knew what else.

Men on the other hand? We'd pretty much come up with only one surefire way of dealing with high amounts of stress.

Sex.

Sure, there might be a few granola dickwads out there, saying running or bicycling was the ultimate stress reliever. But, for most of us, a hot and ready female would always win over a 5K any day.

After my little rendezvous with Morgan behind the curtain and multiple shots of whiskey, I felt like a ten-pound weight had been lifted off my shoulders. Like any red-blooded male, I'd kept my stress from going postal with self-maintenance sessions in the shower, but there was nothing like a little one-on-one action with an attentive female.

But I wanted more—as in, more than one—and Morgan was only more than happy to oblige my request. Feeling greedy and cocky on my one night off from business ownership, we left our little sanctuary and headed out to the dance floor. I wasted no time in scoping out the sea of bodies, searching for just the right woman.

I could see Morgan doing the same. Anticipation was evident in her eyes.

Damn, I'd truly outdone myself with her. If I had the time, I might actually keep her around for a bit of fun and extended stress relief.

Hell, I might still. It had been a while since I'd had a reliable fuck buddy.

We were several songs in, the bass thumping through my chest, as I continued my search. There was no lack of gorgeous women in the club—the bouncers made sure of that—but I just wasn't feeling it. I wanted something specific.

What? I didn't know. But I'd know the minute I saw it.

The rhythm suddenly changed as the DJ shifted gears. The crowd went wild, recognizing the popular song that had been playing over the radio for weeks. Morgan moved closer to me, and I grabbed her waist, loving the way her body felt against mine. As her hips moved against me and the music beat on, I was drunk.

Drunk on the power I had. Drunk with the pleasure I felt and the pain I constantly carried. It was all the same in the moment.

My eyes shut for a brief moment, and I let my head fall back, the world tilting slightly.

How much had I drank?

The moment my lids lifted and settled on the dance floor, I saw *her*.

With beautiful brown hair that effortlessly fell down her back in tousled waves, she patiently waited by the bar for the attention of the Broadway-bound bartender, tapping the tip of her toe against the floor in rhythm to the music. Wearing a sexy emerald-green dress that clung to her figure and glittery gold heels, she was flawless.

But none of that entranced me. She was gorgeous, but every single female in here could be described as such. What made her stand out was that she was trying to be invisible in a crowd that was desperate for attention.

Still dancing with Morgan, I watched as the nameless beauty kept her head low, tucking a loose strand of hair behind her ear. She appeared nervous or maybe anxious as she balanced on one heel and then shifted to the other, like she was late.

Or bored.

The whole scene had me completely transfixed.

"I think I'm going to go try my luck at the bar," I announced loudly in Morgan's ear, hoping to be heard over the music.

"Are you sure you don't want my help?" she asked, a mischievous grin forming around her lips.

I shook my head. "I think my luck is about to change. Meet me behind the curtain?"

Her grin widened as she agreed to my plan.

As I took my time moving toward the bar, my eyes enjoyed every raw inch of her as I drew closer—the curve of her hips, the way her dress accentuated every curve. I was nearly vibrating with anticipation.

"You know, I've heard, if you flirt a little with him," I started off, pointing in the direction of the idiotic bartender, who was currently throwing a wide-eyed grin at a group of college girls, "he'll be yours for the night."

Her back was still turned to me, but I saw a shake of her head.

"I'm good!" she hollered back, barely making the effort to turn her head.

I caught the side of her face. Tiny freckles dotted her flushed cheek giving her an innocence I hadn't quite expected.

"I kind of enjoy the entertainment," she said.

Feeling emboldened by the whiskey swishing around in my belly, I took an eager step forward. "Well, if it's entertainment you're looking for, then please, look no further. I've got an empty couch in the VIP lounge, an endless wallet for drinks, and… hell, I'll give you the party of a lifetime."

Her hand met the tender flesh of my cheek so fast that I was seeing stars before I knew what had hit me.

"Does that crap actually work on women in this city?" she roared. "Because, if so, I feel sorry for my gender for falling for stupid, boneheaded idiots like—oh, shit!"

Her rant was cut short as I straightened myself—or tried to, removing my hand from my jaw long enough to even out my shirt and grab the corner of the bar for balance. The endless shots of whiskey were starting to make their way back to the surface and the room started to spin. The moment she saw my face, she went as white as a sheet and bolted for the crowd.

And that was the moment I chose to black out.

CHAPTER FOUR

CARA

"I still can't believe you decked your boss!" Tyler laughed into his cup of coffee, feeling rather chipper, despite our late evening.

"For the tenth time," I said, shaking my head, as I rummaged around the kitchen, looking for something remotely edible, "I did not deck him. I slapped him. Hard."

His laughter increased, so much so that I swore I heard the old Bulgarian woman next door curse in her native tongue as she shuffled around her apartment. Another great thing about New York was, you could make what would be considered a ton of money anywhere else in the world and still end up living in a crappy hole-in-the-wall apartment with paper for walls.

I was in a foul mood.

A crappy hate-the-world type of mood. It was a rarity for me.

After coming home from what was one of the oddest days of my life, I'd just wanted to kick off my heels and dive into a pint of Ben & Jerry's, but Tyler and the guys from his work had had other plans. One of their clients had been in town, and apparently, that'd meant an evening out. He said he did that a lot.

In Nebraska, accountants were boring and mundane people, but then again, so were most of us. They crunched numbers and worked in small offices. Client meetings were held between business hours, and the only time they wouldn't make it home for dinner was during tax season.

When I'd imagined my life with Tyler, I guessed I hadn't fully prepared myself for the glamorous life he'd set himself up with. I was willing to make a go of it, but right now, this country girl was exhausted.

And possibly fired.

My nerves were already rattled from just thinking of it. As I rifled through the kitchen, I started to wonder if food was really such a good idea.

Better not.

"I'm going to head into work," I announced with as much confidence as I could muster.

Placing his hands on my shoulders, Tyler leveled his dark brown eyes with mine. "Okay." He smiled. "Good luck, and remember, he hit on you. You're not in the wrong."

Only able to nod as my stomach turned at the mere memory of my hand colliding with my boss's face, I headed for the door.

"Babe, your purse," Tyler called out.

I turned to see him holding it out in front of himself.

He was no doubt used to this party-and-work atmosphere. Waking up this morning after only two drinks, I'd felt like I'd been run over by a garbage truck. My eyes felt gritty, my face looked puffy, and my legs had protested every step between our bed and the shower, like I was taking my last.

I'd done my share of late-night study sessions in college, and yes, I'd even had a few all-nighters when I had finals, but that was then.

This was now.

"Thanks," I said quickly.

He grabbed my arm, halting my steps. My eyes turned to meet his. I could sense his concern in his gentle expression and warm gaze.

"I'm sorry," I finally confessed. "I'm grouchy and taking it out on you. It's completely unfair."

"It's okay."

"No, it's not," I replied, sinking into his embrace. "I'm just experiencing a bit of growing pains, I guess—in the metaphorical sense, at least."

"I know, and I'm sorry I dragged you out after your first day at a new job. That wasn't the best idea. I just wanted to show you off," he apologized as his hands ran up and down my spine.

"At least you bought me a pretty dress and shoes," I said, remembering how frustrated I'd been when he announced our plans for the evening and then brought out the wrapped box. It was an incredibly sweet gesture, and I'd probably thanked him a dozen times since then even if the shoes had given me blisters the size of Gobstoppers.

"I did," he said, pulling back just enough so that I could see the dimple forming in his cheek. "Just remember that on your way to work," he suggested.

"You had to mention work, didn't you?"

He turned me around to face the door. The sound of the TV next door now blaring through the walls, we walked arm in arm to the front of the apartment. With my hand on the door handle, I turned.

"Good luck, babe," he said, fixing the strap of my purse so that it lay flat on my shoulder. "And, hey, there are plenty of other great jobs in the city!"

"Thanks," I said, shaking my head. "Thanks a lot."

I was *so* getting fired.

I TOOK THE LONG WAY TO WORK, GETTING OFF AN ENTIRE subway stop early just so I'd have time to think. What I hadn't anticipated was how much it would hurt to walk that far in heels and how oblivious every other female on the street seemed to be to this revelation.

Also, the blisters. The freaking blisters.

By the time I reached Cavenaugh Investments, my feet were screaming. *Why couldn't Tyler have gone to school on the West Coast where casual attire was the norm and flip-flops were considered fashionable?*

I'd thankfully left early enough and had the blessing of the subway gods to arrive to my second day of work on time.

No grim looks from the evil woman at the front desk.

Finding my way to the glass elevator, I entered the code I remembered from yesterday and made my way up to the top floor.

I was nearly shaking by the time the elevator dinged, and the doors pushed back. I looked around, like a convict on the loose. I didn't know where I expected to find *him*. Maybe lurking in that dodgy plant in the corner? Or maybe underneath my desk?

I was perhaps a bit paranoid.

He was the owner of a mammoth company. I was sure he had better things to do than stalk his soon-to-be former assistant.

Oh God, when will this be over?

This was worse than the time my dog, Casper, had shown up in my living room during one of my first dates with Tyler, proudly dropping a used pad he'd managed to dig out of the bathroom trash.

I'd thought for sure my life was over in that moment.

But, nope, I'd managed to live on... until this very moment.

Awesome.

I tiptoed my way to the small desk just outside Mr. Cavenaugh's office. I tried peeking under the door to check for signs of life. If there were any, I couldn't tell.

So, for now, I waited.

It was well past lunch before I heard any noises coming from the opposite side of the door. Since I hadn't planned on staying beyond morning coffee, my belly was rumbling something fierce, and I was hopped up on so much caffeine that I thought I might catapult into space the second I heard the crashing noise coming from the large office next to me.

Had I slept through his arrival? Or had he come in so early that I'd missed it?

Either way, Mr. Cavenaugh was here, which meant our inevitable encounter was forthcoming.

I just hoped it happened sooner rather than later. At this point, with no breakfast and only liquid fuel to keep me going, even the desk furniture was starting to look appetizing.

Forty-five minutes and five games of Solitaire later, he finally emerged. I'd been on pins and needles since hearing the first inkling of him moving about his office, and the second the door handle began to turn, I jumped.

Feeling my face flush almost automatically, I closed the tabs on my computer, realizing the action was fruitless in my current predicament. Dressed in a similar dark suit with matching tie, his appearance seemed to match more closely to the gruff, short tempered man I'd briefly met yesterday afternoon.

The smell that followed him though?

Definitely the other guy.

The one I'd slapped right across the face a split second before realizing he was my boss. My very attractive, scary boss.

Crap.

The cool, collected demeanor he'd had in spades was gone, and instead, I found myself completely befuddled as I watched him stagger out of his office, tripping over his own feet, as if taking a single step was a monumental event.

If I'd had as much alcohol as he had, it probably would be.

Why hadn't he taken a sick day, like a normal person?

And was he ever going to notice me sitting here?

As I was finally gathering the courage to speak up, the words forming in my mouth, he turned. Our eyes met, and I saw it.

The exact second he recognized me.

First, his gaze tightened, and a bit of annoyance seemed to sweep across his features as he remembered Bethany's departure. Then, like a two-by-four had smacked him across the back of his head, his expression lit up like a Christmas tree, and that was when everything hit the fan.

"Motherfucker!" he cursed as his hand flew up to his face, grazing the skin where my palm had hit him.

What do you say to the guy you slapped across the face the night before, who also happened to be your boss of the past twenty-four hours?

Was there a guidebook for this sort of thing? Maybe an introductory course I could take because this kind of stuff just didn't happen in the Midwest. Cheating, backstabbing or a good old teenage pregnancy? Sure, it wasn't a nunnery by any means, but it usually never went any further than a bar brawl and a few bruised egos.

I inwardly snorted.

I guessed I'd had my first bar brawl.

My dad would be so proud.

I looked up to find Mr. Cavenaugh still staring at me, as if he was trying to figure out why I was sitting here.

"Listen… things got out of hand last night," I explained, surprised I'd managed to speak actual words.

Now, I was the one who was proud.

"You're here…" he said, looking at me with big, wide eyes.

"Yes," I managed to say, the brave face I'd had just a moment earlier dwindling under his speculative stare.

Should I not have come in at all? Was my pink slip a foregone conclusion the second my hand had come into contact with his face?

Oh my gosh… had he hit on me, knowing who I was?

Did he sleep with all of his employees?

"Why are you here? How did you find me?"

Before my rambling thoughts got away with me and tears began to form in my eyes, I stopped, realizing what he'd just asked.

How did I find him?

He still didn't recognize me!

"I work here!" I said with force, the fire and spunk finding its way back into my voice because I was now angry. Angry he only recognized the version of me in mile-high shoes and a short dress. Angry because I'd sat here for nearly two days, waiting for some sort of direction and help, and all I'd gotten for it was a cheesy pick-up line and a few hours of Solitaire.

Pieces of the puzzle must have finally started to settle into place as he sat back into a chair at the foot of my desk, the smell of alcohol and cheap perfume following him.

"You're my secretary," he said finally as he slumped back, his hands cupping his face, as if the weight of the world rested there.

"It's 2016. We prefer the term *assistant* now," I responded flatly.

"Jesus," was all he said.

He sat there for what seemed like an eternity, but in reality, it was most likely three minutes. I listened to the wall clock above me tick by and silently wondered if he'd fallen asleep in the plush dark leather chair, but just as I was about to begin another round of Solitaire, he rose, wobbling slightly.

"I have a meeting on Wall Street. I won't be back for the rest of the day," he announced, looking slightly green around the edges.

"Okay," I said, waiting for further instructions, wondering when that final gauntlet would be thrown down.

He disappeared into his office for a brief second and reappeared, carrying a laptop bag and jacket. As he barreled past me, I rose, chasing after him. He had quite the stamina for someone who looked like he was going to be sick at any given moment.

"Sir?" I hollered as he pressed the button for the elevator.

He turned, surprise written all over his face, as he waited for me to continue.

"Am I fired?" I asked.

"No!" he said rather loudly. "Why would you think that?"

"Well, given the events that transpired…" I stumbled out an explanation before he stopped me.

Mr. Cavenaugh took a step toward me. The depth and heat of his stare nearly had me retreating.

"Never happened," he said firmly.

Before I could get out another word, perhaps an apology or more groveling, he repeated himself, this time a bit firmer, "It. Never. Happened. Understood?"

The warmth of his body, so close to mine made me weak in the knees. I could almost reach out and touch him.

Bad idea… bad idea.

"Yes, sir," I answered, almost choking on each word.

"Good." He turned toward the doors, effectively ending our conversation, as if I'd been erased from his memory once again.

"Oh, Mr. Cavenaugh?" I called out on my way back to my desk, my legs still shaking.

"Yes?" he answered, his eyes meeting mine, a bit of surprise hidden in those glittery green irises.

"You might want to take a shower before that meeting of yours. You smell like a hooker."

CHAPTER FIVE

ROMAN

It was well past dark by the time I made it home.

After leaving the office in a haze of regret and disillusionment with an extreme hangover, I'd found myself being driven around the city in a loop as I silently watched the meter of a beat-up taxicab while it moved in and out of traffic with ease. City monuments and endless tourists had passed by in a blur. Families had been walking, hand in hand, and businessmen and women had trekked with sheer purpose and determination down the congested walkways, determined to get to their next meeting or lunch date. Their tight young faces had held fire and determination; they were the kings of their domain—or they were damn ready to be.

I knew that feeling well. It was one I carried with me nearly every day of the week.

But not today.

Today, I felt weak, insecure, and damn stupid.

I hadn't had a meeting on Wall Street this afternoon. I'd

made that lie up in a desperate attempt to flee the building when the walls began to close in around me.

It was that or lose my nonexistent lunch all over the floor.

I'd hit on my assistant. A damn employee.

What a fucking nightmare.

Would she file a sexual harassment claim against me? Could she? It wasn't at work, so did that count? Damn it all to hell, I should probably know these things.

Jude would.

I'd let that dark thought ping-pong back and forth in my mind as the city crept by my taxi window.

Jude seemed to have an answer for everything. When Dad had gotten sick and was scared of the company tanking, whom had he reached out for? Jude. It hadn't mattered that Jude had basically disavowed us and the family name when his fiancée died in a car accident, choosing to live in California rather than where he belonged. No, when things got rough, Jude was always the man everyone trusted.

It was for that reason alone that I would not call my brother. Despite what many might think, I didn't hate the guy. I might roll my eyes at his outdated beliefs on love and the gag-worthy family he'd created, but he was my blood, and as much as it pained me to admit it, I respected him.

No, I would figure this out by myself.

I just needed a plan—and a fucking shower.

AFTER SEVERAL GLASSES OF WHISKEY AND A FEW LAPS AROUND my apartment, I was still drawing a complete blank.

"What a complete clusterfuck," I sighed under my

breath, ending my mini marathon around the sofas as I sank into one instead. My head fell against the soft cushion behind me as I let the dull buzz of the alcohol work its way through my tired bones.

I'd worked major multi-corporation deals. I had sat at the head of conference tables, arguing over hundreds of millions of dollars, and never once had I broken into a sweat.

But this?

This incident with a temporary employee had caused me to flee the office, like a scared little girl running from the bogeyman.

I needed to get my shit together.

And fast.

I just had to approach this like any other problem in my life—with rational thought and little emotion. It was emotions, after all, that had gotten me into this mess.

Sitting up straight, I took another large sip from my glass, nearly emptying it.

I could involve HR and contact them before the girl did.

But what if she didn't? Then, I'd just be compromising myself for no good reason. Best if I just stayed quiet. If it ever did come up, I'd just feign innocence. She'd be gone in a few months anyway.

I could ignore her for that long.

"Okay, problem one solved. Moving on," I said out loud to no one. I thought back to the days leading up to the night before... the endless nights, the forgotten meals. "Too much stress leads to irrational decisions," I told myself.

Like going out to a nightclub and getting so incredibly drunk that I couldn't see straight. I wasn't twenty anymore. This type of behavior wasn't exactly cute.

"Cute but dumb."

The words hit me like a brick.

I couldn't reduce the stress, and I couldn't keep working at the pace I had been going without losing my shit now and then. And that obviously wasn't an option, given the disaster I'd left behind at the office.

So stupid…

"Okay, stay focused," I said, rising from my spot on the sofa to resume my leisurely pace around the room. I felt like a caged lion, desperate for fresh air. I needed an outlet, a way to let go of this pent-up stress that was constantly coiling around in my gut, messing with my head and keeping me up at night.

"Jesus, I'm an idiot."

I just needed sex. It was what I had gone out seeking in the first place last night. That feeling I'd had mere moments after my encounter with the sexy redhead was exactly what I needed.

Everything else, I could do without.

There had been a time in my life when I could balance work and sex in my life, like a beautifully choreographed dance. Too much work? Add a little more sex. Too much sex? Okay, that really never happened.

When Jude had left, the balance had tipped.

I'd never been on my own before. In the past, there had always been Jude or my father—someone to fall back on. But, now, it was just me. Sure, Jude was there in the background, ready to bail me out if needed. But he had a family, and I couldn't be that guy anymore. The slacker. The wanderer.

So, I'd stepped up, and suddenly, that scale—that perfect scale—had gone to shit.

And so had I.

I needed to find harmony again.

It sounded shallow, but I was a guy after all. And a Cavenaugh.

Pulling my phone out of my pocket, I began skimming through my contacts, looking for one specific number.

"Found it."

I could feel the stress already falling to the floor as I hit Send.

"I'M SURPRISED YOU CALLED," JO SAID, HER BODY STILL stretched out across mine. "It's been a long time."

"Just needed a break," I replied, running my hand down her side.

Her skin felt like silk and smelled like some sort of exotic fruit. It was exactly how I remembered her. She hadn't changed since the last time we'd been together, and honestly, I had known this when I called.

It was one of the reasons I never let go of her number.

She was constant while the rest of us were on the go, ever changing.

Jo pushed up onto her knees, lifting one over me, until she was straddling me around the waist. As she bent down, covering my bare chest with tiny kisses, I watched her long blonde strands as they brushed along my torso. Her hair was naturally blonde, nothing fake about those honey color strands that tickled my chest.

When I saw her for the first time on stage, a short black wig covered all that blonde hair. It wasn't until I'd paid for a more private show that I'd discovered it was all a ruse.

During the day, Jo was a single mom, supporting a little boy in a city of millions. Sometimes, I wondered how she did it. Sometimes, I wished I could be the man who swept her off her feet and took care of her and that little boy.

But I wasn't.

I couldn't.

Because both of us were too selfish, too real. We knew things like that just didn't happen in a city like this.

At least, not for people like us.

So, I would give her this, and she'd give it back in return.

A few stolen moments, a brief period of closeness, before the world caught up to us again.

It was enough.

Slowly, Jo made her way up my chest, quickly giving a soft bite to my nipple, before moving up to my chin. Just as our lips touched, a phone began to vibrate on the nightstand.

"Shit, I'm sorry," she said, rolling off me as she reached for her phone. "I set an alarm, so I wouldn't be late to pick up Ben."

Nodding, I sat up, watching her scramble around the room. With swift efficiency, she threw on her clothes and finger-combed back her hair into a knot at the base of her skull.

"Call me again? Maybe sooner this time? I figured when I stopped charging for these little visits, my phone would be ringing off the hook," she said with a small smirk.

"Yes," I agreed.

No good-bye kisses, no promises of plans. That was how we did this, and it was exactly what I needed.

Now that I had a clear head, I knew exactly how to handle my new assistant.

CHAPTER SIX

CARA

I'd been a resident of New York City for two weeks, or thereabout so far, and I'd failed at just about everything the city had offered me. I could barely walk a block in heels, and I hated the subway. And, on a Thursday night, when the rest of the city, including my live-in boyfriend, were out enjoying a night on the town, I was drowning in a pint of Ben & Jerry's.

Karamel Sutra—my favorite.

When I marched up to the counter of the convenience store, holding the precious pint of ice cream and a cheap bottle of wine, the elderly man at the counter had given me one of those looks—the kind that tried to convey empathy but had judgment written all over it.

Can't a girl just have a bad day?

I'd made my way back to our apartment, too moody and upset to even notice the old wrought iron fences that lined our street. I usually loved to run my hand along them, wondering who else had done the exact same thing over the years.

That was why I loved history—the connection it brought to the generations that followed.

It was comforting, knowing those that came before us had struggled, laughed, and loved in much the same way we did even now. Maybe there had even been a young woman who lived in this very apartment many years ago, dealing with a bad day of her very own.

And what a bad day it had been.

The nervousness that I was going to be fired had nearly eaten away at me, when Mr. Cavenaugh had finally made an appearance. I'd planned on standing proud and explaining exactly why I deserved to stay. Instead, I'd stood there, like a trembling idiot, focusing more on his to-die-for looks than his inappropriate behavior. I was a mockery to feminism everywhere.

But, by some miracle, the asshole hadn't fired me, and tomorrow, I'd return to work for another day.

Joy.

"It wasn't a miracle," Tyler had said when I returned home, still gainfully employed. "He screwed up, babe. He hit on you in a public place. If he fired you now, he'd basically be admitting fault. Keeping you employed is the only option he has. Right now, he's probably praying to every god there is that you don't file charges against him… which, you could, by the way."

I'd thought long and hard about that tiny fact.

I'd only known Roman Cavenaugh for a total of twenty-four hours. In that time, he'd been gruff and remote in the office and anything but outside of it. Based on his reaction today—the almost frantic look in his eyes as he'd rushed toward the elevator—I just couldn't see him as the type of man who slept around with his employees. Or tried to. Calling him out on his indiscretion would end him and bring me into a bright spotlight.

I didn't want that.

But how would I go on working for this man?

Letting out a long sigh, I scooped up a large spoonful of ice cream and slowly sucked it off the spoon, letting the caramel and cream hit my taste buds in tandem.

What had people done before ice cream? Take my phone or iPad away any day. But ice cream? That was something I wasn't sure I could live without.

As if it heard my thoughts, my iPhone began vibrating on the coffee table, disturbing the Zen-like calm I'd created for my party of one.

Picking it up, I smiled immediately when I saw the caller ID. *Did parents have a built-in radar that detected when their children were in distress? Was that installed during delivery?* If not, my mother was just naturally gifted because she seemed to be able to sense my mood, even from a thousand miles away.

"Hi, Mom," I said after stuffing another bite of ice cream in my mouth.

"Did I catch you in the middle of supper? I always forget about the time difference. Isn't it kind of late there?"

I looked at the clock on the cable box and shook my head. "It's eight o'clock, Mom."

"Well, I know. I just meant that it's a little late for supper."

I could hear the concern in her voice.

"I'm fine. It just took me a while to get home after work, and Tyler had dinner with a client."

"You didn't go?"

More concern.

"No," I answered, trying to sound light and happy. "I went with him yesterday, and I am still a bit tired from being out late, so I thought I'd stay in. His job really is exhausting."

"And how is your job? First day go all right?"

I let out a small sigh as I pictured her sitting in the kitchen of our old house. She'd no doubt be fiddling with the long cord, winding it around her fingers, as she spoke and listened. I'd tried to talk them into getting a cordless phone over the years, especially around the age of twelve when the phone had become increasingly important to my social life, but they'd never budged.

The wall phone worked perfectly well, so why buy a new one?

But I knew that was a little white lie of theirs. They'd liked seeing me on the floor of the hallway or curled up on the chair of the kitchen table, talking to my friends, rather than hiding in my bedroom. It'd kept them close to me during my teen years, and I guessed, in return, I'd stayed close to them.

"It went as good as could be expected. I think I might be a little in over my head."

"Why do you say that?" she asked.

As I closed my eyes, I could picture her dark eyebrows furrowing together. She'd never been overly pleased with my decision to move to the East Coast. It wasn't that she didn't want me to grow or explore other parts of the world; she did. It was the idea that I had moved here solely for Tyler, she'd argued.

I'd tried to sell her on New York and its many advantages, and sure, she and my father understood a large city had a lot to offer someone my age, but they'd never quite given their blessing.

"My boss," I began, trying to find just how to explain Mr. Cavenaugh, "he's"—*intense, insanely hot, kind of an asshole*—"difficult."

There was a pregnant pause as I waited for my mother to gather her thoughts. I knew what she was doing—

trying to decide the proper course to take and exactly what should be said to comfort her distraught daughter. I'd experienced this particular bit of silence many times before.

"Well, I did look him up on the computer."

Not the Internet. Information was always gathered on "the computer," according to my parents. And it was painstakingly gathered over a dial-up Internet connection and a computer that probably predated the dinosaurs. Our neighbors had had DSL when I was in high school. Me? AOL dial-up. It was maddening.

"Oh?"

"He's…" she spoke slowly.

I smiled, just thinking of my mother using Google.

"Well, he's quite handsome."

"Mom!"

"Oh, sweetheart, as if you didn't notice," she nearly scolded me. "You'd have to be blind not to notice that man, and even then, I think he'd still be able to charm the panties right off a woman."

Shaking my head, I didn't even know where to begin.

"He's kind of mean," I retorted before licking a glob of caramel off my finger.

"Maybe he just needs a little help."

"From the looks of it, he had the best assistant anyone could ever ask for. And, now, he has me, an overpaid work-study student," I huffed, sinking further into the sofa.

"You are not a student anymore," she reminded me. "And you have to stop thinking like one. You told Daddy and me that you wanted new experiences. You wanted to move to that great big city to discover the world and become an adult. Well, get out there and do it."

"But—"

"Not buts, Cara. So, your boss is mean. Figure out why. Maybe he's really just plain mean, but you'll never know if you don't figure it out."

"You're telling me to research my boss?" I asked, a little more interested. I liked research. I liked research a lot.

Get to know him? Roman Cavenaugh?

That didn't sound exciting. That sounded downright terrifying.

THE NEXT DAY, I DECIDED TO SHOW UP TO WORK BRIGHT AND early.

I'd awoken before the alarm, causing my slightly hungover boyfriend to curse obscenities, as I raced to the shower. Tyler hadn't gotten home until late, like wee-hours-of-the-morning late. It had been like this since I'd arrived.

Constant late nights. Constant clients to impress.

I knew it was a process, a race to the top, but I honestly worried about him. How long could he carry on this routine before he burned out?

Before we burned out.

I didn't want to think about that.

He had still been in bed, willing himself to get up, when I gave him a quick kiss good-bye.

I'd like to say, in the last several days, I'd figured out the subway system in the city, but sadly, I still looked like a disheveled tourist trying to make my way from one end to the other of the city. Everyone else seemed to meander about without even looking up, texting and talking on their phones or reading a newspaper, dodging and weaving, to their destination.

I, however, remained standing in place—looking at the

map, pointing with my finger at signs overhead, and talking to myself like a nutjob—as I tried to remember exactly what train I was supposed to catch.

After nearly taking out a stroller and toppling over an old man as I exited the train, I headed to work with little to no trauma, and I'd even managed to stop on the way and grab breakfast.

And I had done it all without being late.

I seriously wanted to pat myself on the back, but I settled for a mental high five instead.

Unfortunately, I wasn't the only one trying to beat the sunrise. Thanks to thin walls, I surmised that my diligent boss had arrived sometime before me and had already locked himself in his office for the foreseeable future.

So much for some friendly chatter and a helpful hand. How the heck was I supposed to get to know the guy if I never actually saw him?

I'd tried the Internet already. Maybe I needed to try my hand at being social for a change. I used to be good at that —talking to people, being a part of the human race.

That was, until I'd moved here.

"Just give yourself time," I chanted quietly to myself.

"What?" a female voice that was definitely not my own answered back.

Looking up, I found myself face-to-face with a beautiful blonde. She had bright brown eyes and cheekbones that rivaled top runway models.

Hell, with that height and minuscule waist, maybe she was a model.

"Sorry," I answered, "I was talking to myself. It gets a bit lonely around here." I immediately felt dumb.

"Just a few days on the job, and he's already driving you mad, huh?" She grinned, displaying perfectly straight teeth that would make any dentist proud.

"What? Oh no. It's not him. I mean," I continued to stammer over my words as she gazed down at me, "I talk to myself all the time."

Lame.

So lame.

"I mean, not all the time. Just occasionally. When I need a little encouragement."

There was a slight pause before I caught the corner of her mouth turning upward.

"I do, too. We all need a little extra encouragement while working here, don't we?"

"Um, I guess so."

"I'm Lauren Drake. I'm an exec over in accounting. I've been holed up in a conference room on a project the last few days. Otherwise, I would have come sooner to introduce myself. Bethany and I were good friends, and I promised I'd take care of her replacement for her," she explained.

"Oh," I said with genuine surprise, figuring that was how she'd managed to get into the secret Batcave, unannounced. "Thank you."

"Don't thank me. It's really quite selfish. I take care of you, you take care of him," she said, gesturing to the closed door behind us, "and we all live much happier lives."

"He's really that bad?" I asked, leaning closer, as my voice dropped to a whisper.

Lauren didn't seem to care if she was overheard, but I certainly did.

"Have you had coffee today?" she asked rather than answering my question.

"Yes," I answered, looking down at my half-empty cup from my breakfast run.

She picked it up, swirled around the contents, and

shook her head.

"That isn't nearly enough caffeine to handle what I have to tell you about Roman Cavenaugh. Come on," she said, motioning for me to get up, "let's go take a walk and get you a proper cup of coffee."

Looking around at my desk and back to the closed door, I shrugged.

I guessed if I couldn't get to know my boss in person, the next best option was the company gossip.

My mom would never approve.

"There are two of them?" I said, dumbfounded, as I stood, hunched over Lauren's phone.

We were huddled together in the break room not too far from my desk—a place I hadn't even known existed until today.

"Yep." She nodded slowly, never taking her eyes off the screen. "That is some damn good DNA, let me tell you."

I looked down at the picture she'd pulled up from an article dated back a few years ago when the Cavenaugh brothers had been photographed leaving their father's funeral together. Roman's eyes were steely, almost void of emotion, as if he'd already mentally checked out for the day. The other brother, Jude, looked as if he hadn't slept in days. Dark lines rimmed the outline of his tired gaze as his shoulders slumped forward. He almost appeared too tired to carry on.

Such a vast difference between the two men, yet... I instantly saw the similarities between them. Same larger-than-life presence and identical green eyes that were mesmerizing, even in a photograph.

"Do you know them?" I asked Lauren as I pulled

myself away from the haunting photo, doing busywork by wiping down the counters and freshening up the coffee.

"Well, sort of," she answered, stuffing her slim phone back into her jacket pocket. "I briefly went to high school with Jude before I ended up transferring. He would never have given me the time of day even if I'd stayed. I was horribly shy back then, and he seemed to be anything but."

Although I'd just learned there was another Cavenaugh, I wasn't nearly as interested in the younger version of Roman. I wanted more details on the original.

"And Roman? I mean, Mr. Cavenaugh," I said, almost choking on my casual reference to his first name.

"Oh God, no," she said, almost laughing out her response. "I mean, he's hot, but he's got the personality of a gerbil."

Stirring the cream into my coffee, I turned. "You mean, he's dumb?"

"No, not dumb. Maybe the gerbil reference wasn't right. He walks around here like he's got a giant stick up his ass, and he doesn't seem to give a rat's ass about his employees. Oh! That's better! He's got the personality of a rat!"

"Hmm," was all I could say in response.

I could tell she wasn't thrilled, and she prattled on as we made our way back to my desk.

"You know the West Coast division? They have company picnics, Christmas parties, and even casual Fridays. I even heard Jude invites the employees to his house for dinner on occasion. Can you imagine? We tried to throw a baby shower for Bethany a few weeks ago, and the man yelled at us!"

"He actually yelled?" I asked, trying to picture the

wealthy executive I worked for shouting at a bunch of women.

"Well, he might have raised his voice a little," she amended as she walked toward the front of my desk and watched me take a seat. She still carried on with the conversation with no regard for who might hear.

Including the boss who sat on the opposite side of the wall.

"Well, it was nice getting to know you, Cara," Lauren said after a moment. Her megawatt smile was back in place as she leaned over my desk. "If you're ever up for lunch, I know a ton of great places nearby, and I'm always up for some new boss gossip," she added with a wink.

I laughed nervously, briefly hating myself and my parents for raising one of those kids—the goody-two-shoes type who always had to stand up for the downtrodden… even if he happened to be the boss who'd hit on me while drunk off his ass.

'Cause I could really use a friend in this city, and I was about to blow any chances of having one.

"Actually, I don't think I can do that," I answered softly, barely able to meet her gaze.

"What? Go out to lunch? Sure you can!" she replied with a touch of humor in her singsong voice.

"No—I mean, yes, I can gladly meet you for lunch. I'd be grateful for your friendship. But, the gossip part, I'm afraid I'm just not that type of person."

Her smile fell slightly. "You remember the part about him being a jerk, right?"

I nodded, still trying to match her confidence, but it was damn hard with her hovering over my desk.

"Yes, I do. And I appreciate the warning. But I work for this man even if it's just temporarily. Whatever goes on in this office is confidential. I can't break that trust. It's not how I was raised."

She shifted, straightening to her full height. "Well, if that's what you believe, I offer you my sincerest wishes for finding someone, anyone, in this city who holds that same belief. Soon, you'll discover, this is a much different world you're living in, Cara Hamilton, and when you do, you'll wish you had a friend like me."

And, with that pleasant closing remark, she disappeared through the door she had come through, her slender hips swaying back and forth with haste, as I tried to calm my ragged nerves.

Looking at the door, still firmly shut, I wondered, *What the hell have I gotten myself into?*

CHAPTER SEVEN

ROMAN

Not how I was raised?

Who the hell was this naive woman? And why the hell was I pressed against my door, listening to the petty conversations of my assistant, rather than working?

Because she was distracting—that was why.

I'd never paid much attention to my assistants before now. Bethany had been working for me for a couple of years, and before that, I honestly couldn't remember.

Jude had always been friendly and personal with his assistants, and my father had been courteous enough to give bonuses and extra days off to his assistants.

But, then again, that was them.

And this was me.

If I couldn't get physical with a woman and we weren't making a business deal, what was the point in talking? This would be considered a sexist comment if I didn't also hold the same policy for men—minus the getting physical part.

I just wasn't much of a social person.

Growing up, I'd always been more introverted than anything. I'd sit on the sidelines of my own birthday parties, watching everyone have a better time than me, wondering how long until I could leave.

I'd become a little more social during high school with the introduction of hormones and the realization that I'd actually have to speak to girls to get them to sleep with me. This practice had continued much through my younger twenties until I had been labeled as the wild child of the Cavenaugh clan.

That had made my dear old dad incredibly happy. Rather than reading me the riot act, he'd turned my misconduct into something he could use, and suddenly, I had become the public face for our company.

I'd felt used and swindled.

I hadn't wanted to be the face of anything, and wasting away at galas and charity auctions had felt like a slow descent into hell. But, for my father, I was exactly where I should be.

"Cute but dumb."

But, now, I had all the time in the world to prove him wrong—if I could just concentrate.

Looking out the tiny peephole in my door—my dad's idea, not mine, I watched my new assistant sit at her desk, staring at a cup of coffee. She appeared forlorn and lost.

Join the club, babe.

With one last glance in her direction, I walked away, back to my desk.

A different man would go out there and tell her to hold her chin up or say something to make her feel he was worth the onslaught of what was to come being a devoted assistant to someone like me.

But I wasn't him.

A better man would have told her to not bother and join the rest of the herd. Defending me wasn't worth her time.

But I wasn't that guy either.

And I had shit to do.

SOMETIME IN THE AFTERNOON, AFTER MY EYES HAD STARTED to go cross-eyed from the complex reporting I was in, there was a tiny knock at my office door.

Having never actually had someone knock on my door before, I found myself uttering out loud, "What the actual fuck?"

Isn't this what I have an assistant for? To keep out the unwanted?

How long does bed rest last?

With anger rising near my temples, I stalked toward the unfamiliar sound and pulled back the door in one swift movement. There, on the opposite side, was my new assistant, looking short and timid, as I nearly breathed fire at her.

"Um, hi, Mr. Cavenaugh. Sir. Yes, I, uh," she stammered on.

My fingers gripped the door harder.

"Phone," I responded.

"Sorry?"

"The phone. There's an intercom button on it. Use it," I said, each word clipped and concise.

"Right. See, that's what I wanted to talk to you about. I have a few notes here and there from Bethany, but beyond that… I don't know what to do exactly. I mean, I've been answering the phone, but without your schedule or a general knowledge of your daily routine, I have no idea what to tell clients when they do call, so I've just been taking messages."

Considering she'd barely been able to get a word out a moment earlier, I was almost blown over by the sheer number of syllables she'd managed to string together with hardly a breath in between.

"You've taken messages?" When I looked down at the stack of pink notes in her hand, my stomach went sour.

"Yes, quite a lot actually," she said, holding up the pile.

There had to be thirty at least. Possibly fifty.

"Jesus. Get in here," I said, stepping aside.

Her eyes widened at my request, as if she wasn't sure I'd actually meant it.

"What are you waiting for?" I snapped.

That seemed to stir some action in her. She scooted past me, and I couldn't help but notice the way her dress clung to her curves. It wasn't the same as the tight green number she'd worn out to the club, but now that I took a good, hard look, I'd recognize those hips and ass anywhere. She was doing a decent job of covering them with that horrible-looking sweater dress, but underneath it, I could still picture every luscious inch.

"Sir?"

"Right," I said, shaking my head, as I shut the door.

She had already positioned herself in one of the heavy leather chairs in front of my desk while I had been busy having an inappropriate fantasy about her in my head.

That didn't make me any more of a jackass, did it?

"Okay, let's get a few things straight," I said, taking a seat in front of her.

She nodded enthusiastically. It wasn't in a bobblehead Barbie sort of way, but it was the kind of nod that would let you know someone was tuned in, and focused, on you.

"Right, so I like as little interruptions as possible.

None, if it can be achieved. Think of this as my private sanctuary. I don't hold meetings here. I don't like it when people 'swing by to chat','" I said, holding my fingers up to emphasize the phrase. "And I especially hate knocking."

Her cheeks instantly reddened.

"I'm so sorry," she started gushing.

I held up my hand to stop her.

"Now, you know. Moving on," I continued.

She pressed her lips together in what I assumed was to halt whatever additional apologies might come, but instead, all it resulted in was my eyes darting straight to her pouty pink mouth.

What would those lips would feel like wrapped around—.

"Now, for these messages you took," I said in a desperate attempt to concentrate, reaching out for the messages.

She handed them over, her fingers grazing my own. Her touch was light, fleeting, but it left a warmth on my palm that I couldn't explain.

Thumbing through several, I nearly laughed. "You took a message from a cable company?" I asked, glancing up at her for a brief moment.

I saw embarrassment blossom across her features as she smiled sheepishly.

"I didn't want to miss anything."

There were several more in the pile similar to the cable company, and I immediately dumped them. I would normally yell at someone for this lack of common sense, but it somehow suited her.

The unaffected nature she seemed to possess.

It made me curious how in the world she'd ended up in a place like this... with a man like me.

"Where did you say you worked before this?" I finally

asked after I'd managed to get the pile of pink slips down to a manageable few.

"I didn't, but this is actually my first job out of college. I just graduated from the University of Nebraska in Lincoln, but I worked for the university president for several years," she added at the last moment.

So many things clicked into place in that moment.

The conversation she'd had with the blonde from accounting, the doe-eyed look she constantly wore, and the skills she obviously needed, both in and out of the office.

And wouldn't you love to teach her a few of those? the devil on my shoulder asked me as a vision of her in that tight green dress crept back into my mind.

Looking up at that innocent face, I let out a sigh.

This was going to be a long three months.

"So Mondays, you have a standing appointment with the VP of Finance. And on Fridays, your lunch hour is blacked out, why?" She looked up at me for confirmation. The day had progressed into evening and I was starting to feel my usual restlessness, as if my body knew it wasn't supposed to be here at this hour.

"I usually eat at my desk unless my mother is feeling particularly needy, so I leave it booked," I explained, paying particularly close attention to my feet as they rested on the edge of my desk. I'd placed them there as an attempt to put space between me and this new assistant. It was the only sanity I could find, having been confined with this woman for so long.

When she'd first arrived, I could have sworn she didn't have an ounce of perfume on, but now that I'd been sitting in this room with her for what felt like hours, watching the sun set long ago, it was like I was drowning in her honey-sweet aroma.

Was it her hair or the scent of her skin that was slowly driving me mad? Or was it just the sheer torture of knowing what delectable curves were hidden under that department store knockoff of a dress?

Letting my feet fall to the floor, I stood abruptly and stretched my sore back. My body didn't like a sedentary lifestyle, and my back had been protesting the overuse of my office chair.

"Are you okay?" a timid voice asked.

I looked to my right and saw Cara standing up as well with genuine concern in her eyes.

"Just a stiff back. This damn chair is killing me."

She was so quiet that I barely heard the sound of her moving around the desk until the warmth of her body was within reach.

"May I?" she asked, holding out her hands toward the spot I'd just been rubbing.

With a suspicious gaze, I nodded, wondering just what my naive little assistant was up to.

"I used to play softball in high school and college—just intramural in college though. Mom and Dad didn't believe that mixing a college-level sport and a major was a great idea, so I managed to get my excess energy out with the intramural team instead," she explained as her hands reached out toward my lower back.

I nearly groaned when the heat of her fingers radiated through the thin fabric of my shirt.

Nearly.

I managed to keep some decency, and instead, I focused on her words even if I found the rambling a bit ridiculous.

"Anyway," she continued as she dug deep into the knot that had formed in my back, "my roommate was the opposite—or at least she had wanted to be. She'd planned on going to state on a full ride for volleyball, but she'd busted her knee in her last season in high school."

"Bummer," I grunted.

"Yep, that's what I said. But it all worked out because she ended up majoring in sports medicine, and she fell in love with it. She's in her first year of medical school now, and she wants to be an orthopedic surgeon. Even though she can't play anymore, she'll be able to help those who do. So, long story short," she said, making me wonder just what she considered a long story to be in her mind, but I let it go, "when I'd come home from intramural, all banged up and bruised, she'd work out all my kinks, and after four years, I managed to learn a few things."

"Brilliant," I replied stoically.

"You should really look into getting a new chair, something with—"

"What the hell?"

I turned to see a man standing by the open door to my office, looking at Cara with a heated expression. I tried to think back to when it had been opened and remembered her taking a restroom break about an hour earlier. Since the office had been cleared out, she'd probably left it open in her haste to return.

And, now, we were being interrupted because of it.

I immediately felt the loss of her touch as I watched her step away and greet the unknown man, "Tyler! What are you doing here?"

His eyes held mine for a brief second before meeting hers. "I was worried. It's after eight, and I hadn't heard from you, so I went looking for you. Some janitor said you hadn't left for the day, and he let me up the elevator."

Someone is getting fired.

She closed the gap between them and took his hand. "I'm so sorry. We were just going over some of my duties and responsibilities, and time must have gotten away from me."

"While feeling your boss up? Is that one of your new responsibilities?" he asked, his voice harsh, as his steely gaze drifted back to mine.

"Oh! No. I mean, I was just being helpful. An old trick Melissa showed me when I'd pulled the same muscle after pitching during my freshman year."

"Right," he replied, nodding slowly.

"Forgive my rudeness," Cara interjected, completely oblivious to the obvious tension in the room. "Tyler, this is Mr. Cavenaugh, my boss. Mr. Cavenaugh, this is Tyler Rhodes, my boyfriend."

He held out his hand first, a slight smirk tugging at his lips, and he waited for me to reach for his outstretched hand. He clearly thought he had something to prove to me —perhaps that he was the better man, the front-runner.

Who knows?

But whatever great competition he'd conjured up in his mind, he believed he'd win the instant I succumbed to his handshake.

"Nice to meet you," I said slowly, gripping his hand as tightly as he held mine. If we were animals, I believe this would have been the part of the intro where we marked out territory with piss or some shit.

"You as well," he replied smoothly. "If it's not too much trouble, I'd like to steal back my girlfriend for the remainder of the evening. She looks a little malnourished." He laughed, glancing down at her with a wry grin.

"I'm fine. Really," she insisted, her cheeks flaming red at his bold words.

"Go ahead," I replied, shifting my stance, as my hands went to my pants pockets. "I insist. We'll figure the rest of this out tomorrow."

"Are you sure?" she asked, her eyes roaming mine for some sign of indecision.

"Yes, quite sure. In fact, I have plans of my own. You'd better be on your way, so I won't be late."

"Oh, yes. Of course," she said, picking up the small pile of messages she would have to return the next day and the few notes she'd taken.

I stood there as she walked toward her boyfriend. His hand went around her waist, a possessive gesture, and they walked side by side toward the door.

She suddenly stopped. "Thank you," she said quietly, "for everything."

Not used to the sentiment of being thanked, I didn't know how to respond. Luckily, I didn't have to. She turned and vanished into the darkened waiting area before I'd had the time to form a single word, and I was left dumb-struck and somewhat disturbed by the feelings swirling in my gut.

Sitting back down in my uncomfortable desk chair, I did the only thing that I knew would bring me back to where I needed to be, back to the man who would get the job done.

Reaching into my pocket, I grabbed my cell phone and punched in the speed-dial number I'd reserved for this very occasion.

"Hello?" the sultry voice on the other end answered.

"Are you working tonight?" I asked.

"No, I'm home," Jo replied.

"Find a babysitter, and be at my place in an hour."

I needed to regain my focus.

It was time to get back on schedule.

"You seem distant," Jo said as we settled back into the sheets, our bodies still slick with the sweat of passion.

"What do you mean?" I asked casually, barely paying attention, as my eyelids began to drift close.

"Well, you're always a little distant. *Removed*, I guess would be a better term."

That got my attention a little, and suddenly, I found myself wide-awake.

Turning toward her, I rested on my elbow. "Are you saying, you didn't have a good time? Because the three orgasms I heard say otherwise."

"That's not what I meant," she retorted, playfully slapping me on the arm.

I fell back on the bed, facing the ceiling once more.

"What I'm trying to say is"—she sighed dramatically— "you're always here physically but not mentally—if that makes sense. And I'm never upset by that fact. Actually, I'm glad for it most of the time," she added. "It makes what we do together a hell of a lot easier. God knows, I don't need any strings, but tonight… I don't know. You seemed even less here, like your mind wasn't just shut off but somewhere else entirely."

I nodded silently before answering, "Work is killing me."

She took my response at face value, not bothering to argue its validity. Why bother? She wasn't here for anything more than what we'd just done.

But it did make me wonder.

Because she was right.

As I watched her re-dress, readying herself to leave, I found myself reliving our evening together, and I came to a startling conclusion.

While I'd been mindlessly fucking Jo, I'd been thinking of someone else.

Someone innocent and sweet. Someone gentle and kind.

And someone completely off-limits.

CHAPTER EIGHT

CARA

"So, tell me a little more about your boss," Tyler said as we waited for our food at a little restaurant around the corner from our apartment.

After surprising me at work, he'd suggested we splurge on a night out, just the two of us.

I didn't really consider it splurging when we ate out practically every night of the week, but I didn't tell him that. Nonetheless, it was a sweet gesture.

"There's not much to tell, honestly," I answered, fiddling with the napkin in my lap.

The lighting was low, mostly candles and a few lamps to help out the waiters. Tyler had said it was supposed to be romantic, but I couldn't see a damn thing. Restaurants like this didn't exist in the small towns of Nebraska. The closest thing to romance Tyler and I had while growing up was a trip to the Dairy Queen to share a chocolate malt.

Sitting here, across from that same boy I used to make those trips to the ice cream parlor with, was slightly overwhelming. I felt like I'd gone from zero to sixty in a matter of minutes even though it had actually been a couple weeks now since I'd left the Midwest.

Sadly, I didn't think *Friends* had truly prepared me for life in the Big Apple.

"Oh, come on, you have to know the guy somewhat. I mean, well enough to give him a private massage in his office."

My eyes jerked up in surprise. "Is that what this is all about? You took me out to a fancy dinner, so you could what? Give me the third degree about my boss?"

He deflated instantly, his shoulders slumping, as he let out a sigh. "No. I'm sorry. I didn't mean to upset you. But I won't deny that it bothered me to walk in and see your hands all over him."

My hands tightened around the napkin in my lap.

"First of all," I began, speaking softly in an effort not to be overheard, "my hands were not all over him. And, second, don't you trust me? Even a little? We've been together forever, Tyler, and most of that time has been spent apart. Do you think, after all that separation, I would suddenly decide that now would be a great time to cheat on you?"

"No, of course not. And you're right. I do trust you. It's just… I don't trust guys like him, especially knowing he hit on you in that club," he said, shaking his head.

I leaned closer, the napkin still tight in my hand, as I caught his gaze. "It was an accident. He was drunk and obviously had no idea who I was. He's been nothing but professional since then. I think he's more embarrassed over the ordeal than I am."

"Let's hope so," he grunted as the waiter neared our table, carrying our plates of pasta.

One thing I could not complain about with my cross-country move was the food. My mom was a whiz in the kitchen. She could take just about anything and turn it into a casserole, and so far, in my twenty-two years of life, I hadn't met a casserole I didn't love.

But moving here, I'd suddenly discovered there was life beyond the casserole.

And, tonight, I was eating one of my new favorites—Italian. Like real slap-your-mama-'cause-it's-that-good Italian, cooked by legit Italians. Half of the items on the menus I couldn't pronounce, and the other half, I probably butchered in my attempts.

As my lips bit into those homemade noodles and as I tasted the prosciutto and lemon sauce, I could have sworn I'd died and gone to heaven.

"You okay over there, babe?" Tyler took a sip of wine from across the table.

"Just having a private moment with my pasta. Sorry, you're not invited," I explained with a goofy grin slapped across my face.

"So, we're good?" he asked, reaching out for my hand.

I nodded as the tips of our fingers touched. "Yeah, we're good."

But, as we finished our food in silence, part of me wondered, *Are we?*

OUR FIGHT IN THE RESTAURANT CONTINUED TO REPLAY IN MY mind, over and over, for the rest of the evening. It was the type of thing I'd usually talk over with a friend, but considering I had been in short supply of those lately, I instead lay awake in bed, staring at our popcorn ceiling—a travesty to the 1920s craftsmanship of the building—and replayed the conversation in a loop, like a broken record.

Since when had Tyler become so jealous?

Had he always been like this, and I'd simply forgotten?

My mother had warned me that there might be a period of readjustment for the two of us. Being apart for so long, we had established our own lives, separate from each other.

"Finding your way back to each other will either be a fight or the failure of your relationship," she'd said.

I hadn't really paid much attention to it at the time, thinking it was one of those things old people said, bestowing all their vast knowledge and wisdom to the youth in an attempt to prevent them from making their mistakes of the past. And, like every other young person of my generation, I'd pretty much just rolled my eyes and ignored her. Because to me, in that moment, as I'd packed up my boxes and prepared for my great move to the East Coast, I had felt invincible.

And so was the love that existed between Tyler and me.

But, now, I wasn't so sure.

Maybe the wisdom my mother had tried to offer wasn't too far off base.

———

STILL FEELING OFF THE MORNING AFTER OUR CANDLELIT dinner, I made sure to be the first in the shower, letting the water slide down my body as I contemplated on what to do about my funky mood.

It wasn't like me to be so confused and conflicted.

Once I made a decision, I usually stuck to it.

Tyler was the first boy I'd ever liked. Once we'd started dating, I had known he'd be it for me. I was one of the lucky ones, the precious few who ended up finding their soul mate at a young age and spent the rest of their lives changing and growing together.

Or at least I'd thought I was.

How could one little fight suddenly rock my certainty?

Before I hastily made my way out the door, blaming my rushed routine on wanting to catch an earlier train into work, I kissed Tyler and said I'd make it up to him later.

There was no earlier train.

I'd just lied to my boyfriend.

But I needed some time to myself, and telling him this would have only caused unnecessary worry, which would have perpetuated the fight that had started the night before.

Knowing I had no one in this entire city I could reach out to, I did the only thing I could think of.

I phoned a friend.

Thankfully, my best friend, the sports medicine ex-roommate of mine I'd talked to Roman about, was an early riser.

"This'd better be important," the familiar female voice answered after several rings.

I was walking at a brisk pace down the sidewalk in an effort to keep up with the rest of the morning travelers. Failure to do so, and I was sure to be mowed down and trampled to death.

That was not how I wanted to go.

"That's not very cheery," I replied with a faint grin spreading across my face.

Just hearing her voice had the ache for home I felt in my chest instantly abating.

"Sorry, I'll try to be nicer next time. It's just… I think I'm getting old," she said in almost a hushed tone, like it was some sort of state secret that she wasn't supposed to share.

I snorted slightly. "What do you mean? You're twenty-two freaking years old."

She sighed, "Am I? 'Cause I think med school has aged me about forty years! Why did I think it would be a great idea to do this?"

"Because you're an overachiever," I reminded her. I paused with a group of strangers, all staring at a no-walking light, waiting for it to change.

"Oh, right. That. I've just always been a get-up-and-go type of person, and nothing—not even four finals in a single day—seemed to get me down. But this? This is brutal."

I could hear the fatigue in her voice, even from miles away. Where there had once been bounce and optimism in every word, there was skepticism and doubt. This was the girl who'd aced every class in her major and gotten accepted to some of the top medical schools in the nation. And now, she wasn't sure she could go on.

"Do you love it?" I asked, crossing the street, as the morning sun winked at me from between the few scattered trees.

"What?"

"You said, it's brutal, and you're tired, but you never once said you hated it. So, I'm asking, do you love it—what you're learning and discovering? The idea that, someday, you'll be able to use these skills to help others? Do you love it?" I repeated, waiting for a reply.

"Yes," she confessed. "Every single minute."

"Then, there is no doubt in my mind that you'll succeed. You always knew it would be hard. You've just never faced something this challenging before, and the fact that you want it so bad makes it even more daunting. But you'll get through it, and when you do, I'll be in the first row to cheer you on as you're handed that diploma."

"You should really consider a career in motivational speaking," she said, her spirits sounding a bit lighter.

I could hear her munching on something. Probably granola—her breakfast food of choice.

"Nah," I replied, shaking my head. "Not unless I could give my speeches in a fancy old building or a museum with cool historical artifacts."

"Oh, that reminds me. I meant to call you the other day and ask, how's the job hunt going?"

I took a deep breath, knowing she wouldn't be pleased with the answer.

Melissa was a go-for-your-dreams type of person. That explained why she was busting her ass at the ripe age of twenty-two in medical school while I was…

"Um, good," I responded. "I actually found something. It's not permanent, but it's a job. Nothing fancy, I mean, but it pays. I'm not flipping burgers, so that's a plus because you know how clumsy I am, and the idea of me working with grease and fire—"

"You're stalling," she said, her voice completely flat as she cut through all the bullshit of my blathering.

"Yes, I am, but it's only because I know you won't be happy with what I have to tell you."

She sighed again. "Cara, all I care about is that you're happy, and if I sound disappointed, it's because I know you're selling yourself short. So, spill it. What horrible, awful job have you gotten yourself into?"

I looked up at the heavens, asking for a little help, as the last ray of sunshine disappeared before I descended into the subway station.

"I'm a temporary assistant to a seriously successful businessman here in the city."

Silence.

"Well, that's not as terrible as I envisioned."

"Oh, stop. Yes, it is," I answered, rolling my eyes. I once again checked the map to make sure the route in my head was indeed the correct way. I didn't want to get lost on the subway because I was too busy chatting on the phone.

"I mean, you're right. It's not flipping burgers."

"Stop," I replied.

"Or driving a taxi. You're a terrible driver," she went on.

"I hate you."

"Oh, wait! I have one more! Exotic dancing! Now *that* would be a horrible job for you!"

"Hey, I think I have pretty nice breasts, thank you very much," I said a bit too loudly.

The guy standing next to me as we waited to board the train suddenly looked down at my chest, as if he were verifying my statement.

I was waiting for a thumbs-up or some sign of approval that he agreed, but unfortunately, he just moved ahead onto the train. I followed closely behind with the rest of the herd.

"I wasn't referring to your boobs. Do you not remember last year when you decided it would be a great idea to go clubbing after midterms?"

"Hey, you said I looked hot!" I retorted.

"A hot mess! Your dance moves are like watching a bad '80s movie. You can't look away; it's just too horrifying."

"You're just jealous." I laughed as my hand wrapped around the slim stanchion pole mere seconds before the train took off. The force pushed me forward, and suddenly, I was wrapped around that damn pole, holding on for my dear life.

Melissa was rolling with laughter after I explained the ruckus of noise that had been heard on her end.

And, no, the irony was not lost on me either.

I FINISHED UP MY PHONE CALL WITH MELISSA RIGHT AS I rounded the corner to the Cavenaugh building. Seeing it rise into the Manhattan summer skyline didn't feel nearly as intimidating today.

Spending the evening with my new boss had given me a bit of purpose in this place, and finally, I felt like I might actually belong—even if only for a little while.

Bypassing the judgy receptionist at the front desk, I went directly to the private elevator that led up to the executive wing. Still dressed in my bargain labels and holding my Goodwill purse, I held my head up high as I pressed in the key code and waited as the elevator rose.

Nothing was going to disrupt my happy mood today.

Before Melissa and I had said our good-byes after I'd voiced my concerns over whether I'd made the right choice moving here, Melissa had said, "Don't be like every other Midwestern girl who moves to a big city and loses her sense of self, showing back up here at Christmastime, looking like a trashy version of a runway model. Live your new life the way you want to, not the way everyone expects you to."

She was so right.

I had spent the last few weeks comparing myself to everyone and feeling nothing but inadequate. From my budget haircut to the less-than-stylish clothes I wore, I'd already singled myself out before anyone else had a chance to.

And why? So that I could prove to myself that I wasn't ready to live here? To take this step?

Well, screw that.

I'd second-guessed myself and my entire relationship with Tyler in the blink of an eye, all because my self-confidence had dropped to an all-time low.

Like my mom had said, it was time to grow up.

If Melissa could make it through the grueling hours of med school, barely catching an hour of sleep, then I could handle moving to a new city with a frigid boss.

Without even realizing it, I'd already made waves—well, maybe tiny baby waves—in that department. Getting Roman Cavenaugh to acknowledge my presence yesterday had been a small triumph, and I just knew, if I kept at it, I could make a difference.

I'd go crazy otherwise.

After a quick stop at the break room, I made my way to my desk, ready to start my day. With coffee in hand, I was a force to be reckoned with.

Or at least, I thought I was...until I saw the door to Roman's office firmly in place and a note on my desk.

No interruptions. No exceptions.

So much for waves.

I'D BEEN STARING AT THE DOOR FOR HOURS, DAYS MAYBE.

What had happened between last night and this morning to cause this sudden change? Had I misinterpreted what I thought was the beginning of a happy working relationship between us?

"You know, if you stare at that door much longer, it might burst into flames."

Blinking several times in an attempt to pull myself out

of the trance I'd settled into, I turned to see Lauren seated on the edge of my desk.

How long had she been there, watching me slumped over my desk, like an obedient lapdog waiting for my master to return home?

"Sorry," I responded quickly, straightening, as I faced her. "Must have been daydreaming."

"Hmm… well, I wanted to stop by and offer my apology."

Staring down at my desk, I picked up a paper clip and began to untwist it with my fingers. "An apology?" I clarified.

"Yes, you see, I think you and I got off on the wrong foot yesterday. I've been told that I can come off a bit too strong, and I feel like that might have happened yesterday when you surprised me with your completely genuine response."

Glancing up at her, I refrained from nervously biting my lip. "I won't change my mind, if that's what you're after," I said, referring to her not-so-subtle attempt to siphon gossip from me, regarding our boss.

"I understand that. And, in the name of honesty, I wanted to tell you, I find the integrity you possess quite refreshing… and I hope you never lose it."

That surprised me, so much so that I didn't know how to respond. Yesterday, I had regarded this woman as an enemy, but today, she was kind of shocking me with her humility.

Was it genuine?

I wasn't sure, but I guessed I owed her the benefit of the doubt.

"Thank you," I finally responded with a brief nod.

"You're welcome. Now that we're back on good terms,

can I interest you in that lunch date again?" she asked, arching her brow. "Just lunch and good old-fashioned girl talk. Promise!" Her hands went up in a gesture of concession.

A smile crept across my face. "Well, I could use a little girl talk," I confessed.

"I knew it. You have the look. Let me grab my purse, and I'll meet you downstairs in ten."

"Sounds great," I said, feeling a flutter of excitement already.

Besides nights out with Tyler and his many clients, I hadn't had a single moment of fun since I arrived. The idea of sitting around a table and laughing over a basket of bread and a few cups of coffee sounded like heaven.

Giving one last look toward the door and the man who had locked himself inside, I decided a note wasn't necessary.

He'd crawled back into his hole.

There was no telling when he'd come back out.

If ever.

CHAPTER NINE

ROMAN

Two weeks.

That was how long it'd been since Bethany left.

It'd been fourteen days since *she* took over and my brain officially stopped working.

My productivity level had since reached an all-time low, and even though I'd managed to see Jo a record-breaking number of times over the last few days, I couldn't seem to block out the sound of *her* voice as it bled through the thin wall that separated us.

I'd gone nearly nine months without noticing my previous assistant was even pregnant, and now, I couldn't go an hour without breaking the tip off my pencil every time *she* answered the phone or laughed.

Was she talking to her boyfriend?

Shut up, Roman.

Staring at a spreadsheet that had been sent to me earlier in the day for approval, I was startled by the vibrations of my cell phone as it danced its way across my desk.

Shaking myself out of a trance, I quickly picked it up and inwardly groaned.

I was in no mood for this.

"Hey, Jude," I said, doing my best to cover any lingering fatigue in my voice.

"Hey, haven't heard from you in a while. Thought I'd give you a call and get an update," he said, his words slightly muffled.

I checked the clock, realizing it was sometime around lunch on the West Coast. He had a tendency to eat at his desk unless he was meeting his wife for lunch.

Why did I know this?

Because these were the things Jude liked to share, which was basically everything.

Ever since he'd gotten his life back on track, he suddenly couldn't stop talking about it. Or maybe I just couldn't stand to listen.

"Things are good," I answered vaguely. "Everyone is still employed, and the board hasn't fired me yet, so there's that."

He laughed at my joke, and then silence filled the air.

"And you're okay?" he asked.

"Sure. Why?"

"Well, you never call and when you do talk, it's to Lailah mostly. I know we aren't super close, but I was hoping you'd be able to make a trip out here and see the baby before she wasn't a baby anymore. You know, she took her first steps the other day," he said, a sentimental resonance behind each word.

My finger wove through my hair as I took a deep sigh. "It's been a busy year," I replied.

"I know," he answered. He sounded disappointed. "Lailah and I had a kid. Remember Meara, your niece?"

"Listen, I—" I began, trying to sever the awkward

conversation, but a knock at my office door came before I had the chance.

Surprise with, I'd admit, a bit of anticipation churned in my gut as I yelled out an okay to enter.

"Hold on, Jude," I said.

I placed the phone to my shoulder as I watched Cara enter.

Or tried to.

Hidden behind a large black chair was my tiny assistant. She was pushing it with force, making a grand entrance into the office.

"What the hell?" I uttered as she finally wheeled the thing up to my desk.

"It's a new chair," she said, her face beaming with pride.

"I see that. But why is it in my office?"

"It's yours," she explained simply, the smile never leaving her face.

"But I didn't order it," I replied curtly, looking at her with equal parts intrigue and hostility and maybe a dash of lust.

"You're right. I did," she said, her big brown eyes glowing, as her hands went to her hips. "You were complaining about your back the last time I was in here, and I wanted to be helpful. So, while you were holed up in here over the last week, I did some research on office chairs. Research is kind of my thing—although it's usually historical research. Anyway, I love to hunt for information, so I made it my mission—since you haven't given me anything else to do—to find you a better chair, and here it is!"

I was so dumbfounded by her sunny demeanor that I'd completely forgotten that Jude was waiting for me on my cell phone.

"Wait a second," I said, holding out a finger, as I dragged the phone up to my ear. "You still there?"

"Oh, yeah," he replied, amusement laced in each word. "And do I have some questions for you."

I rolled my eyes.

"I've gotta go."

"I bet you do." He nearly laughed. "Call me back, brother. Otherwise, I'll tell Lailah, and you know what that will mean."

Jesus.

"Fine," I grunted, not wanting a nagging call from my sister-in-law, whom I had a soft spot for.

When it came to me, Lailah tended to overanalyze, scrutinize, and hope for far more than I was ever willing to give.

I quickly hung up, dropping the phone on my desk, before turning my attention back on the petite brunette who'd stumbled into my office just minutes earlier.

She was dressed oddly once again, and her dark chestnut hair was pulled back into a high ponytail, which only highlighted the fact that she was light-years younger than me. The shoes she wore, although technically a high heel, were chunky and scuffed, probably something she must have bought years ago. Even in the frumpy heels, her legs went on for miles.

What a man could do with legs like that.

"Exactly how did you pay for this?" I asked Cara, hoping to redirect the thoughts in my head from the asshole in the room who was checking her out back to the asshole in the room who happened to be her boss.

"That's where I needed a little help," she confessed. "Since no one was around to help me figure out interdepartmental accounts, I went to Lauren Drake. She works in accounting. I think she's a VP or manager or—"

"I know her," I said flatly. "Go on."

"Right," she stuttered slightly, her eyes meeting mine for a quick second before darting away. "She helped me figure out how to charge it to the right account. And the rest is history! It took some time to get here because I had them assemble it rather than have me try. I'm horrible at that stuff. I once tried to put together an IKEA desk in college. It ended up being a botched bookshelf." She laughed.

I just stared. "So, you decided I needed a chair—without asking me. Then, you bought something and charged it to the company—again, without asking. And you expect me to be happy?"

"Well"—her fingers nervously wrung together—"not yet. You haven't even sat in it."

I looked down at the chair with a heavy amount of doubt. I didn't know how one black leather chair could possibly be any different from another, but I found myself agreeing to take it for a test drive.

She jumped with excitement, moving my chair out of the way before putting the new one into position. I would have offered to help, but I was still a bit miffed.

And if I were being completely honest?

I enjoyed watching her sexy little ass as she bent over, checking the height and removing the random sales stickers that still clung to the leather.

Yeah, I knew it; I was going to hell.

"Okay! It's ready!" she announced, holding her hands out, as if she were one of those models on *The Price Is Right*.

I took a hesitant couple of steps forward before turning and lowering into the chair. An involuntary groan escaped my lips as my body melted into the plush leather back.

"See? It's good, right?"

"Fuck, how much was this thing?" I said as my eyes closed in bliss.

My back had been in knots for weeks—a combination of stress and lack of physical movement. My body was used to moving, either from regular workouts or just the hustle and bustle of life. This solitary existence was taking its toll, and I didn't think I'd experienced any real kind of relief until I'd slid into that chair.

"Not much, I promise. Not everything amazing has to cost a fortune," she replied. "It's like being hugged by the Stay Puft Marshmallow Man, huh?"

I lifted one eyelid. "How do you even know who that is? Aren't you, like, twenty?" I asked.

"Twenty-two," she answered, her arms wrapped tightly around her waist. "And I watch movies."

"I used to love that movie. All the ghosts and the green goo everywhere. Totally disgusting," I said, my head resting against the back of the chair. "I don't know why I just told you that."

She smiled. "It's because you're finally relaxing. Maybe now you can get some work done," she said, patting my shoulder.

She walked toward the door, taking my old chair with her.

The door clicked closed moments later, leaving me alone.

The four walls that surrounded me were completely silent.

Peace at last.

But now instead of feeling comfort, I just felt lonely. And cold.

"Who's the girl?" the familiar voice asked as I sank into the sofa.

I'd barely made it into my apartment before my phone started ringing.

"He said he wouldn't say anything," I growled, rubbing my tired eyes.

"There are no secrets in marriage," my sister-in-law scolded.

Even without seeing her, I knew she had a smile painted across that angelic face.

Lailah Cavenaugh was one of the few women to ever break through this grizzly exterior of mine and see something worth rooting for. There was a time I'd thought my brother might have been jealous of the strange relationship that had blossomed between his lovely bride and me, but now, I thought he had come to appreciate it.

Or he just liked the fact that I couldn't drift too far away.

Lailah always made sure of that.

"I'm not sure that's true," I answered, hearing the faint cry of my niece in the background.

"It should be," she responded absently. "At least for the important things."

"And who I happen to be talking to in a private conversation is considered important to your marriage, how?"

"Well, first of all…" she began, her words muffled, as if the phone was pressed against her cheek.

She was the queen of multitasking now that the two of them had a kid, so I could only imagine what she was doing—laundry, yoga… nursing. I inwardly shuddered.

"It wasn't a private conversation," she reminded me. "You had Jude patiently waiting for upwards of five minutes."

"It wasn't that long. God, he's dramatic."

"And, second, you are very important to our marriage, so yes."

I sighed. "I don't think I'll ever understand you and that bleeding heart of yours."

"Hey, my heart is awesome. My cardiologist told me so. And I think you understand perfectly. You're important because you're family, and we love you. I know, in your own weird little way, you love us, too."

I rolled my eyes.

"I can see that eye roll from here, buddy."

"Is there a point to this call? 'Cause I could really use this time for much more important things," I reminded her.

She ignored my icy demeanor, as usual.

"You haven't answered my question."

"And I'm not going to," I replied.

"Why?"

"Because you're not my mother, Lailah!"

"So, if I got your mom on the phone, would you answer?"

I could hear the humor bleeding through each word.

"She's my assistant," I finally answered, caving to what I knew would be an endless barrage of questions ending in the same results.

"Jude said you sounded… different with her."

"Different? What is that supposed to mean?" I asked, replaying what he might have heard while Cara had been in my office. Besides the weird comment about my childhood, which I'd said after hanging up with my nosy brother, I thought I had been fairly professional.

At least on the outside.

Inside, my head had taken a trip to the fucking strip club. And Cara had been my ultimate fantasy come to life.

"He said you were, um… nice-ish to her," she said, phrasing each word with a bit of uncertainty.

"Nice-ish?"

"His word, not mine. But he basically said you weren't as big of a jerk as you normally are. In Roman terms, that means you were actually kind of nice. So, this brings me back to my original question. Who's the girl?"

"I told you! And I can be nice. I'm nice to you."

"Yes, you are," she said fondly. "Now, we just need to work on the rest of the world."

There was a scuffle and a laugh, and suddenly, the sweet voice of my sister-in-law was replaced by the husky deep one of my younger brother.

"Sorry, she was taking forever, and if I had to hear her flirt with you one more time, I might have just lost my dinner."

I chuckled silently.

"Can't help it if your wife recognizes the true stud in the family," I said with ease.

He, as expected, ignored my comment and proceeded to ask, "So, what my wife was trying to say is, who's the chick, and how long have you had a thing for her?"

"Since when do you say words like *chick*?"

"Stalling tactics. Nice. But that shit doesn't work with me."

"Like I said, she's just an assistant."

"Picturing her naked yet?"

"For fuck's sake!"

He laughed. "Just trying to get to the nitty-gritty here. Okay, interesting. It's just that I've never heard you so worked up over another human being before."

"The only reason I'm worked up is because it's eight o'clock here on the East Coast, and I haven't eaten since noon."

"Testy."

"I'm hanging up," I warned him.

"Okay, but call back when you want some advice."

"Never happening," I growled back before hitting End on the phone.

I looked around the room, still dark from me stumbling in the door as I'd answered the phone.

Gazing out the windows, I took in the skyline of Manhattan. The lights flickered like stars from apartment buildings and late-night employees burning the midnight oil in corporate office buildings.

Life went on.

Even three thousand miles away, in a house somewhere on the beach, my brother and his family snuggled in for another blissful night together.

But, here… life stalled.

Here, it was stagnant. A void.

Just like me.

Are you proud of me, Father?

THE NEXT MORNING, RATHER THAN DOING MY USUAL disappearing act, I decided to try something different. If yesterday had taught me anything about Cara, it was that she didn't handle boredom well. If I left her on her own much longer, I'd find myself with an entire office of new things.

And, as much as I was currently enjoying my new chair, I didn't want to explain that one to the board.

Why did you spend such a large amount on an office redesign?

Well, you see, gentlemen… I got this new assistant, and she's got this ass…

Right…

So, in the name of being an effective boss, I took one last sip of the lukewarm coffee I'd grabbed on the way in and summoned Cara.

The look on her face was priceless.

It was like a deer caught in the headlights of a semi-truck. Having never actually used the intercom to speak with her, except a few phone calls that just couldn't wait, I realized I'd probably spooked her.

Looking beyond her face though was a bad decision because the effective boss attitude I'd had vanished in milliseconds as my eyes collided with her body.

Long gone were the shabby sweater dresses and bargain-bin finds she'd been wearing ever since she started. Today, she was sleek and sophisticated in a heather-gray pencil skirt and sapphire-blue blouse. It was unbuttoned just enough that she still looked professional, but it was low enough that I suddenly found myself instinctively leaning forward.

"You asked for me?" she said, her words coming out hushed and hesitant.

I coughed quickly, desperately trying to clear my throat.

"Yes, sorry." *Why was I apologizing?* "I thought it would be a good idea to continue what we started late last week and make you a bit more comfortable with my daily activities… so you aren't stumbling around to keep busy."

A small smile crept up her face. "That would be great. Thank you."

"Why don't you have a seat?" I offered, hating myself for how polite I was being.

She was my employee. A temporary one at that.

I watched her move across the space, her toned calves

flexing as her hips swayed with a femininity and sexual presence she probably didn't even realize she possessed.

I heard my brother's voice in my head.

"Picturing her naked yet?"

I tried to think of the number of employees I'd actually visualized in my bed.

There was the blonde in accounting, who'd tried to seduce me, but I'd dealt with the likes of her before. My dick might have wanted a ride, and I might have done a cursory glance at the goods—I wasn't dead—but that was the end of it.

Nothing more.

Cara though?

She was quickly becoming an obsession I couldn't seem to shake, and sooner or later, I'd have to figure out why.

Only problem?

I wasn't sure I'd like the answer.

"Do you want me to order some lunch?" Cara asked after watching me lean back in my chair, rubbing the sleep from my eyes.

"What?"

"Well, I noticed you never seem to eat when you're here, and I thought it would be nice for you to actually consume food at a decent hour for a change."

"I consume food," I replied. "Occasionally."

"What was the last thing you ate? And when?"

"Does coffee count?" I asked wryly.

"No!" She laughed.

"Fine. Let me think," I began.

"You have to think? That's a bad sign."

"I'm a busy guy. Not all of us live such a leisurely life," I said, grinning.

Jesus, now, I was smiling like a freaking idiot.

"With all that money you have, you should be. What's the point otherwise?"

What was the point indeed?

"Turkey sandwich. Last night around nine o'clock," I finally replied.

"It's one!" she said, shaking her head. "In the afternoon. The day after!"

"I'm aware."

"You're going to waste away."

"Doubtful. But I appreciate the concern. I've made it this far, and I don't think I've wasted away yet." I caught her eyes roam down my body for a split second before she realized what she had been doing.

"From now on, I'm going to make sure you're fed while you are here. Lunch and dinner, if needed. This isn't healthy," she rambled, feverishly taking notes, as her cheeks flamed red.

I contemplated whether to argue, but I knew it would do no good.

She was on a mission now.

At least it wasn't another chair.

I listened as she quickly and efficiently placed meal orders for the two of us. I was acutely aware of the level of professionalism she held, despite her age and lack of experience. She handled herself well, but she was extremely polite and well mannered.

Something I probably lacked.

"Can I ask you something?" she said, drawing my attention away from the monotony on my computer screen.

I looked up to find her eyes dead set on mine. It was unnerving.

She usually tried to avoid direct eye contact with me. Maybe I intimidated her. Perhaps she found me attractive, and the idea of lusting after her boss bothered her.

Believe me, it bothered me, too.

In a very physical way.

"Go ahead," I answered, unwilling to break the intimate connection she'd started.

"When you saw me… at the club that night," she said, her eyes wavering just slightly, "what was it you saw in me? I mean, was it just the clothes?"

My eyebrows furrowed in confusion. Even though I'd said we'd never speak of what had happened that drunken night two weeks ago, I saw something in her eyes that said she needed an answer.

That she needed something more.

"Why are you asking?"

"It's nothing. Sorry. I'm being stupid," she backpedaled as she began fiddling with the hem of her skirt.

Looking back at our few interactions, I noted the difference in how she'd been acting today. Her normal never-ending stream of word vomit was there, but behind it, there was an internal struggle going on. The hemline wasn't the first thing she'd fidgeted with. I'd watched as she pulled at the collar of her shirt, and then, as if she'd realized what she'd done was wrong, she'd quickly laid it flat again.

"Does this have something to do with the way you're dressed today?"

Pink tinged her cheeks. "You noticed?"

I simply nodded, not trusting myself with words in that moment.

Because I'd more than noticed. It'd been damn hard not to think about anything but.

"A gift from my boyfriend," she replied. "He said my old clothes didn't fit in with our new lifestyle. It was a very generous gift," she added, never forgetting that politeness she'd no doubt been taught since birth.

"But?" I questioned, waiting for her to continue.

"But… I don't feel like me anymore," she finally admitted.

"And I'm guessing the night in the club was another gift from him as well?"

It was her turn to nod.

I could see the indecision and worry gnawing at her. Someone like her—sweet, honest and good—was meant for better things than a life with a man who didn't appreciate her.

Leaning forward, I made sure she saw the sincerity burning in my eyes as I spoke, "That night in the club, I'll admit, it may have been the dress I saw first."

She opened her lips to speak, but I held up my hand to stop her, wanting to make my point.

"And, today, when you walked in, I couldn't help but give a second… or third glance at the way that new skirt hugged your ass."

Her eyes widened at my blatant honesty.

"So, yes, the way the clothes clung to your body might have caught my attention for a moment or two. But every moment after that? That's been you, Cara. All you."

And, just like that, I'd crossed the line.

I'd hit on an employee.

And there was no going back from that.

CHAPTER TEN

CARA

"That's been you, Cara. All you."

It's all me.

It's all me...

His words had been replaying in my mind for the last five hours. Like one of those annoying microwave trays my mother always made me clean or a ceiling fan—circling around, on repeat until I thought I might go mad from the repetition.

I couldn't even remember what we'd talked about for the rest of the day or how we'd even managed to make it through lunch. I could have sat there with a giant leaf of spinach wedged in my teeth, rambling on about interoffice nonsense, and I would have never known.

Because my boss had said he was into me.

Or had he?

He hadn't directly said it, but he had mentioned my ass. And I did have the memory of him that night in the club—his voyeuristic eyes roaming my body as drunken words had tumbled out of his mouth in an ill attempt to take me home. I thought his fixation with me had only lasted the few seconds it took for his head to hit the floor, but seeing the way his eyes had darkened as he spoke today had me wondering just what I'd missed over the last couple of weeks.

Melissa had always said I was a little absentminded when it came to the opposite sex. It was why I was always so thankful for Tyler.

Tyler.

He'd be home any minute, and here I was, sitting on the sofa, in the apartment we shared, thinking about my boss.

In a very unprofessional way.

This was not how I pictured myself adjusting to New York life.

Getting up, I began fluffing the pillows. Then, I folded the blankets and stacked the magazines on the coffee table. I spent nearly ten minutes in this mindless cleaning mode before I even realized what I had been doing.

"Mom, what are you doing?" I asked, watching her buzz around the living room, picking up my shoes and backpack mere seconds after I'd dropped them by the couch.

Our house was always well kept. It had that dated '90s look to it—worn oak cabinets, flower wallpaper that peeled at the seams, and weird knickknacks that collected dust but reminded us of all the places we'd visited or would like to someday.

My mom hated dust. Some days it seemed like it was her life mission to get rid of it. I'd always come home to find her in the middle of polishing or dusting one thing or another.

But today was different.

Today, she seemed almost manic, as if the Devil himself were tailing behind her.

"Cleaning, dear. The same thing I do every day," she answered, seeming to find my question comical.

"I see that, but what's the rush? Did you accidentally mistake one of my Adderall for a vitamin again?"

She rolled her eyes, still darting between the kitchen and the living room, rearranging pillows and scrubbing counters like the pastor was about to show up for Sunday night supper.

"No, and that's not funny. You don't take Adderall."

"I know, but I got you to slow down for half a second. Seriously, what is up?"

She shooed me into my bedroom for afternoon homework, claiming she had loads to do, never answering my question for her erratic behavior, but I didn't have to wait long to figure it out.

When my father got home, sparks flew.

And not in the gross parents-kissing kind of way.

In the way that made all children nervous. When words were spoken too loudly and tears were shed. The kind of sparks that could ignite a forest fire of doubt.

I never found out what the fight had been about or how long they had stayed mad at each other. All my young teenage mind had cared about was that everything remained the same, that my status quo held firmly in place.

Looking back, I realized it wasn't the first time I'd come home to find my mother in the midst of that type of behavior. Just the first time I'd realized it for what it was.

Guilt.

Everyone processed it in one way or another. Some would bury it in a bottle, others in food. My mother cleaned.

And I guessed I did, too.

Because, by the time Tyler got home... the apartment was spotless.

"You have nothing to feel guilty about," Melissa said, an obvious attempt to comfort me after I'd called her a second time this week, rambling on about what had happened the day before.

Including the extreme cleaning of my apartment.

"But don't I? Tyler got home, and I said nothing. Nothing, Melissa! That's the telltale sign of a guilty person! This is the part of the movie when I'd be throwing popcorn at the screen, yelling at the stupid heroine to stop being… well, stupid."

"You're not stupid. You're just in shock. And, honestly, I think you made the right choice in not telling Tyler. It would only end badly for you anyway," she said, sounding more chipper today than the last time we'd spoken.

I was hoping she'd taken my advice and stopped feeling sorry for herself.

God knew I could stand to use that same bit of advice myself.

"Why?"

"Well, for starters, you mentioned Tyler wasn't exactly thrilled about meeting your boss in the first place. That things felt a little frigid?"

"Like the Antarctic on a summer day," I replied dryly, remembering the exchange between the two men. Or lack thereof.

"Exactly. He was wary of you going back to work for the man after he'd hit on you in the club. And this would only solidify that. No doubt, he wouldn't be satisfied until he had you pressing charges against the man for sexual harassment in the workplace. And that's fine, if that is indeed how you want to proceed, but from the rambling way you started this conversation and the fact that you're headed to work as we speak, I'm guessing that's a no."

I took a deep breath, looking down at the grimy subway floor, and shook my head. "No. I don't want to press charges or go to HR or do anything else that would showcase him poorly."

Silence followed until she finally spoke up and asked, "Do you have feelings for this guy, Cara?"

"No."

"That was a little too quick. I'm not your mom, asking if you got into the liquor cabinet while I was out of town. I'm your best friend. I can tell when you're purposely replying with the answer you think you're supposed to give just so you can avoid the truth."

"Am not," I answered childishly.

"Are too. And, before you can follow with a rebuttal, another *am not*, let me just say, *are too*, and be done with it. So, can we move on now?"

Feeling the train come to a stop, I gripped the bar next to me and stood, following the rest of the morning commuters out.

"Fine," I replied. "I might be slightly interested," I confessed. "But interested how, I'm not sure. He intrigues me—that I'm sure of. And I would have to be blind not to notice his looks, but it's more than that. And it could just be the simple fact that he's attracted to me, and I find that odd."

"You find the fact that a man is attracted to you… odd?" she said, repeating my words for her amusement.

"Well, yes, actually. I started dating Tyler when we were kids. The fact that he liked me out of all the girls in our school—"

"All the girls?" she questioned.

"Okay, there weren't many, but still, that's not the point. He liked me, and I found that adorable and charming. I wasn't the most popular girl or the prettiest. I was just me. But I guess he was kind of the same, you know. We fit."

"And Mr. Cavenaugh?"

"He's just completely different than me. Worldly, classy, elegant, and I'm the strange girl who shows up with an outdated purse from Goodwill and says *thank you* way too much."

"I still remember when we got that purse. Good day," she said nostalgically.

"Stay on topic," I warned.

"Right. So, here's the deal, Cara. You know I love Tyler. I've only met him a few times, but I've known him for years now. What you two have is special, but that doesn't mean it's forever. I'm not saying you have to cut the cord or anything. But, just know that if your heart starts to lead you somewhere different, don't be afraid to follow."

"But Tyler is why I'm here," I protested.

"No," she argued. "Tyler is what brought you to New York. You are why you've stayed. Make this adventure what you want it to be. Sorry, I have to get to class."

We hung up just as I climbed the final step onto the street. Clouds covered the sky today, making the air feel sticky and humid. Back home, this type of weather would signal thunderstorms and make everyone edgy because with thunderstorms came tornados.

I'd been fortunate never to encounter one close-up, but the fear was always still there even if the Midwest was long behind me. It made my pace quicken and my heart rate rise as the first raindrop hit my nose.

"Make this adventure what you want it to be."

This city would only become home if I chose it to be.

I might finally know my way around a subway and the route to work like the back of my hand, but it didn't provide any comfort as the tiny raindrops fell from the sky. Hell, I didn't even have an umbrella.

Thunder cracked above me, and I flinched, my heels clattering against the paved sidewalk faster and faster, as people pulled out umbrellas from briefcases, purses, and God knows where else.

No one offered assistance as I walked helplessly in the rain, the water pouring down on my bare head, soaking into my top and bra. The click of high heels transformed into a squishy thud.

"Make this adventure what you want it to be."

Melissa's words echoed in my head once again, and I stopped dead.

People trudged past me with their umbrellas and water-wicking jackets, as if I were nothing more than an empty void on the sidewalk. Something to bypass.

No one even looked at me.

Why was I here? Why had I even come?

Some moronic idea of love and a few reruns of *Friends* had had me packing up my entire life. And for what? So, I could be a drowned rat on the side of the street?

Well, screw—

A car suddenly pulled up to the curb in front of me.

People actually noticed that. It was a sleek black sedan. The type I saw executives being chauffeured in all the time. The exact type my own executive used.

"Need a lift?" Roman asked, his dark head peeking out the window, not a drop of water daring to touch it.

All I could do was nod as water fell from my chin and dripped onto my shoes.

I took a few steps toward the car and stopped. "I'm a little wet," I said.

"More than a little, I'd wager." He grinned.

A chauffeur appeared, not seeming to mind the fact that rain was pummeling his perfectly pressed uniform, and he pulled the back door open for me. I didn't think I could remember the last time a car door had been opened for me. Senior prom maybe? And I'd laughed at Tyler's ridiculous notion.

But it wasn't ridiculous now.

And, as I took his hand and let the stranger guide me into the car, like I was a proper lady in my soaked clothes, I didn't feel the slightest twinge to organize or fluff anything.

I just looked into those bewitching green eyes and smiled.

"Salad again, Miss Hamilton?" Roman said, raising an eyebrow in my direction, as I sorted through the food delivery.

When I'd phoned him to inquire about lunch ideas, he'd told me to make sure I included something for myself if I planned on eating at my desk every day.

I nodded, setting his chicken salad on wheat that I'd ordered from a deli onto his desk. He speculatively eyed me before taking the wrapped sandwich and iced tea.

"You don't really strike me as a salad girl," he said before I had the chance to turn around.

Instead, I stood there, awkwardly holding my strawberry and walnut salad in one hand and an empty bag in the other.

"I don't really know what that means," I admitted shyly.

He slowly unwrapped each corner of the wrapped sandwich, like a present. His face was passive, as if he were wisely choosing his next words.

"Your boyfriend, the clothes he bought you… it's not altering the way you feel about yourself, is it?"

I thought back to the night Tyler had come home, arms laden with packages and bags as he tried to fit through the small opening of our apartment.

"What is all this?" I asked, amazed by the sheer volume of material goods he'd acquired since his departure to work just a mere nine hours earlier.

"I bought you an authentic New York wardrobe, Cara!"

"What?" I asked, completely blindsided by his announcement.

"You've seemed so down and out since you arrived, roaming around the apartment and barely leaving unless it's for work or to follow me to a function. We might have been apart these last few years, but I know you—the real you—and I know this move has been harder than you've let on. So, I've been beating myself over the head, trying to come up with a way to help acclimate you to your new home, and when I mentioned it to one of the girls at work, she suggested this!"

"And what is this?" I asked hesitantly.

"Clothes!" He laughed. "I went to Bloomingdale's and gave one of the consultants your sizes. And here I am!"

He was so damn excited. He'd blown half his savings on it. I knew he'd make up the cash in a matter of weeks with the way he was going, but as we sat down and went through the various patterns and textures, I felt nothing but distance growing between us.

Yes, he knew me well enough to know I had been struggling

to find my way. But, rather than talk to me, he'd asked for advice from a virtual stranger.

Did we really know each other at all?

"Cara?" Roman said.

I realized I'd gone quiet for far too long.

"Sorry," I answered quickly. "And, no, I like my new clothes."

He eyed me carefully before offering the seat across from him. It was a place I was beginning to grow rather fond of. It was also a place where I found myself sweating nervously, thinking impure thoughts about the man in front of me, while trying to keep my fingers from fidgeting with anything in sight. But I somehow liked it all the same.

There was something about this man, this boss of mine, that intrigued me. What was hidden behind all those grumpy layers of protection he'd built to keep everyone in the world at a distance? And just how would someone break through?

"How's your salad?" Roman asked, watching me from across the desk. He popped another piece of bread into his mouth.

"Good. Great actually. I'd never really tried fruit on a salad until I moved here. I mean, we have fruit salad back home, but that's an entirely different thing than this," I said, motioning to the fresh pieces of ripe strawberries that dotted my plate.

"And where exactly is that?" he asked. He'd finished his sandwich and leaned back in his chair, holding his glass bottle with both hands.

"Nebraska. I'd tell you the town, but you wouldn't recognize it. It's about as big as a thumbtack. It's one of those towns where everyone knows everyone else, no one locks their doors, and children run around without supervision because nothing bad ever happens."

"That explains a lot," he simply replied.

"What does that mean?" I asked, setting my fork down to catch his mischievous gaze.

"It just means, there's a lot of good in you. Too much sometimes. Hearing you talk about where you grew up, the *Leave It to Beaver* lifestyle—it all makes sense."

"Does it bother you?" I asked, sitting back in the chair.

"No," he instantly replied. "I find it oddly refreshing. But I worry that you'll lose it, living here."

"Why do you say that?"

"I have a sister-in-law. Very much like you in fact," he said, "Good, kind, but very—"

"Naive?" I said, guessing his next word.

"No," he said sharply. "Not the word I would have used at all. I don't see you or Lailah as a fragile bird. But I think others might. *Targeted* is maybe the word I would use. You see, Lailah had an unusual upbringing. Vastly different than yours but with some of the same outcomes. She sees the world through a different set of eyes. She has yet to inherit that jaded view of the world we all seem to get, and something tells me you haven't quite gotten there yourself."

"And?"

"And it makes you rare. As much as I roll my eyes and mock Lailah for her sunshine-and-daisies attitude, it's one of the reasons I love her so much."

"And you think I'm like her? Your sister-in-law?"

"In your own way," he clarified. "No one is quite like Lailah."

"She sounds like someone I'd like to meet one day. But, I've got to ask, why are you telling me this?" I said, enjoying the conversation, especially the fact that he was once again opening up to me but I couldn't understand why he was opening up.

What was the point?

I'd quickly learned that when it came to Roman… he always had a point.

"I overheard you speaking with Lauren Drake last week."

I nodded, remembering our lunch. She'd kept her promise and managed to keep Roman completely out of the conversation, instead recommending restaurants and local thrift shops I might try. I would never have pegged the tall model-like beauty for a thrift-store junkie, but she'd just smiled and reminded me of how expensive New York was. We'd laughed and had a great time. It had made me rethink my initial opinion of her.

Until now.

"Yes?" I responded.

"I know I can't tell you what to do on your own time, but consider this a friendly suggestion. Steer clear of Miss Drake. If I know anything about her type, she's got her own agenda when it comes to you, and it's definitely not braiding hair and bonding over clothes."

I smiled and politely nodded as I gathered trash and leftovers from lunch.

As I exited, leaving Roman to his afternoon tasks, I sat down and looked at my schedule for the next day.

Lunch with Lauren. Noon.

I picked up the phone, intent on canceling. It would be easy to explain. Roman needed something. I had errands to run. There were a hundred excuses to cancel a lunch date.

But I didn't.

"He wants you to go where?" Tyler roared after I'd broken the news to him.

Oh God, this was bad.

You knew it would be bad the moment you said yes.

Shut up, brain.

"He wants—*needs* to go check on how business is going on the West Coast. Having his assistant with him is a perfectly legitimate requirement," I said, feeling like I was backpedaling up a creek.

Shit creek, to be exact.

But everything I'd said was actually true. Roman had asked me to go with him to California to check out operations on their new West Coast business holdings, and it was completely normal for an assistant to travel with his or her boss.

But the gnawing guilt in the pit of my stomach wasn't.

I really needed to clean something.

And the fact that I hadn't told Tyler about Roman admitting he had some sort of attraction to me definitely wasn't normal.

"I thought his brother was in charge of the West Coast. Why does he suddenly need to fly over there to 'check things out'?" he asked, putting air quotes around his last three words, signifying his disbelief in Roman's motives for this last-minute trip.

"He's frantic about his upcoming meeting with the board. I think he just wants to make sure, with his own eyes, that things are running smoothly, so when he meets with the board, there are no hiccups. You should see the poor man. He's at that office all day, practically all night. I had to start ordering him meals because he was wasting away over this."

He warily eyed me, those deep irises I'd fallen for gazing deep into mine for some sort of olive branch. He wanted to trust me, but I could tell it was killing him to give in to Roman's demands.

"I need this job," I said, my tone almost pleading.

I watched his features soften ever so slightly.

"Fine," he sighed. "But keep that slimeball at a distance. I don't trust him."

"I will," I assured him, wrapping my arms around his waist. "Besides, he's harmless."

Famous last words…

CHAPTER ELEVEN

ROMAN

"Is that what you're wearing?" I asked.

Cara nearly tumbled out of the elevator, looking frantic, as she toted a small suitcase behind her. Dressed in another pencil skirt and heels, she was all business today, right down to the tweed jacket that she had draped over her arm.

"What? Why?" she said in alarm before taking a look at me. "Is that what you're wearing?"

I nodded, looking down at my casual denim and crisp white shirt.

"We're traveling for ten hours," I explained, leaning against her desk. I took another sip from my coffee. "I'm not spending it in a stiff suit and tie just so everyone around me knows I'm traveling for business."

"Oh, well… I didn't think of that," she stated, straightening, as she stopped in front of me, clearly agitated. Her hair was windblown, and her cheeks were flushed from exertion.

"Tell me you took a cab to get here?" I said, annoyed that she hadn't let me pick her up this morning.

She'd flat-out refused, saying she'd just meet me at the office, as usual. It seemed ridiculous and unnecessary.

"I took a cab," she repeated my words nearly verbatim, obviously not even attempting to convince me of the fact. She sighed dramatically and finally fessed up, "I took the subway."

"The subway?" I nearly roared. "Why? When I offered to pick you up? In a hired town car?"

"I just didn't think it was that big of a deal," she explained.

But she wouldn't meet my eyes, and I knew she was sidestepping around the truth.

"You didn't want me to pick you up, did you? Because of what's-his-name? Your boyfriend?"

"His name is Tyler," she replied, her voice betraying the anger stirring in her veins. "And, yes, okay? He's not exactly thrilled with the idea of me traveling with you, so I didn't really want to dangle it in his face by having you show up bright and early at our apartment."

"Okay."

"Okay? That's it? Why are you smiling?"

I couldn't keep the grin from spreading across my face as I watched her growing more hostile by the second. I'd grown accustomed to her soft-spoken demeanor. But this side or her? It reminded me of the girl in the club… the one that had rebuffed me in seconds without a second glance.

"You're angry. I like it."

She rolled her eyes, turning on her heels, obviously expecting me to follow. "The town car is here, waiting for us."

"It can wait. I'm not done with my coffee."

"Jerk," she whispered under her breath.

I laughed.

She turned back around, tapping her foot in those sexy high heels. I took my time, sipping the last few drops of cold coffee in the bottom of my cup. It was awful, but I liked testing her patience.

"Okay, I think I'm done," I announced, dropping the cup into the trash. I took a few steps toward her and motioned to her bag. "Need help with this?"

"Bite me," she answered, pivoting around toward the elevator.

"Gladly," I whispered, shaking my head, as I watched her walk away.

This was going to be the longest two days of my life.

My father was right.

I was the dumbest man on the planet.

Making the hasty decision to rush out to California with Cara in tow had to be one of the most dim-witted ideas I'd ever concocted.

And that was saying something. I'd made some epic mistakes in my past.

But this one? It was a doozy.

Sitting on a plane with the woman who was quickly becoming something bordering on an obsession as her body grazed mine and her scent permeated the air around me, I thought I might surely go insane. By the end of our flight, I was sure I'd gone mad from the sheer will it had taken to keep my hands to myself.

I could have made this trip by myself. Hell, I could have done this trip in a thirty-minute phone call to my brother. But hearing Cara speak about my sister-in-law, smiling as she'd said she hoped she'd get the chance to meet Lailah one day, had been all I could think of for the rest of that day.

Before I knew it, I had called her back in my office as my fingers danced across the keyboard, booking our first-class seats to LAX.

I hadn't even confirmed the dates with my brother.

By the time I'd gotten around to calling him that night with the news, the response I had gotten was expected.

"You're coming here? With her?*"*

The emphasis on the word her was not lost on me.

"Yes," I replied. "She's my assistant. That's what assistants do. They assist."

"And when was the last time any of your previous assistants traveled with you for business?"

I cleared my throat, buying time. "Bethany had a husband, kids."

She did have more than one kid, right?

I honestly had no idea.

"And the one before that? What was her name?"

"I don't know. Shut the hell up."

It had taken several minutes to dull down the laughter on the other end of the line, especially when he'd told Lailah. They'd both eventually promised to be on their best behavior when Cara and I were in town or else I wouldn't bother coming around at all. There were plenty of nice hotels, after all. And they'd both understood this was a threat I would be very good at keeping.

Family had always been important to me, so much so that I worked my ass off for the company we'd built. Spending time with those family members though? I could usually go without.

Although I was slightly interested in seeing this tiny human my brother and Lailah had created. I'd glanced absently at the half a billion pictures Jude had sent over, and even I had to admit, the kid was pretty cute.

I hoped she was giving my brother hell.

"You ready?" Cara asked as the row ahead of us began to deplane.

I hid my smirk, nodding, as I remembered the moment we'd sat down, and I'd noticed the way she'd looked around like a wide-eyed child at Disney World.

"What?" I asked.

"I've been on a plane only once," she admitted, "and it was the back row, right next to the lavatories. It smelled like sewage, and people were lined up next to me, pushing and shoving into me the entire time, as they waited their turn for the restroom."

"So, this is different then?"

She looked around once more, admiring the ample legroom and the soft blanket that had been handed to her upon arrival after they'd taken our drink orders.

"Yes, much different," she answered with a gentle laugh.

I didn't think she'd lost that dopey grin the entire flight. I'd watched her look down at her plated food with wonder, picking up the real silverware, as if she'd never seen such a marvel. With amazement, she'd sat back and enjoyed a movie with the high-quality headphones the flight attendant had provided, like it was positively the best day of her life.

It made me happy.

The kind of happy I'd felt only a handful of times in my life, but this time, I also felt something else.

Fear.

Way back when, when I'd walked into that dress shop in California and first met the strong-willed girl who had fallen in love with my brother, I'd felt that same type of happiness. When I'd convinced her to hop on a plane to go to New York with me and fix my brother, it had simply been out of commitment to my family.

Lailah? She was just the bonus.

This though? This was purely selfish.

And the only one who could end up hurt was me.

"We're staying with your family?" Cara asked as I followed behind her.

I bent over to tuck myself into the backseat of the town car that had met us at the airport.

"Yes," I replied passively, trying to sound aloof. "My brother insisted."

"Oh, okay. I mean, I get *you*. You're family. But me? I can stay in a hotel, so you guys can catch up. I'm sure it's been a while."

"Your presence was insisted upon as well," I said, staring straight ahead, missing the look of surprise that was surely spreading across her face.

"Well, all right. That's very generous of him. And I did say I wanted to meet your sister-in-law. What's her name? Lailah?"

"Yes." I smiled briefly, impressed she'd remembered Lailah's name.

"She seems like a fascinating person."

"She is," I simply stated as the driver finished loading our luggage into the back.

We quickly pulled into LAX traffic, and I paid close attention to Cara as she experienced LA for the first time.

Although the views you experienced when leaving the airport were hardly what one might expect when thinking of Hollywood, the Pacific Ocean, and rows and rows of palm trees.

"Is that a—" she asked as we passed a particularly gross part of Center Street.

"Gentlemen's club? Yes. Although you won't see many gentlemen entering a place like that," I said, watching her shoulders slump in disappointment as we passed a Taco Bell and several other nondescript fast-food places. "Just wait. It gets better. I promise."

And it did.

About thirty minutes outside of the dreary streets that surrounded the airport, past the greasy-food joints and the clogged freeways, we were greeted by the crystal-blue water of the Pacific.

"Wow," she murmured, her face nearly pressed flush against the window.

"I take it your last trip aboard a plane wasn't to come here?"

She turned, scrunching her nose, as a small laugh escaped her lips. "No, definitely not."

"Are you ever going to tell me where you went? I'm starting to believe it's some sort of state secret you're carrying around. Let me guess—New York to visit the boyfriend?"

Her attention had already drifted back to the window, but I could see her shoulders rise as she shrugged.

"No, I only visited Tyler a few times, and I drove. In fourth grade, my father broke his right ankle while bowling, and rather than make our usual twelve-hour drive to visit my grandmother in Texas, we flew there and back. At the time, it was the most exciting moment of my life. I couldn't believe how fast we got there. I begged my parents to allow us to fly again the following year, but Dad's ankle was better, and he could actually drive again, so there was no need."

"How does one break their ankle while bowling?"

She snorted, her dark brown eyes meeting mine once more.

"I think there was a lot of beer involved. Plus, those shoes are slippery. Haven't you ever noticed?"

"I've never played," I admitted.

I watched her expression turn from playful to downright astonished.

"Never?"

"Nope."

"Not even once?" she asked, her eyes still wide with disbelief.

"I believe that's the definition of never." I laughed.

"That's ridiculous," she said, her head shaking back and forth in complete shock, as if I'd just told her I'd never used modern plumbing or had a haircut. "We're going to rectify this. Before we leave," she announced with conviction.

"If you say so, but it's really not that weird."

"It's weird, Roman," she retorted, instantly realizing her slip.

It was the first time she'd ever used my first name. Usually, she didn't address me at all, which I'd always found unusual, considering her immaculate manners. But seeing her reaction now? The instant flush, dodging my gaze… it was obvious she was conflicted.

"I'm sorry," she said quickly. "I didn't mean to—"

"Don't apologize. I'm Roman, Cara. To you… I've always just been Roman."

Her breath caught for a moment, and time seemed to stand still. The sound of the tires against the pavement, the cars around us… everything stopped. For just one moment

And then it was gone.

"Sir, we're here," the driver announced as we came to a stop.

She looked at me for the briefest of time and then blinked, and it was as if the world reset itself. She gave me a polite smile, grabbed the formal tweed jacket she'd been carrying around with her all day, reached for the handle of the car, and was gone.

And the world suddenly seemed louder because of it.

—

"So, Cara," Jude chimed in as we were all gathered around the living room, munching on chips and salsa, while dinner cooked. "I've always wondered… how big of a dick is my brother to work for?"

I nearly choked on my tortilla chip. Quickly giving him a dirty look, I washed it down with a large gulp of cheap beer, cringing as the pungent flavor hit my tongue.

Clearly, my brother's taste buds hadn't improved with time. His time as a "commoner," as I liked to call it, working in a hospital as a nursing assistant for several years while coming to terms with the death of his fiancée, had changed him. In more ways than I could ever comprehend.

He'd not only met Lailah, gotten a few tattoos and life experiences, but his whole demeanor had altered in those precious few years.

We had both been trying to fight the inevitability of our lives back then, I guessed. I had lashed out, trying to be someone I wasn't, and Jude had transformed into the person he was always meant to be.

Looking at everyone in the room, so relaxed and comfortable, I wondered if I was still searching.

"Mr.—Roman, I mean," Cara said, correcting herself mid sentence, "isn't actually that bad. He has his surly moments, and he was a bit difficult to warm up to, but in retrospect, he isn't the worst boss I've ever had."

She didn't look at me as she spoke. Instead, she paid particular attention to the half-empty glass of beer she'd been nursing since we arrived, but I did see her cheeks flush as she spoke, and it gave me great pleasure, knowing I created such a response in her.

How I'd love to create a plethora of responses in her, in so many ways.

"You hear that, brother? You're not the worst boss she's ever had. That's got to be one of the best compliments you've ever received from an employee!" Jude said, slapping me on the back, as he wandered into the kitchen to check on dinner.

"Do you want to book that hotel room yet?" I asked, shaking my head. I took another swig of tasteless beer.

"No." She laughed. "He's great. They're both great."

I nodded, agreeing mostly, as I tried to cover my disappointment. I had known this would happen. It always did. People would meet me and then meet Jude, and suddenly, I was invisible under his hero-like personality. It was like being the stepbrother to Superman. Who would honestly care about that guy?

"I knew they'd be great," Cara said softly.

I looked up at her, preparing myself for the barrage of hero-worshipping that would follow.

"Why?" I played along.

"Because they're related to you," she replied, briefly placing her hand on mine, before she rose from the couch and headed toward the kitchen.

I sat there, dumbfounded, speechless, and silent for I didn't know how long, trying to remind myself of all the reasons I didn't get involved with others. Especially employees.

But the only thing I could hear was her melodic sweet voice while still feeling the warmth of her touch.

I was so incredibly screwed.

"I CAN'T BELIEVE YOU MADE ME BORROW MY BROTHER'S CAR for this," I muttered, already feeling cramped and uncomfortable behind the wheel of Jude's trendy electric car.

"First of all, it's not as small as you think it is," Cara pointed out, gesturing toward my slumped shoulders and surly posture. "Jude seems to fit himself in it fine, and he's definitely... well built. And those tattoos? Sexy."

I threw her a look of disdain before she continued on, completely unaware, "Secondly, showing up at a bowling alley in a hired town car is just ridiculous, in my opinion. It completely ruins the entire experience." Her head was adamantly shaking back and forth as her arms flailed around with the passion of her words.

Since leaving New York, she'd seemed to become more and more comfortable with me. With each passing minute, I was becoming less of a boss in her eyes and more of a person.

It should have been a warning sign, but instead, my heart raced with complete satisfaction.

"Yes, well... witnessing my driving skills in the middle of LA traffic might ruin the entire experience for us permanently," I growled as I pulled out of the driveway with surprising agility I hadn't quite expected from the tiny car.

"You realize that this is kind of like a date," I announced as we drove away from the small exclusive neighborhood where Jude and Lailah lived.

It bordered the Pacific, giving them impressive views of the ocean from almost every room in the house. My brother had specifically designed the house for that purpose. To say I was a little jealous would be a giant understatement.

"It is not!" she squeaked, squaring her shoulders, as her arms wrapped around her midsection in defiance.

"Well, you did ask me, and bowling isn't exactly work-related. And, besides, I don't see anyone else in this car with us." I didn't bother hiding the wolfish grin spreading across my face.

"It's not my fault that Lailah and Jude couldn't come," she fired back.

"Not that I've ever been, but I'm guessing a bowling alley isn't baby-friendly."

"Probably not," she huffed. "But they didn't seem like they wanted to go."

I caught a glimpse of sadness in her eyes.

"My brother's sad attempt at a setup," I said, catching her eyes jerk toward me.

"A setup?"

I nodded. "He's a hopeless romantic. What can I say?"

"Oh," was all she said in response.

"So, are you going to pay for my food then?" I asked, hoping to lighten the mood once again.

She tried to maintain her annoyed exterior, straightening in her seat, as her chin held its proud stance. But I could see the slightest upturn of her pretty pink lips before an all-out grin broke free.

"Fine. One giant soft pretzel and a Coke. But that's all you're getting out of me tonight!"

I smiled in return.

That was just fine with me. There was always tomorrow.

It took about fifteen minutes to get to the bowling alley Cara had found online. She'd spent an unreasonably long time researching it after she'd discovered the sheer volume of places she had to pick from.

"You're in LA," I'd reminded her when she showed me the list of places.

"Back home, we had one—in the entire county."

"You're not in Kansas anymore," I had responded, knowing full well she wasn't from Kansas. But it was a hard line to resist.

The place she'd picked was new, clean, and extremely popular, especially for a Wednesday night. I mostly knew what to expect, having watched TV before. But, stepping inside, I was immediately hit by the smell. Cara explained it was a typical bowling-alley smell—the combination of floor polish, shoe cleaner, and food. It wasn't unpleasant, but it was definitely unique.

Cara seemed to find it comforting.

She also seemed to be giddy over the idea of me having to trade in my three-hundred-dollar shoes for a pair of used bowling shoes. I'd forgotten about that particular part of bowling.

God, how I'd forgotten about that part.

"What size are you?" she asked as we got to the rental counter.

"Thirteen," I answered.

"Thirteen?" she gasped as the man behind the counter chuckled. "That's—"

"Huge?" I grinned, suggestively lifting an eyebrow. "Why, thank you."

"Dirtbag." She laughed, playfully slapping my arm. Turning back to the employee, she asked, "Can you grab my friend here the circus-clown size and me a seven and a half?"

"Sure thing," he answered.

"What size shoe does Tyler wear?" I asked as we waited for our smelly shoes to arrive.

"I'm not sure," she answered passively.

"Yes, you are," I prodded.

"Fine. An eight. Happy?"

My grin grew. "You have no idea."

"I hate you."

"No, you don't," I said as our shoes were delivered.

Grabbing both pairs, she turned swiftly toward our assigned lane, expecting me to follow.

And I did.

I was beginning to believe I'd follow this woman anywhere.

Even into the depths of hell.

And that was where I was surely headed.

CHAPTER TWELVE

CARA

"**I** do believe, Miss Hamilton, that I am kicking your ass," Roman announced as he swaggered back to his chair, looking equal parts hot and ridiculous in his bright red-and-blue bowling shoes.

I guessed I'd never noticed his feet before, my attention usually stolen away by other parts of his anatomy. His mesmerizing eyes or those broad shoulders of his and how his arms must feel wrapped around you. The way he raked his hands through his hair when he was frustrated, which was a lot. It would give him this permanent unruly hairdo that would look laughable or foolish on most men of his status.

But on Roman?

Nothing but pure sex on a stick.

Not that I should notice.

No…

Definitely not.

Because he was my boss.

My sexy, sexy boss.

"Cara? Are you still in there? Did the salt from the pretzel do you in? It was the nacho cheese, wasn't it? I told you not to eat it," he said jokingly.

I rolled my eyes, rising from my seat next to him to take my turn.

In the few hours since we'd arrived in Los Angeles, he'd changed completely.

His hair was still unruly and unkempt but not from the overwhelming duties of the day. Today, he seemed stress-free and happy.

It was an entirely different side of him.

One that I was finding hard to resist.

"I'm fine," I replied with a small smirk tugging at my lips. "And that cheese was delicious. You totally missed out. Now, if you'll excuse me, I have to get back to kicking your ass again."

"Again?" He looked at me with a dubious grin. "I don't recall that ass ever actually kicking mine."

"Oh, yeah?"

He stood swiftly, and our bodies nearly collided from the close proximity. I could feel the heat from him rising off his chest, like it was reaching out for me, asking me to lean in.

And I wanted to. I really, really wanted to.

"Yeah," he answered.

"Want to bet?" I replied. Swallowing a gulp of air, I took a step back, instantly feeling the loss of heat.

"What kind of bet?" he asked with a hooded expression that made my stomach flip-flop.

"I don't know," I backpedaled, suddenly feeling like I'd just stepped into uncharted waters and I was about to be eaten alive.

"You can't offer up a bet and back out, Cara," he teased.

"Okay, fine," I replied, squaring my shoulders. Turning, I bent down and grabbled the polished pink ball I'd claimed as my own for the night and let the solid weight of it settle into my grasp. "I win, you… have to wear those shoes to work for a week."

He silently groaned, looking down at the funky bowling shoes that really did make his size-thirteen feet look insanely large.

That only reminded me of the comment he'd thrown out about men with large feet.

Don't look down, Cara. Don't look down, I chided myself.

But like most things lately that concerned Roman… I really, really wanted to.

"That's cruel, Cara," he replied, shaking his head, as his hands casually went into his pockets. He took a step forward, so we were nearly touching again. "But, since you're not going to win, it doesn't really matter."

"Oh, really?"

He smiled that wolfish grin I was becoming so fond of.

"So, what will you have me do?" I asked.

His eyes went wide. I feigned innocence, tilting my head to the side, like a child.

"What?"

"If I lose." I laughed, loving the fact that I'd made him stumble.

"Right," he answered, clearing his throat. His eyes traveled from my mouth and slowly up to my eyes. "If you lose, which you will… I want you to show up to work on Monday, wearing that horrible bargain-brand sweater dress or whatever weird frock makes you happy."

Confusion instantly hit me.

"But I love that sweater dress," I said, not understanding his rationale at all.

"I know." He smiled.

I turned away from him, taking my time to line up my shot, as my mind went over the conversation a hundred times in a matter of seconds.

Why would he do that?

As I let go of the ball, watching it fall effortlessly from my fingers, heading for the center, it dawned on me.

"Tyler," I said suddenly, spinning on my heels.

"Sorry?"

"The bet. You're doing it to get back at Tyler," I said as the puzzle pieces all began fitting together.

"And why would I do that?" he asked, his eyes set dead ahead.

"The clothes," I answered. "He bought all those clothes for me, and I went on and on about them to you. You want me to purposely hurt him."

His jaw twitched before his gaze met mine.

"I want you to be comfortable in your own skin, Cara," he said with ferocity. "And, if that means wearing some old, frumpy sweater dress or a pair of jeans, then by all means, wear it. No man, including Tyler, should ever dictate what you put on your body. So, no, I didn't do this to hurt him. I'm doing this to empower you. Wear your clothes, or don't. Just be happy—with your own self. But, in the process, if I teach that jackass you live with a lesson, then so be it."

Then, he pointed to the scoreboard above us. "Also, you just made a strike," he added.

I looked above and saw that he was indeed correct. In my mind haze, I'd somehow knocked down all ten pins and scored my first strike of the game.

Go me.

I sat in silence and watched as Roman lifted the shiny black ball and stalked up to the lane. If I hadn't seen his expression when we walked into this place, I wouldn't have believed he'd never been bowling before. He'd looked around like he was stepping foot onto another planet for the first time.

A planet filled with giant green aliens and snow-cone machines.

It was in that moment that I'd finally realized just how different our lives must have been while growing up. Mine was drive-in movies and trips to the city for school clothes in the summer. His must have been private tutors and trips to Europe.

Yet here we both were, bowling.

Together.

The muscles in his back and shoulders flexed as he bent down, angling his shot just right. And then he struck. Like a predator.

In high school, Tyler and I had gone bowling more times than I could count, laughing over sodas and pretzels with our friends.

I'd never once looked at him throwing a ball down the lane the way I looked at Roman.

And that thought alone made me nervous.

"You know, Tyler isn't a bad guy," I said, unable to meet Roman's gaze as he turned around, waiting for his ball to return so that he could bowl his second turn.

He'd knocked down all but two pins. Not bad for a beginner.

A beginner who was currently beating me by twenty points.

"I never said he was."

"He's nice and sweet and good. And he's been incredibly patient with me while I've been going through this process of settling in."

"I'm sure he has been," he answered passively.

"Then why don't you like him?"

"Why do you seem to care? I am, after all, just your boss," he pointed out, sitting down next to me rather than taking his turn.

He'd turned the chair and straddled it, so rather than sitting side by side, he was looking at me head-on. I could see every random color of green that lived in the depths of his eyes—from the darkest hints of clover to the vibrant tones of moss and sea-foam. He seemed to capture my soul in that solitary glance.

"You're more than a boss," I confessed.

"And you deserve more than a good guy," he answered. "You deserve the right guy. Figure out the difference."

And then he was gone. The heat from his body, the words from his lips.

I watched him take his second turn, lost in thought and wonder.

In my twenty-two years of existence, good and right had always been mutually exclusive. In church, they'd always taught us that being good was the right thing to do.

Love was gentle. Love was kind.

It was the way I had been raised.

Had I fallen in love with Tyler for all the wrong reasons?

"You went bowling? With your boss?" Tyler's groggy voice asked as I paced around the guest bedroom in Jude and Lailah's coastal home. I could hear the waves crashing outside my window, calmly reminding me of the late hour. That made me only that much more aware of the time difference in New York.

"Yeah, it was fun. We needed to get out of the house

and blow off some steam. Especially Roman. He's been so busy and stressed. It was good for him."

The line went quiet as I waited for him to respond. I nervously fidgeted with the little bow on my pajama pants, as I paced around the room.

I shouldn't have called. I should have waited until morning. Telling your boyfriend you'd been out late with another man, especially one he already loathed, at this late hour was bound to be nothing short of a disaster.

"Roman?" he finally said.

"What?"

"You called him Roman. Since when do you call him Roman?"

More fighting, more nervousness.

"Oh, um… I guess since today. It became a little cumbersome to refer to him as Mr. Cavenaugh all the time."

No reply. No explosion. No yelling or name calling. Nothing.

"Listen, it's late. I've got to get up in a few hours for work. I'll talk to you later, okay?" he said simply. There was little anger in his voice. It was as if he'd switched to autopilot.

"Oh, okay. I'll let you get back to sleep then."

The call dropped, and I was left with my twitchy hands and an untied bow, wondering what had just happened.

I'd expected an outburst of words, an epic exchange of dialogue where he laid it all out on the table, professing his never-ending love for me and how much it hurt to know I'd spent the night with another man.

I knew it was cruel, but tonight hadn't started out as a test. I hadn't purposely sought out the company of another man to see how Tyler would react. But, standing here now, I realized something. He'd just failed a very important test.

Did he even want me anymore?

I felt raw and shattered after my talk with Tyler. Since sleep was no longer an option, I found myself wandering the halls, lost in thought, wondering how we'd ended up like this.

Life with Tyler had always been easy.

In our eight years together, that was the one word I'd use to describe it.

Easy.

Even when we had been half a country apart, we'd managed to make it work seamlessly. He'd started his own life at NYU, and I'd done the same in Lincoln. We'd barely seen each other, but when we had, we'd always picked back up right where we'd left off.

It was effortless.

Our friends and family were always so proud of the way we managed ourselves. We never got caught up in the whirlwind romance, like so many others. We'd stayed firm on our individual paths, and somehow done the impossible—stayed together.

But had we?

As my mind went over and over each detail of the conversation, I continued to slowly roam around the darkened hallways until I heard the faint sound of singing.

The gentle lullaby called to me, and I found myself instantly gravitating toward it.

At the end of the long hall, I could see a soft light seeping out from underneath the door. Noticing it wasn't fully closed, I quietly knocked, seeing Lailah's silhouette in the open space.

"Do you mind if I join you?" I asked, sticking my head in.

Rocking back and forth in a comfortable chair with Meara in her arms, she motioned me forward and nodded. "It gets a bit lonely in here sometimes. I wouldn't mind the company."

I crawled onto the daybed across from her, making a spot between a giant panda bear and a plush pink elephant. The bedding was soft and warm, and I instantly felt at home in this space.

"We brought in that bed a few weeks after she was born," Lailah said, fondly pointing to the bed with a look of nostalgia in her tired expression. She was just a few years older than me, maybe mid- to late-twenties, but she held herself with the grace of someone with more years. "She was so small, you see. I just couldn't stand the idea of leaving her alone."

Her hands smoothed out the wisps of hair that curled around her baby's cherub face.

"Was she a preemie?" I asked.

She nodded. "She spent quite a long time in the NICU. And even when they swore she was ready to come home, I was scared to death. I don't know that any parents, especially those who have spent days and weeks in the NICU, are fully prepared to bring their child home for the first time. I just kept watching her, waiting on every breath.

"We used the bassinet for several weeks until we realized that it resulted in neither of us getting any rest, and that didn't work at all. So, that's when the idea of the bed came to be. The pediatrician swore she'd be okay on her own, told us to just rely on a baby monitor, like normal parents. But I couldn't do it—at least, not at first. We'd been through so much."

"So, you slept in here? For how long?" I asked, enthralled with her story.

I'd always been fascinated by children, especially babies. Growing up, I'd done my fair share of babysitting, but it had mostly been for our neighbors who had toddlers and young grade-school kids.

"A couple of months," she answered with a bit of embarrassment. "But it wasn't just me. Jude and I would trade every other night. I tried to take more than that since he was working, but he refused. He didn't want me to overdo it. He's a bit overprotective," she explained.

"Roman told me about your heart transplant," I said, hoping I wasn't overstepping. He hadn't explained everything, but had mentioned on the way here that his sister-in-law and brother had met in a hospital, while Lailah was waiting for a new heart. They'd fallen in love within the walls of that small hospital room.

"Yes, hence the reason for the overprotectiveness." She laughed quietly.

"You're a very brave woman."

She shrugged, looking down at her daughter with warmth and tenderness. "Bravery comes in all different shapes and sizes. I was given a certain hand in life, and I dealt with it. Sometimes, I'd handle it well, and sometimes, not so well. We all have ups and downs. Shoot, yesterday the grocery store was out of my favorite kind of cereal, and I thought it was the worst day ever. It's all about perspective."

"I don't think anyone can really compare their life to yours," I said, thinking back to my hall-wandering just a few minutes earlier.

"And they shouldn't," she said softly. "Life isn't about comparing one's strife to another. It's about making the most of what you've been given. If I sat back and thought about all the hardships I've had to endure to get here… right here, it would be overwhelming. Some days, it is overwhelming. But I'm here. I'm living, and I love my life. That's what it's all about—loving your life."

I nodded, watching the rhythm of the rocking chair, as she slowly moved.

"Do you love your life, Cara?" she asked after a few minutes had passed.

"I…" I stumble, trying to find the answer.

Am I happy?

Just as I was about to answer, bloodcurdling baby cries tore through the room as Meara woke.

"Saved by the bell—or baby, I guess I should say." Lailah laughed. "Would you mind getting me a bottle from the fridge? She fell asleep before I could get her evening feeding in."

"Sure," I answered.

"Jude is downstairs in the living room. He'll give you instructions on how to warm it, if you don't know how." Lailah said, trying to soothe the hungry little one.

"I babysat for a few neighbors who still gave bottles. I remember." I smiled before quietly slipping out of the room.

Was I happy? It was a simple question.

It should be a simple answer.

Yet, as I walked down the long hallway and to the stairs that lead to the kitchen, I couldn't come up with an answer.

As I approached the open kitchen, expecting to find a tired Jude up, alone, watching TV or reading in the nearby living room, I instead found both Cavenaugh brothers, deep in discussion.

"You like her, don't you?" Jude said, a wicked grin

spreading across his face, as he leaned back against the sofa.

I pulled back into the shadows, realizing the conversation they were having revolved around me.

"You're incredibly annoying, you realize that?" Roman fired back before sipping brown liquid from a crystal glass.

Whiskey probably. I'd seen vintage bottles high atop the shelves of his office, dating back to his father's days, and that night in the club, he'd reeked of it.

"And you're evasive and a little hostile. We all have our things. So, fess up, and then I can give you some proper brotherly advice before you screw it all up."

"Screw it up? Who says I'm going to screw it up? And since when does the little brother give the advice?"

"Since the little brother seems to have his shit together, the little brother gives the advice. Okay? And I'm not little, jackass." Jude laughed.

"Could have fooled me with that joke of a car you have," Roman growled.

He was still annoyed I'd made him drive the clown car for the evening. But he hadn't bothered covering up that gorgeous smile of his when he was effortlessly weaving in and out of LA traffic. He'd never admit it, but he'd enjoyed the ride.

"That car is called being responsible. I know it's a word you're unfamiliar with—"

"Now, who's being the jackass?" Roman grinned back before letting out a huge sigh. "She's my employee, Jude. My fucking employee."

"And Lailah was my patient. What's your point?" Jude asked, raising a speculative eyebrow.

"My point? What's my point? That's the whole fucking point, Jude. She's off-limits. No dating the employees. Isn't that a rule? I'm pretty sure it's even written in the handbook."

Jude shrugged casually. "I'm pretty sure it wasn't exactly kosher for hospital employees to fool around with patients in their rooms either, but Lailah and I did that plenty of times."

Roman held his hand out in protest. "That's my sister-in-law. Please stop. And if this is what you call brotherly advice, it sucks."

Jude laughed, a deep masculine laugh that filled the room. "Look, brother, this is all I'm going to say. I've only been around the two of you for a few hours, and I know you've got the hots for her. More than the hots, I'd say.

"I've seen you with other women. They were disposable. Frivolous encounters. But Cara? She means something to you, and I don't think you've quite figured out what that is yet. But you owe it to yourself to do so.

"Yes, she's your employee. Yes, she's even your assistant. But she's temporary. And I can't believe I have to tell you this because I always thought of you as the cunning one, but do yourself a favor. Check out the HR file. She was most likely hired by a temp agency, which means she's not our employee to begin with."

Roman's head whipped around, meeting Jude in shock.

"You really didn't think of that, did you?" He laughed. "There's always a way, Roman, if you want there to be."

"It doesn't matter what I want. She has a boyfriend."

"Then, why is she here with you?" Jude asked.

I looked down at the half-tied bow on my pajama pants, remembering the way I'd kept fighting with it as I spoke with Tyler.

Why was I here? Was it really for work?

Or was it for something more?

Someone more…

CHAPTER THIRTEEN

ROMAN

"**G**ood morning, sunshine!" Lailah teased, a bemused smile upon her lips, as she danced around the kitchen at the ungodly hour of five in the morning.

"Why are you so chipper? Aren't new parents supposed to be tired and grumpy all the time?" I asked, shuffling toward the coffee pot in a daze. It wasn't that I was unused to getting up at this hour on a routine basis, but it was usually three hours later.

At my regular time.

Eastern time.

Not at five in the morning, Pacific time, after I'd stayed up until midnight listening to my younger brother ramble on about destiny, fate, and love.

And a bunch of other bullshit.

"If you paid attention or actually came to visit every once in a while, you would notice that Jude and I aren't exactly new parents anymore. Meara is nearly a year old.

She eats solid food. She's walking. We're solid pros at this gig by now."

I'd finished pouring a fresh cup of coffee, and I could already feel the stiff black liquid warming up my veins. As a man who pretty much lived on caffeine, I was proud of myself for having heard half of what she'd just said, considering my buzz still required a few more cups until it was safely in place.

"Pros, huh? Well, Mrs. Professional, if you're so good at this gig, where's the little one now? She's usually attached to you, in one way or another." I gestured to her and the baby she was currently not sporting on her body.

Instead, she wore a frilly apron and held a worn spatula in her left hand. There was a stack of piping hot pancakes next to the stove, and the smell of bacon in the air was making my stomach growl with desire.

"She's outside," Lailah answered, pointing to the large deck just beyond the kitchen.

The sun was beginning to rise, casting a halo of light over the murky blue water.

I caught the faint smirk of my sister-in-law as I wandered toward the slider, and then I instantly froze. Outside, Cara was slowly bouncing my niece in her arms, looks of pure contentment upon both their faces. A small giggle broke the silence as Meara laughed, causing Cara to smile from ear to ear.

Jesus.

"They've been out there for thirty minutes or so," Lailah whispered, standing next to me.

I hadn't even noticed that she'd moved. I'd been completely rendered immobile by the scene playing out in front of me.

"I bet, if you went out there, Cara would teach you

how to hold her," Lailah said with an impish grin before meandering back to the kitchen.

I knew she was goading me, egging me on, like I was some insolent child who didn't know any better.

But I went anyway.

Sliding the door back, I caught Cara's attention almost immediately.

"Good morning," she greeted me, settling her gaze back down on her tiny charge.

Normally, I'd feel dismissed by the sudden loss of eye contact, but seeing her attentiveness to my niece did something to me.

I felt like that damn Grinch who stole all the Christmas presents but then ended up growing a heart in the end— the sudden rush of emotions overwhelmed me.

Desire, longing, and something innately primal.

A need to make her mine.

"Did you sleep well?" I asked.

Clearing my throat, I lifted a shaky hand toward my niece's tender head. I'd never actually touched her. The uninvolved, careless bachelor in me said it was against the rules. Men like me didn't touch things as precious as her.

As precious as both of them

My hand fell back to my side.

I didn't deserve any of this.

"Yes." She smiled weakly. "As well as could be expected with jet lag."

"Mmm," I agreed, looking out toward the waves in hopes of gaining some clarity.

There were a few stragglers on the beach. Runners, walkers… some just strolling down the shoreline, staring into the endless ocean.

For answers? Peace? Serenity?

It made me wonder how many of us had peered at

these same waves year after year, wishing for all the holes in our lives to be filled. *How many hopeless dreams had been wasted on these swirling tides?*

"Do you want to take her? I need to go get ready," Cara announced, holding Meara's fragile body out toward mine.

The little child glanced up at me with raw curiosity, her bright green eyes assessing me with a peculiar sense of awareness.

"No." I held my hands out, stepping back toward the open door.

I turned and fled.

Fled the beautiful child who hadn't been sullied by the harsh realities of the world, all the pain and suffering, like I had.

And I fled the woman who could make it all go away.

"Nice shoes."

Cara was sitting behind her desk, dressed in the heather-gray sweater dress she seemed to love more than life. Her scuffed chunky heels were back as well as the tight ponytail that made her look years younger than she already was.

"Nice dress," I answered back, surprised to see she'd beaten me to the office.

I was usually the first to arrive on Mondays, the most hated day of the week. While most people were sluggish and tired from their weekend spent with family and time in front of the TV, I found myself recharged, hopped up on caffeine, sex, and sleep.

And most of that was still true today.

Minus the sex.

I'd been an absolute nightmare for the remainder of our trip to California, feeling like a lunatic, as I tried to sort out my feelings for Cara. I was like an out-of-control pendulum, agonizing over my desire for her one minute and pushing her away the next.

After an entire day of meetings with Jude and our West Coast division, I'd decided it would be in my best interest to stay focused and just keep my eye on the prize. I'd busted my ass for this company, and in less than two months, our entire board would be arriving. This wasn't the time to become overly besotted with my assistant.

But then the pendulum had swung again.

This time, it wasn't a baby or sweeping emotions that had pushed me over the edge.

It was just *her*.

We'd said our good nights and good-byes, knowing that Cara and I would be catching an early flight out the next morning. With Jude and Lailah's crazy baby schedule, I hadn't wanted to wake them when we left, so I thought it would be better if we hired a driver and let everyone sleep.

As I meandered through the house, collecting phone chargers and random items that still needed to be packed, I found myself face-to-face with Cara.

Wearing very little clothing.

"Oh!" she nearly squeaked.

A look of surprise painted her red cheeks as my eyes moved up and down her body. She must have thought she could sneak to the bathroom, unnoticed, because she was in only a T-shirt and panties.

And damn if I hadn't caught her.

"I was just running to the bathroom to grab my toothbrush," she explained, awkwardly trying to pull the hem of her T-shirt

down. It barely grazed the top seam of her panties, exposing a bit of tender flesh around her abdomen.

God, how I wanted to lick her. Right there.

Everywhere.

I took a bold step forward without even thinking. A slight gasp escaped her mouth as she looked up at me, her warm breath against my neck.

"Then, I guess you'd better do it," I whispered.

Time stopped.

For the second time in my life, it stopped. And I never wanted it to start again.

I felt her lean in as her breath faltered. Her eyes fluttered closed for the briefest moment.

And then reality stepped back in.

She stepped back, her eyes wide open, filled with emotion. "I can't."

The next morning, as we'd both groggily gone through the motions of flying back home, the incident was never spoken about. Cara had gone about the day as if it'd never happened, and after a while, I'd found myself wondering if I'd dreamed it.

But, every so often, I would catch her looking at me… as we'd fixed our morning coffee or when she'd thought I was sleeping beside her on the plane.

And now we'd returned to the normalcy of the office. She might have started the morning off with a joke, trying to maintain the status quo we'd once had, but deep down, she knew.

We were anything but normal.

DAYS HAD TURNED INTO WEEKS, AND NOTHING HAD HAPPENED.

The glow of our trip slowly faded… and nothing happened.

Our flirty banter continued but still…

Nothing fucking happened.

I wasn't a man used to waiting. I got what I wanted, and when I didn't, I simply just took it.

She wanted me. She wanted us. I could see it in her eyes when she thought I wasn't looking. I could feel it in the air, pulsating around us, as she'd delicately maneuver around me, plainly trying to avoid my touch.

She felt it just as much as I did, and that only furthered my desperation.

The only question was, *Why is she denying it?*

Anyone with half a brain could see that she wasn't happy with Tyler. I knew I was a biased bystander with much to gain from their inevitable breakup, but it still brought nothing but pain to see her traipse into work each day with the color and life draining out of her.

What was she holding on to?

"You look rough today," I finally commented, looking up from my morning coffee. I watched her drag herself from the elevator before plopping onto the chair.

"Thanks," she answered halfheartedly, her eyes barely leaving the top of her desk. "You're pretty ravishing yourself." She huffed before meeting my gaze. "I'm sorry. That was rude."

"Bad morning?" I guessed, gesturing to the cup of coffee I'd made her before she'd arrived.

She stared at it with a bemused expression before returning her attention to me.

"Bad morning, bad evening. Just bad altogether."

"Ouch." I didn't know what else to say. I wasn't exactly the warm and fuzzy type. I didn't have a go-to speech for empowering others, and I definitely wasn't known for motivational talks.

But I also didn't want to be a jackass—at least, not to her.

Never to her.

So, I stood there, in front of her desk, like a fucking statue, waiting for her to say something.

Anything.

Jesus, I was turning into a pussy.

"He went to a strip club," she finally said.

I barely made out the words as they left her lips. She stared at the cup in her hands as the steam rose, and I could see her reliving it. Like a victim of a senseless crime, she sat there and recalled every terrible moment, and while it happened right in front of me, I was powerless to stop it.

And it was all because of *him*.

"What happened?" I asked, instantly moving toward her.

Grabbing one of the extra chairs near her desk, I pulled it close and settled in next to her. There were no tears, but her eyes were still swollen from those she'd shed hours earlier.

"He says that nothing happened, but how would I know?" she pleaded, her voice heavy with emotion. "This isn't us, Roman. This isn't how we're supposed to be. We're supposed to build a life together here, not continue two separate ones simultaneously. How do I trust a man I don't even know anymore?"

"I don't know. I honestly don't. But I'd be happy to kick his ass for you," I said, hoping to lift her spirits because mine definitely were. This was exactly what I'd been hoping for. Not that I enjoyed seeing her hurt. I'd gladly make good on my words and track that bastard down this second, if it meant making her happy again.

"No, that's not necessary. It's something we need to work out on our own. I'm sorry. I shouldn't have dumped this on you. You've got enough to deal with," she said, suddenly shifting into gear. She turned away from me, gathering loose papers from her desk, and she frantically tried to organize the lack of a mess in front of her.

I sat there, dumbfounded by her words. "You're not leaving him?"

She briefly glanced at me, placing a paper clip on a report I'd given her the day before. "No. Why?"

"Why?" I muttered under my breath, setting down my coffee. "Why? Because the guy is a douche bag who doesn't deserve you. Why? Because he treats you like you're nothing more than typical when you're anything but. Why?" I repeated, feeling my fists tighten at my sides.

"Sorry," I said, backing down.

Without realizing it, I'd jumped up and began pacing around the small space in front of her desk, like a caged lion, as I'd loudly listed off the many reasons my assistant should leave her boyfriend.

It was completely unprofessional.

And worthless because she'd obviously made up her mind already.

"You're right. This isn't something I need to be dealing with right now. Excuse me," I said, retreating quickly. I slammed the door shut behind me, letting out my first full breath in minutes.

What was this woman doing to me?

And how did I make it stop?

My brother's words echoed in my head as I worked.

I'd given up on actual work long ago. What I was doing could only be categorized as crazy.

But that was what Cara made me feel like.

Fucking crazy.

Life had been easy before her.

Lonely. Lifeless maybe, but easy.

I'd gone to work, put the hours in, seen results, and when I could, I'd reaped the rewards. When things had gotten rough, the rewards were few and far between, but that wasn't a big shocker. I ran a Fortune 500 company. People like me just weren't made for anything else.

It was what I had been raised to do after all.

My legacy.

But she made me want more.

More nights of bowling and talking over cheap salads. I wanted to spend time with her outside of this godforsaken office—without the excuse of work or job duties.

I just wanted her.

All to myself.

And, somehow, I was going to make it happen.

I'D BEEN THINKING ABOUT IT FOR DAYS.

It was dirty and wrong, and if she ever found out about my involvement…

But I needed to know what it felt like.

I needed my chance.

Otherwise, this obsession would eat me alive.

I was done waiting.

It was time to take.

I WAITED UNTIL THE FOLLOWING WEEK WHEN OUR PATHS would naturally cross. Seeking Lauren out, as cunning as she was, would only put the leggy blonde on high alert that much faster.

I needed this to be casual, calm, and anything but deliberate.

Luckily, we had an upcoming acquisition, and with that came meetings. I usually loathed meetings. They were long, boring, and involved far too much talking for my taste.

But today I was actually looking forward to one because of the possibility it held.

One step closer…

I slipped into the conference room a few minutes early, something I wasn't known for. I pulled out my laptop and pretended to be working. A complacent boss tended to cause turmoil among employees. *Why isn't he working? Doesn't he have anything to do? Oh God… are we shutting down?*

That was how rumors started.

It was also why I kept the janitorial and coffee budgets well funded. Nothing like a break in the java supply to cause mass panic regarding job retention.

"You're here early."

Just the voice I'd wanted to hear.

Looking up from my laptop, I took a moment to take her all in. She was still as striking as the day I'd first noticed her. Same gorgeous looks with a rack men would weep over.

My body had taken note of her before, but today… nothing.

I only needed her for one thing, and it didn't involve my dick.

"Lauren," I replied with authority, ignoring her earlier comment. "I actually have a question, and you might know the answer."

"Sure," she answered, her voice obviously shaken by my abrupt tone.

Besides our back-and-forth banter that night in the lobby, I didn't think we'd exchanged more than a few words to each other.

But I could say that for the majority of people who worked in this building.

I was, after all, the evil overlord.

"My assistant, Cara, mentioned to me the other day that her boyfriend works for a prominent accounting firm here in New York. I want to know the name."

"Of her boyfriend?"

I stared blankly.

"Sorry, I'm just a little confused as to why you would ask me," she said, her voice recovering its normal confidence.

"I've heard the two of you talking outside my door. I don't work in an iron vault, unfortunately."

"No, of course not. Um, she doesn't really talk about him much, but I believe the company is called Blythe."

"Great."

"Can I ask why you want to know? Another acquisition? Need an accountant?" She laughed at her own joke.

I settled my steely gaze upon her.

"Right. Never mind."

I had the name. Now, all I had to do was the dirty work.

Lucky for me, I excelled in all things dirty.

CHAPTER FOURTEEN

CARA

The leaves on the trees had finally begun to turn all over the city, giving it that classic postcard look New York was known for. Central Park was filled with families bundled in wool coats as dedicated runners flew by, hoping to get in a few more runs before the first frost appeared.

It was a part of the year I was used to—the changing of seasons. In the Midwest, winter was always the highlight of most conversations from about mid-September on.

How much snow will we get? When do you think it will start? How will the crops fare?

And, although the conversations might be slightly different here, in my new home, I could still feel the antici-pation as November swiftly took root. The holidays were just around the corner. Summer was well behind us, and soon, the streets would be blanketed with fluffy white snow.

Just like it was supposed to be.

It gave me a sense of peace, knowing at least one thing in my life was still predictable. Still normal.

Especially when everything else in the last few weeks had gone topsy-turvy, leaving me hollow and confused.

"I'm thinking we should have chosen a table inside," Lauren said, rubbing her arms to work off the chill that had settled there.

I nodded in agreement. "I guess that's why they had immediate tables open out here."

"Lucky us."

"Oh well," I replied. "Nothing a little coffee won't fix, and at least we'll get back to the office in an hour."

"Very true," she sighed, leaning her slight frame back in the seat.

She was dressed warmly today in heavy dark wool pants and a fashionable cashmere sweater. Even in the bulky fabrics, she still appeared glamorous and sophisticated, her buttery-gold hair pulled back into a simple but elegant bun, while mine was just hanging loose and lifeless.

"So, how are you? You weren't exactly in the best frame of mind the last time we met," Lauren asked.

I slowly sipped on my glass of water, wishing it were something hot and caffeinated. The restaurant was slammed. Most places in this area were at lunchtime. It was why I usually just took Roman up on his offer and ate in the office.

But sometimes, I just needed to get out.

Away from work.

Away from him and all the confusion he brought.

"I don't know," I confessed. "One minute, I think I'm okay, and the next, I'm not. I didn't exactly envision my life going this way when I moved out here."

"Have you talked to Tyler?"

Have I talked to Tyler?

What a loaded question.

My mind flashed back to the moment when he'd crawled in bed, smelling of cheap perfume and cigarette smoke. *I flipped on the lights, abruptly turning around.*

"What the hell?" he groaned, his eyes squinting at the sudden onslaught of brightness.

"Where have you been?" I asked, looking him up and down for some sort of clue. I didn't know what I expected to find. A giant sign on his forehead that proclaimed all of his horrible crimes in plain English?

"I had a thing with work. I told you about it," he replied lamely, collapsing down onto the mattress with an exhausted grunt.

"Since when do your work things include women hanging all over you?"

"What?" His eyes popped open.

Well, at least now I had finally gotten his attention.

"You smell like a brothel."

"A brothel? What the hell, Cara? This isn't the 1800s. We don't have brothels anymore. Grow up."

That hurt. I swallowed my pain, sticking my chin out in defiance. "You would know."

"Look, not everything I do for work is exactly classy, okay? Until I'm higher up, I do what the clients want. That's how it works. I'm pretty much a gopher. Some want expensive restaurants. Others want to go to the clubs. Tonight, the guys wanted to go to a strip club, so that's what we did."

"That doesn't exactly explain why you smell so... up close and personal," I said through my teeth.

"The guys bought me a lap dance as a thank-you. Can we drop this? I'm tired."

"Yeah, we can drop this," I said quietly, turning off the light.

I left the room.

I fell asleep that night on the couch in a puddle of my own tears while Tyler slept like a baby.

We'd barely spoken since.

"Things are tense," I said finally, glancing up at Lauren.

Her eyes rounded in compassion. "Then, why are you still with him? You know you have a place to stay. Just say the word, Cara. Don't keep putting yourself through this."

I nodded, greatly appreciative for her friendship. Roman had said to steer clear of Lauren, but I thought his assessment regarding her was all wrong. She'd been nothing but a steady rock for me over the last few weeks, offering friendship where I had none, courage when mine seemed to be failing, and a helping hand, even when I was too afraid to take it.

"Thank you," I said. "But I don't think I'm ready for that yet. And I know you think I'm crazy for staying, but you've got to understand. This is the only relationship I've ever had, and I know it might seem naive or childish, but a part of me still believes that we are meant to be. That the eight years we've put into this is worth it. I know he's made some mistakes, but so have I. I can't walk away without at least trying to mend what is broken."

"I understand," she stated. "I might not agree, but I understand."

"Thank you."

She smiled sweetly just as the waiter came. We each ordered coffee and a warm bowl of soup, opting out of our usual salads, going for something warmer instead.

As we waited, she naturally moved onto another subject, obviously noticing I needed a change of pace. Things settled back on office gossip, and even though I wasn't a fan of it, I let her prattle on, enjoying the simple fact that I wasn't the only one in the universe who had issues.

"My boss just got hair plugs. I don't think he wants us to say anything about it, but it's super obvious. He's the VP of Finance, so it's not like he's invisible. Even Cavenaugh noticed."

"Roman notices everything. He just likes everyone to think he doesn't," I said, instantly regretting my words.

"Really? I guess that makes sense. He did know my name the other day," she said before taking a sip of coffee.

"What day?"

"Tuesday maybe? Before that acquisitions meeting earlier this week. He asked me a question but actually said my name first. I just figured he referred to all of us as Peon Number One, Peon Number Two…"

She snickered as I shook my head at her horrible joke.

"What did he ask you?"

"Oh, it was something about Tyler."

"Tyler? What would he want to know about Tyler?" I asked, my heart skipping a little faster at the mention of Roman and Tyler in the same sentence. My hands began twirling the napkin in my hand as I nervously listened.

Why was I so anxious?

"It wasn't about Tyler exactly. Cavenaugh wanted to know what company he worked for." She shrugged. "Something business-related, I guess."

"Oh," I responded, my fidgety fingers slowly relaxing.

"Why do you look so worried?"

"What? No, I'm not. It's just that Roman can be very intense sometimes," I explained, hating myself for even mentioning his name. I felt like I was breaking some sort of confidentiality rule.

"Intense how?"

"Well, he told me to steer clear of you once," I said, the words coming out like vomit.

God, I couldn't even stop them. I'd been holding too

much in. With Melissa's late nights and my inability to talk to my mother about grown-up problems, I felt like a volcano ready to erupt. If Lauren prodded too much more, I'd end up telling her everything.

Like the fact that I had a big, fat crush on my hotter-than-sin boss.

And my relationship with Tyler was the only thing keeping me from climbing Roman like a tree.

"He told you to stay away from me? That's insane! I mean, first of all, why would he even care?"

I laughed awkwardly. "I know. It's so weird."

"And, second, it's none of his business."

"It's not," I agreed.

"Listen, you've got enough to deal with right now besides a pushy boss. Just focus on yourself, okay? And I don't care what Cavenaugh says. I will continue to be your awesome friend. Sound good?"

"Great," I said, breathing out a sigh of relief.

I needed to talk to my boyfriend. And I needed to do it soon. Otherwise, I really was going to explode.

And that just sounded all sorts of bad.

I was used to the loud noises at night now. Even though Tyler made vain attempts to be quiet, the alcohol still pumping in his veins always made him clumsy and awkward, even in his own space.

I tried to ignore it.

I tried to tell myself he was doing his job.

Paying his dues.

But this was not how I'd pictured our life together. This was not how it was supposed to be—our happily ever after.

So, I did the only thing I could. I sank further into the covers, burying my head in the blankets, and I pretended I was somewhere else, anywhere else, other than here.

I'd tried to talk with him over the last few days—to bring us back to the happy young couple we'd once been. But nothing seemed to work. The search for common ground between the two of us was like the hunt for Amelia Earhart all those years ago. After a while, you wondered when it was time to call it quits and move on.

But this wasn't just some history lesson I was studying. This was my life.

A life I'd drastically changed for the man stumbling into bed next to me.

The shuffling abruptly stopped as his warm body closed around me. A hand caressed my hip before I felt the full weight of him behind me. I tried not to recoil from his touch as the whiff of perfume and booze wafted toward me.

His arms tightened around me, and suddenly, he began to tremble.

Turning quickly, I found myself face-to-face with the man I thought I'd spend the rest of my life with… and he was broken beyond measure.

"Tyler? What happened? Are you all right?" I asked, frantically reaching for the lamp on the edge of the night-stand. When I finally found it, the room went ablaze with the glow of the lamp, as I searched him from top to bottom, trying to find some sort of clue or physical injury that would cause such anguish.

He was still drunk. I could tell that much. His eyes were glossy, his hands were clammy, and he was sweating so much he was already sticking to the sheets.

"I've destroyed everything," he mumbled, his eyes finally finding mine. It was as if he'd just realized I was in the same room. It sobered him greatly. He sat upright as he wiped tears from his eyes.

"You have to go," he said flatly.

"What? What are you saying, Tyler?" I said, reaching out to comfort him.

He put a steady hand out, keeping a safe distance between us… as if the very idea of touching me disgusted him.

"I slept with another woman tonight, Cara. I didn't mean to, but things got out of hand. You should go. Please, just go. I can't—just go."

His confession hit me like a battering ram. My worst fear had been confirmed.

I'd been trying to convince myself for weeks that we'd make it through this, that it would just take time to find our way back to each other after so long.

But now it was all over.

In the blink of an eye.

I couldn't even stand to look at him anymore.

"I guess I should go," I said softly, grabbing what I could in my haze.

I managed to snag a change of clothes and a toothbrush. I'd have to come back for everything else.

Oh God, where would I go?

Stopping by the door to our bedroom with my small bag of things I'd stuffed inside, I turned one last time. He was lying on the bed, his eyes shut tight, like he had to force them to stay closed

"Are you going to tell me why you did it? Do you even feel the least bit guilty?" I asked.

"Please. Just go, Cara."

Nodding, I pushed myself past the door, hating the tears streaming down my face. He wasn't worth them.

He wasn't worth any of this.

Three o'clock in the morning… and I'd just been kicked out of my apartment.

Standing on the street corner, holding a bag with barely a night's worth of things, the reality of my situation came barreling down on me.

And so did the rain.

New York was never quiet. There was always movement and lights, but at certain times, it could be oddly peaceful.

As the rain beat down on my head, mixing with the salty tears falling from my eyes, I took a moment to appreciate the almost Zen-like calm happening around me. No cars, no footfalls from impatient pedestrians shuffling off to work. It was calm and eerily serene.

It also freaked me the hell out.

I was a lonely girl, outside, in the middle of the night, about to lose her mind.

I looked at the heavens and begged God to do me just one solid favor and send a friendly, non-creepy taxi driver in my direction. Apparently, the big man was listening because about five cold, wet minutes later, a single taxi appeared.

"Need a lift, sweetheart?" he said, his window rolled down just enough for him to speak to me.

"Yes, please!" I said gratefully, opening the back door and hopping in before he changed his mind.

Tyler had been bugging me for weeks to program the numbers of the major taxi companies in my phone in case I ever needed one.

But my response had always been, "Why? They're on every street corner."

Well, I guessed I'd learned my lesson now.

Not that I'd ever tell the cheating, lying bastard that.

The truth of his deceit was still raw in my mind. It felt foreign and wrong—like finding out the world was round when, all along, you'd believed it was really, truly flat.

Tyler had cheated on me.

He'd cheated.

After all this time…

In all those nights he'd stumbled in, reeking of cheap booze and women, I'd never once thought he'd cheat on me.

We were Cara and Tyler.

We made it four years, long-distance.

Four long years.

Why would he choose now to mess it all up?

"Do you have an address for me, sweetheart?" the driver asked, looking back at me through the rearview mirror.

"Um…"

Lauren had vowed to be there for me more times than I could count. She'd seen this coming even though I swore we'd make it. I knew I could come to her anytime of the night, and she'd take care of me.

But did I want her to?

I rattled off an address, one I probably shouldn't know, but did, and watched the car shift into gear.

Rainwater beaded up and slipped down the glass windows, like tears falling from the sky. As the small apartments disappeared, giving way to grand historic skyrises, I felt the sway of my stomach lurch.

"We're here," the man said.

With apprehension, I stared up at the building.

"Thank you." I quickly paid and stepped out.

"You okay, sweetheart?" he asked, his window cracked open once more.

"I think so," I answered.

"Okay, you take care of yourself. I don't want to find a sweet girl like you out on the curb at this late hour again, you hear me?" His words were fatherly, but it was the warm smile behind them that gave them meaning.

I gave him a sad smile. "I will, and thank you."

My heart skipped a beat as the old man pulled away from the curb, leaving me alone once more. Soon, that beat turned into a full gallop as I made my way toward the elevator and then down the hall, slipping in with a nice elderly couple arriving home late from the theater.

My hand shook as I lifted it to knock.

And my breath caught as the door cracked open.

"Hi," Roman greeted, looking devilishly handsome in a pair of pajama bottoms and nothing else. I gulped audibly.

"Hi," I replied.

He pushed open the door, never asking for an explanation or a reason for my late arrival.

Like he'd always expected me to wind up here eventually.

I guessed he did know everything after all.

CHAPTER FIFTEEN

ROMAN

Everything had worked out perfectly.

I'd planned out every detail until the execution.

It was devious.

Calculating and deceptive.

But then again… when had I ever gotten anything in this world by being honest?

As Cara slowly walked through my apartment, looking from one spacious corner to the next, I couldn't help but notice her swollen eyelids and the heavy posture she held.

I'd done that. I'd caused that pain.

No, he did, I reminded myself.

I'd only offered the bait, and now, I was going to be the one to bring her back to life.

Back from the misery and solitude he'd driven her to because of his own selfishness.

Jo had reported back just a few hours earlier, telling me it had taken little effort on her part to convince the asshat to a private dance. And, from there, it had been like taking candy from a baby.

He hadn't even put up a fight. Just handed over his hard-earned money and taken her for a ride—obviously with little thought to the woman waiting for him at home.

Jo had had so much fun that she'd offered me a refund, saying how rare it was to find such an eager cheater.

"Keep it," I'd demanded. "God knows I feel guilty enough."

"You don't feel guilty." She'd laughed. "You don't even know the meaning of the word."

Our conversation had left me cold.

I watched my newest houseguest become acquainted with the space. I'd left most of the lights off, preferring the soft glow of the city to the harsh fluorescents of the kitchen.

Maybe it hid my guilt, making me appear to be the shining white knight she so desperately needed.

But then again, according to Jo, I didn't feel anything close to the word.

Or did I?

"Breakfast?" Cara greeted me in the kitchen as the bright morning sun cascaded through the windows, nearly blinding me.

I nodded, catching my first glimpse of her. Dressed in an oversize T-shirt and a pair of shorts I'd loaned her the night before, she looked nearly as homeless as she probably felt.

Yet I'd never seen anyone so beautiful.

Her hair was loose and tousled, framing her high cheekbones and mesmerizing brown eyes that no longer held the tears she'd arrived with. She smiled, and although I could tell it was somewhat forced, it was something.

She'd make it here without him.

I'd make sure of it.

We'd gotten off to a bit of a rough start last night. My usual self-assured, levelheaded persona had seemed to take a vacation the minute she arrived, and I had suddenly found myself tripping over words and stumbling over what to do. Generally, I'd just lacked any kind of grace.

I'd offered her a drink and nearly dropped the entire glass on the floor. When it came to figuring out sleeping arrangements, the normal me wouldn't have hesitated at the opportunity to invite her into my bed.

But this new adolescent version of me? I'd chickened out, offering her the guest room instead. I'd chastised myself the entire night as I lay in bed, knowing her body was mere feet from my own.

She'd come here, to me.

On her own.

And I'd done nothing but treated her like a buddy.

Good God, I really was turning into my brother.

"Did you get any sleep?" she asked.

I took a seat at the breakfast bar, watching her move about my kitchen like she owned it.

I'd never seen a woman in my house before—outside the bedroom, that was. The kind of dates I had would leave early in the morning, never staying for pillow talk or meals. It was the type of life I'd enjoyed and needed to survive the stress of my job.

But seeing Cara, in her goofy clothes and her unkempt hair, tossing pancakes and pouring coffee, made me realize that I might have been missing out on something major.

Something vital.

I'd always known I wanted Cara for more than a fling. She wasn't Jo or any other girl I'd bring home for an evening or two.

She was special.

That was why I'd tried so damn hard to stay away.

For a man who didn't believe in love beyond obligation, the very idea of her made me want to run. Even now, I could feel myself fighting the pull to stake my claim, after everything I'd done to make this moment a reality. Because once I did, there'd be no turning back.

"Tossed and turned," I replied, taking the cup of coffee she'd offered.

Our fingers briefly touched before she pulled away and busied herself once again. I wondered if she could feel the heat of my touch seeping into her skin.

As she was seeping into my goddamn soul.

"I've got to get ready for work," I announced, rising suddenly.

I couldn't help the look of alarm that washed across my face. I felt in over my head.

I needed space.

Nearly running toward the master bedroom, I slammed the door shut, seeking shelter and silence.

Dear God, what the hell had I done?

Bent over with my hands on my knees, I tried to breathe, but even that felt like a luxury I shouldn't be allowed.

I'd done a lot of terrible things in my life. I'd lied, cheated, and stolen to get to where I was. Being a businessman at the level I was… it was inevitable. Sure, we could say it was legal.

Taking over a small company and providing them with the stability to move forward for generations to come?

Fine.

But what it really was... was stealing. I'd stolen the livelihood of countless people for a profit. It was something my brother and father had only dabbled in.

We were an investment company. We invested money where we thought it would profit the most. But I'd taken it one step further and started buying out companies that had been succeeding and mowing them over.

My brother believed we were bringing them into the Cavenaugh family. But really we were just adding to the bottom line. At least, that was all I cared about.

And, now, I'd done the same thing with Cara.

I'd treated her like she was just another gain, an addition to my bottom line.

I'd gone after something that wasn't mine, and all I could envision was the end goal—her in my arms.

So, I had taken.

I had stolen.

I'd cheated.

And now, here she was.

The problem though?

I'd pictured all the obstacles—Tyler and her grief over the breakup.

But I'd never imagined I'd have to deal with the biggest obstacle of all.

Myself.

I snuck out of the apartment while Cara was still in the shower. The breakfast she'd left me on the counter—pancakes, eggs, and bacon—had gone untouched as my new guilty conscience and I headed for work.

I knew what I had to do.

As soon as she came into work, I'd have her make

arrangements for her to move her things into a hotel until she could figure out new housing arrangements.

I'd help her as much as I could.

As much as a friend could.

But, for now, that would be all I could offer. All I should offer.

Because, if it weren't for me and my meddling, she wouldn't have been in this mess.

She wouldn't have had to hail a taxi in the middle of the night with swollen red eyes, carrying the pain of a failed relationship, all the way to my door.

And she wouldn't have had to move on—unless she'd wanted to.

I followed my usual routine into work, going through the motions, as my mind relived the last twenty-four hours over and over.

Grabbing my cup of coffee, I found my way into my dark office and closed the door.

The silence that used to greet me now felt more like a prison sentence.

Powering up my computer, I stared out the large windows, out onto the city.

I thought back to the many hours of my teen years when I'd looked out the very same windows, wondering what the people down below were doing. My father would tell me to stop fooling around and pay attention. This was a place for work. Nothing else, nothing more.

But I knew the truth.

He couldn't hide his true nature from me.

Like recognized like, and no matter how hard he'd tried to raise Jude in his image, he'd hated the fact that I'd turned out to be just like him.

Cold and manipulative.

I just chose not to hide it.

"You left without saying good-bye?"

I turned to see Cara standing in the doorway. She'd been so quiet stepping in, I hadn't heard the door open.

Dressed plainly in black pants and a pink sweater that had seen better days. The shoes she wore were the same ones she'd had on when she arrived at the apartment, soaked and dripping wet. I'd offered to toss them in the dryer, but she'd declined, saying it was too late. They were probably still damp on her feet.

"Wanted to get an early morning start on the day," I said lamely, knowing she could see through my lie.

I didn't have anything important on the calendar that would have warranted the need to sneak out of the house. I was just making up excuses.

And hurting her in the process.

Again.

"What is going on, Roman?" she asked, pushing the door closed behind her.

It clicked shut with a resolute finality. As if everything before this moment—the flirting and the tired excuses to spend time with her—was then.

And this?

This was now. It was all about to change.

I might have stolen her like a thief in the night, but she was here now—with me. And damn if I wasn't going to take advantage and lay all my cards on the table.

"I don't know," I confessed, taking a step forward.

She leaned back against the door as I stalked toward her.

"I don't know, but damn it if I don't want to find out."

I stopped less than an inch from her. I could smell the scent of my shampoo in her hair. My hand nearly shook as I lifted it to her face. "I want you, Cara. I want you more than I've ever wanted anyone," I said, my voice barely louder than a whisper.

She parted her lips to respond, but I stopped her.

"I want you, but I need you to want me back. I've seen your eyes following me around the room. I know the way they linger, but it's not enough. I can't be with you, knowing you're still hurting over someone else. So, believe me when I say this, I will wait, but please don't take too long. For both our sakes."

And to remind her of exactly what she'd be giving up if she walked away, my lips met hers for the very first time. I hoped it wasn't the last.

It was everything I'd imagined it would be. Heat, passion, longing, and tenderness all wrapped up into one life-defining kiss. Her lips parted, and I felt her gasp as our tongues collided, like the merging of two souls.

And, fuck, maybe it was.

For the first time, I was losing myself in another human being, and I wasn't scared.

For the first time, I didn't feel like my father or my brother.

I just felt like me.

CHAPTER SIXTEEN

CARA

How could I move on after a morning like that?

How could I move on, period?

I'd somehow managed to peel myself off Roman's office door and find my way back to my desk, going through the motions of the morning, all the while still picturing my boss's hands on my body… his mouth as it devoured me.

Holy shit.

My thighs involuntarily squeezed together as I just thought about it.

He wanted me.

He wanted me to want him.

Well, news flash, Mr. Cavenaugh… that was not a problem.

Every neuron in my body was currently fine-tuned to his unique signal, and had he continued to kiss me like that for much longer, I was fairly certain I would have just died right there in his arms.

Could women actually die of orgasmic bliss?

Something else to research… maybe later.

But something was stopping me from running back into that office, locking the door, and doing the nasty with my boss.

Something important.

And it most definitely had to do with the crater of emotional baggage currently lodged in my head. Shacking up with another man, right after my boyfriend of eight years had cheated on me, sounded like something out of a daytime soap opera.

And I was better than that.

The way Roman had looked at me, I felt like he truly believed I was better than that as well.

So, when I came to him—which I thoroughly planned on doing and soon—it wouldn't be a knee-jerk reaction to Tyler's misdeeds.

It would be because I wanted to.

Hell, it would be because I damn well needed to.

My internal monologue of confidence lasted about an hour.

By the time lunch rolled around, I was a basket case.

Holding back tears, I rushed out of the building, seeking the shelter only an overpopulated, overly self-involved city could provide. Getting lost in the crowd, I let my tears loose, knowing no one around would dare approach me. Not when they had their own boatload of drama to deal with.

Rounding the corner, I made it to the deli Roman loved and prepared to brave the line that had already formed. Lunch in this particular area of town always meant a line.

Even for the assistant to Roman Cavenaugh.

Deli meat favored no one.

As I became like the rest of my line dwellers and began putzing around on my phone, I was surprised to see an incoming call from Melissa interrupting my endless search for funny cat videos.

"Hello?" I answered, curious as to why she would be calling in the middle of classes.

"Cat videos? Again? You could at least do something useful with your time, like research a cure for cancer. Oh, wait, that's me."

"How did you—" I began to say, suddenly looking up with frantic eyes.

It took mere seconds for me to settle on that familiar petite frame. She'd cut her hair since the last time I'd seen her. The sandy-brown locks now barely touched her shoulders, but those effortless waves I'd envied for years were still there.

Along with her beautiful smile and open arms, waiting for me to hug her.

"Oh my gosh!" I screamed, not caring one bit that I'd stepped out of line and lost my spot. "What are you doing here?"

"You called me, remember?"

I thought back to the night before—Tyler dropping his cheating bomb, me grabbing a few articles of clothing before I'd disappeared into the freezing rain. Somewhere in between all that mess, I did recall leaving a somewhat cryptic message for Melissa.

"Now you remember." She laughed, seeing the realization spread across my face.

Her arm draped across my shoulders as we began walking away from the deli. Where to, I had no idea, but there were too many people to just stand around.

"I missed your call because it happened to be the one

night I actually managed to get some sleep. Between exams and roommate drama, it's been a precious commodity. Have I told you lately how much I love you? If not, I do. So very much."

"Is it bad?" I asked, remembering her mentioning her roommate the last time we'd spoken.

She was a perky girl from Colorado. She sounded nice enough, but apparently, their personalities just didn't mesh well. Melissa was ready to kill her.

"Bad," she answered. "She's just too happy. No one can possibly be that happy, Cara. No one. And I lived with you."

"Hey!"

"I mean that with love. Lots and lots of love. Anyway, you called, and I was sleeping."

"Sorry about that," I said.

She shrugged, looking around at the city like it was a zoo. It kind of was. "It's okay. I got your crazy message when I woke up to work out. But, instead of going to the gym, I went to the airport. I figured I needed a little break from the roommate, and you needed… well, me."

I sighed, leaning my head on her shoulder, as we walked. "I do. Thank you."

"Good. Now, where am I staying? I took the train into the city from the airport, and left my bags in a locker there, so I need to go back and get them. But I need to know where I'll be sleeping."

Oh, crap.

"So, here's the thing."

She stopped dead in her tracks, turning to me with her hands on her hips. "We're homeless. This is what you're about to tell me, isn't it? Oh God, Cara Hamilton, you did not sleep on the sidewalk last night, did you? If so, I am going to march right over to wherever that douche canoe works and give him a piece of my mind. Kicking you out in the middle of the night," she began to mutter incoherently, her temper taking over.

"We're not homeless!" I nearly shouted, grabbing her shoulders to gain her attention. "I'm staying with Roman."

"Roman? Your hot boss Roman?"

I nodded, my checks instantly inflaming.

A devilish grin spread across her face. "Nice, Cara-saurus. Didn't think you had that in you."

"Cara-saurus? Really? You said you wouldn't call me that after graduation! You promised," I whined as she headed back down the street.

"No, I didn't. You only thought I did."

"Cheater," I muttered, crossing my arms over my body like a five-year-old child.

"You love me. Now, are you going to tell me where we are, or am I going to have to pull out a map?"

"Dear God, no." I flinched at the very idea of her pulling out a gigantic old map in the middle of lunch hour in Manhattan.

Grabbing her hand, I pulled her back toward the deli line.

"Just follow me, and I'll get us a hotel for the night."

"No hot boss?"

"Not for you!"

"You're no fun," she laughed, garnering the attention of several suits as we passed by.

"Yes, well, you called me Cara-saurus, so I win."

"You're just jealous you could never come up with anything to call me in return."

"Asswipe."

"Clever."

I couldn't hide the smile that spread across my face as

we bantered back and forth. We hadn't seen each other in months, but it was as if not a single day had passed.

"I missed you, Mel," I said.

"Right back at you, Cara-saurus."

I rolled my eyes and punched her in the arm.

Because that was what best friends did.

TRUE TO MY WORD, I BOOKED MELISSA AND MYSELF A HOTEL not too far from work. At exactly five o'clock, I made a beeline for the elevator, knowing I was chickening out of explaining my absence to Roman. I hadn't exactly said I was moving in, and although he'd been gracious enough to take me in for one night, the idea of moving in with my boss was… well…

Enticing.

Exciting.

Inappropriate.

Yes, there was the word I was looking for. *Inappropriate.*

I might have been sticking my tail between my legs and running away, but I had things to attend to. Friends to entertain. A mangled life to repair. A hot boss with an equally hot body and a set of lips that could set a forest ablaze.

Well, that would just have to wait.

For now…

Knowing I had limited time with Melissa, I relied on old standbys to get us through the evening. I knew she'd never been to New York, and she would probably enjoy a night out, seeing the sights and enjoying a crazy expensive meal or maybe even visiting a club, but this was my night.

My only night with her.

And I was being selfish.

So, armed with candy, pizza, and copious amounts of beer, I arrived at the hotel, prepared to keep her indoors if it was the last thing I did. Not having a hand free, I knocked on the door with the tip of my shoe. As pain radiated through my toe, I quickly realized it wasn't the smartest idea I'd had to date.

"Ouch," I mumbled, balancing several bags and a pizza box in my hands.

"Think you've got enough stuff there?" she asked after opening the door.

I looked her up and down. She was in a ratty shirt she'd had since freshman year and a pair of scrub bottoms.

"You don't want to go out?" I asked.

She took the pizza box and began to dive right in.

"No," she answered, a slice of pizza already halfway to her mouth. "I came here for you. Not the city. I can come back anytime. Preferably when you're happier and not a freaking disaster. We'll do the touristy crap then. For now, I'm trying to put this train wreck back together again."

And by train wreck she meant me.

I had the best friend ever.

"Thank you," I said, dropping the bags on the sofa to envelop her in a hug.

"You did it for me when Jeremy broke off our engagement."

"I know," I said, "but that was then."

"And?"

"And I didn't know if things had changed."

She rolled her eyes, sitting down on the spot of the sofa that wasn't covered in bags. "Things between us will never change. For four years, we managed to live together and not kill each other. Believe me, that's a huge success. We're friends for life now."

I snorted, reaching out for a piece of pizza to call my own. "She must be really horrible."

Melissa sighed. "She's not that bad. She's just not you."

"Well then, maybe you should give her a chance," I suggested with a wink.

"I don't wanna," she whined, grabbing another slice.

I'd always been envious of Mel's amazing metabolism. She could sit down, eat an entire pizza with a side of ice cream, and wake up the next morning, weighing a pound less. But then again, she was also the one running five miles or more every morning while I was stuffing down a bagel and considering my three-block walk to the subway a workout. But it was that get-up-and-go attitude that always kept her motivated and pushing forward, and because of that, I knew she'd someday make an incredible doctor.

Whether she currently believed it or not.

"So, tell me more about the hot boss," she requested after we'd finished scarfing down the pizza and moved on to dessert, which consisted of basically every single kind of candy I could find.

"Would you stop calling him that?"

"Why? Because it offends you? Or because you agree?" she asked.

She dug into the bag of M&M's. They were her favorite, especially the kind with peanut butter. I didn't know how many times we'd sat around, talking about boys, homework, or God knew what else, while I watched her squash a bright little morsel in between her thumb and pointer finger before popping it into her mouth.

"Your silence is answer enough," she said with a smirk. After a moment, she added, "And I happily agree."

Shaking my head, I replied, "How would you even know? You haven't met him."

"I have a computer. And hello? Google! You think I didn't look up the guy after hearing the way you talked about him over the last few weeks?"

"I haven't talked about him that much, have I?"

"Remember when I first started dating Jeremy our sophomore year, and I couldn't stop talking about his hair and the way it looked in the morning—"

"And after he ran," I added.

"Exactly. I swear, I had a love affair with that boy's hair alone. I could have written sonnets about it in that first month. I was obsessed."

"It really was disgusting. But you were in love. That's what we do when we're in love. But I'm not," I said, thinking back to those first few months with Tyler and comparing them to now. I might not have been obsessed with Tyler's hair, but I'd had an affinity for his smile.

I still did.

Or at least, until last night, I had.

"You might not be sonnet-worthy yet, but if you were me and you had a chance to hear yourself, you'd see it."

"See what?" I asked.

"The pull he has over you. The connection that's there. The way you include him into a conversation without even realizing it. You've become infatuated with this man, and it has nothing to do with work, Cara. When you finally stop denying the truth to yourself, just do me a favor and make sure he's deserving of you."

I had no response, but I gave a small nod.

"Oh, and one other favor, as a friend."

Our eyes met.

"When you do, you know, decide to seal the deal... take pictures. Please? 'Cause that man is... *damn.*"

Laughter burst out from both of us and didn't cease for the rest of the night.

It was good to have my best friend by my side once again even if everything in my life was lopsided.

She was my constant.

Melissa decided to prolong her stay by another day when she discovered I wasn't kidding about having nowhere to stay beyond Roman's.

"Nowhere?" she yelled loud enough for the entire hotel floor to hear.

"Well, there is this coworker who said I was welcome to crash at her place, but I don't think it was an offer to move in indefinitely."

"We need to find you a place and fast," she said, already pulling out her phone and tapping away.

For a Midwestern girl, she was incredibly tech savvy and pushy. Something told me she'd fit in better in this city than me. Within seconds, she pulled up nearby apartments, complete with ratings, rent, and openings.

"Wow, I'm impressed."

"Be more impressed when I can actually get you into a place. We have our first viewing in a few hours. These places go fast. Let's get over to Tyler's and start packing up your stuff. Maybe we can get in and out of there before the cheating dickwad gets home."

"Good idea," I said, thankful for once for Tyler's grueling work schedule, which happened to include weekend hours.

And very late evening hours.

Good to know my bitterness was firmly intact.

After a wholesome breakfast of leftover pizza we'd somehow managed to cram into the small fridge along with whatever candy we hadn't eaten, we packed up and headed out to my—*Tyler's* apartment.

The tension was palpable as we drew near. I was so fidgety by the time we turned the corner that I was nearly jumping out of my own skin.

"Could you let us off here?" Melissa softly asked the driver.

He pulled over to the side of the street and Mel paid as I calmly waited, feeling like the worst friend on the planet.

She'd flown out here on a moment's notice. God knew how much money she'd spent that she probably didn't have. Plus, she'd blown off important classes, and she was probably now behind on hours and hours of homework.

"Thank you," I said after we'd climbed out of the taxi.

"For what?"

"Everything. Coming out here, talking me off the ledge, being here with me now."

She turned to me as yellow cabs zoomed by, passing each other in a race to get their customers to their destinations on time.

"Listen," she said, "I didn't have to talk you off any ledge. You were doing fine all on your own. You would have figured this out without me. I just like to think that you do better when I'm around." She laughed.

A gust of wind raced through the trees, making our teeth chatter.

"You don't give yourself enough credit, Cara. I know you think I came out here because I didn't believe you could do this on your own, but that's far from the truth. I came here because I heard the pain in your voice and couldn't imagine being anywhere but by your side. So, yes… I might be a little bossy and demanding, but that's only because that's how I handle these kinds of situations."

"That's not how you handled Jeremy," I reminded her, shoving my hands into my pockets for warmth.

"Sure I did. After several weeks of self-loathing and wishing harm and ill-will to several parts of his lower anatomy, I eventually got up and took care of things."

"Mmhmm," I agreed, rolling my eyes.

She grabbed my arm, tightly linking us together. We began the one-block stroll toward my apartment. How she knew what direction to go, I'd never know. She'd probably Googled it while I was in the shower. It was what I would have done.

We were oddly similar in that way.

"Let's just consider my experience with getting over Jeremy a crash course for you on what *not* to do. Don't sit around in your pajamas for weeks on end. Don't blame yourself, and definitely don't convince yourself that chocolate is a major food group before trying to fit into your skinny jeans. It's not good for the ego."

"Duly noted."

"On that note, let's go get your stuff, and find you a place. Then, if we have time, maybe you can take me out to dinner?" she said with a flicker of hope.

"Sounds like a plan."

<hr>

As we'd predicted and hoped, the apartment was quiet and dark when we entered.

"What the hell?" I found myself saying immediately as my eyes scanned the empty walls, the bare floor, and the nearly barren kitchen.

"Does it always look like this?" Melissa asked as she took a walk around the living room where the couch used to be.

"No," I said in a daze. "Not at all."

My first thought was that we had been robbed, but as I

looked around, I realized that the only things missing were Tyler's. The afghan my grandmother had given me on the day of my high school graduation was folded neatly on the floor by the rug I'd found at the flea market just a week earlier.

"Cara?"

"Yeah?" I choked out.

"There's a note."

When I looked up, Melissa was holding a handwritten note in Tyler's familiar angular penmanship. He'd written it on the back of a cable bill, obviously in a hurry.

> Cara,
> The apartment is paid for through June of next year.
> I'm truly sorry.
> Tyler

"He left," I said, still not believing the words as they fell from my lips.

"Well, I figured that much out for myself. The note wasn't very long. Are you going to stay?"

I looked around, remembering the brief time I'd spent in this place. I'd only lived here for a couple of short months, barely enough time to even consider it a home. But, in those short few weeks, I'd laughed with Tyler, made love to him, and hoped for a future with the one man I'd thought would be with me until the end.

Was it enough to haunt me if I stayed?

"I don't know," I answered honestly. "Should I?"

Her footfalls were audible against the aged wood as she took a look around the small apartment. It wasn't much. A small front room made up what we'd considered the living room, and the kitchen could barely hold both of us, but we'd made it work. The bedroom was big enough to hold a bed and basically nothing more. I'd shoved as many clothes into the closet as I could, and the rest had gone into storage bins under the bed.

It had been a hard adjustment, but I'd done it. It wasn't the ideal life I'd pictured when I watched *Friends* or *Sex in the City* reruns, but it was mine. I'd thought it would be something Tyler and I would share together, but I could see now that it would be my adventure alone.

If I still wanted it.

"I think it's a great place—or at least, it could be if you allowed it to be. Want some help?" she asked, taking another glance.

"Absolutely," I said.

"Great. Let's get started."

I was slowly starting to realize that life was never what you intended, but as my best friend and I went from Goodwill to every thrift store we could find to decorate my first apartment, I discovered this unpredictable new life had left me a little scarred and perhaps a tad bitter, but also full of hope.

And that was the most beautiful thing of all.

CHAPTER SEVENTEEN

ROMAN

I'd never been a lonely person.

Silence didn't bother me. Stretches of time when it was just me was pure bliss in my opinion. Where others felt lost and alone, I found the life of a loner calm and peaceful.

Until Cara.

When I'd left the office on Friday night and found her gone without an explanation and her things vanished from my apartment without a trace, it was the first time the real definition of loneliness had finally sunk in.

Without her, the silent apartment I used to love so much now just felt empty and cold.

Like the man who occupied it.

After a hopeful hour of believing she might indeed return, balancing bags and dragging suitcases behind her, apologizing profusely for leaving me in the dark about her plans, I had given up and dived into a fresh bottle of scotch.

Let's face it, who'd want to move in with this cluster

fuck? After all, I had sabotaged her relationship to get her here in the first place.

What kind of sane person did that?

Jo had briefly questioned my sanity over the phone after I'd explained to her what I wanted, asking if maybe all I needed was a little time-out, which she'd be happy to give. When I'd blatantly turned her down, she had known I meant business, especially when I'd offered the substantial cash to back it up.

Having Jo seduce Tyler hadn't been as hard as I'd thought it would be. Jo had said he was like every other stressed out young suit who walked in there—eager, hungry, and teetering on the edge. No doubt, he'd been tempted to jump more times than he could count, but a faithful girlfriend half a country away had always stopped him.

But now that she was here…

Now that she was real and things weren't as he'd expected, it was the ideal time for him to stumble.

And he'd done so perfectly.

I'd thought I'd be the one to pick up the pieces of her broken heart and show her that he hadn't been worth it in the first place. But she hadn't even given me twenty-four hours, and I'd run like a coward—hiding in my bedroom rather than seeking her out like I should have.

Friday had bled into Saturday, and now, the first rays of light were just starting to break over the horizon on what was one of the longest weekends of my life. While I usually had no problem with occupying myself—either bringing work home, finding an old movie on TV, or making a late-night call to Jo—the hours that dragged on before a new workweek seemed endless.

I'd already drunk my way through the bottle of scotch, the reminder of it drilling its way into my head. But even that hadn't lessened the sting of loneliness I felt, and the longer it lasted, the angrier I felt about it.

Since when did I walk around, moping over a girl?

Especially one I'd barely touched.

But, God, when I had…

Her body had been like putty in my hands, her lips had felt like velvet, and she'd tasted like fucking cream.

I put the memory deep in the back of my mind because even the slightest flashback would have me hard in seconds, which only reminded me of the fact that she'd left.

Without saying good-bye.

For all I knew, she'd gone back to the bastard. After everything he'd done, she could be cozied up to the big, dumb ox right now, wasting away their lazy Sunday, watching movies, as they cuddled under blankets in bed.

"Damn it!" I shouted, pushing myself off the couch. I stalked toward the kitchen in search of my next liquid meal.

Maybe this one would actually do the trick.

After an exhaustive hunt, tossing open every cupboard and drawer, I managed to find one miniature bottle of peach-flavored vodka and an empty bottle of tequila.

Where did that even come from?

Guess I had an errand to run.

Throwing on a pair of jeans and a T-shirt, I grabbed a baseball cap to control the Mohawk that was starting to form from sleeping on the awkward sofa, and then I headed out.

A sharp yelp met me at the door.

Glancing up, I found a pair of familiar dark brown eyes staring back at me.

"I've never seen you in a baseball cap," Cara said in a rush, obviously embarrassed by the terrible girl noise she'd just made in the hallway. It'd been so loud that I was surprised old Mrs. Fenton wasn't sticking her nose out from across the hall to investigate.

"Well, I don't wear suits all the time—something you probably would have discovered if you'd stayed around long enough."

She blanched instantly, her eyes widening, and then she turned away from me.

Rather than the cool and aloof approach I was known for, apparently, I was going for direct and a bit desperate today.

Good move, Cavenaugh. Good move.

"I'm sorry. That was rude," I said, softly touching her shoulder. "Let me start over." I cleared my throat as she slowly turned back toward me. "Hi. How are you?"

A small smirk tugged at the corner of her mouth. "Better. Thank you for asking. But I didn't mean to interrupt your weekend. I can come back."

"No, come on in. I just realized I don't need anything anyway."

"Okay, good. Because I was lying. I didn't want to come back. I brought enough breakfast to feed a family of five, including teenagers. So, I hope you haven't eaten."

She held up her arms, each hand bearing a large bag of food from a bagel shop down the street. The smell of bacon, eggs, and freshly baked bread hit my nose, and my stomach instantly groaned in protest of its maltreatment.

"Starving," I answered, stepping back to allow her entry.

"Perfect."

I stood at the door, watching her walk past, and I took a moment to just stare at her.

In my house.

Twenty minutes ago, I'd felt alone and lifeless in this place. And, now, I couldn't imagine being anywhere else.

She seemed to have this effect anywhere she went. She brought life to everything.

Maybe even me.

CARA WASN'T KIDDING ABOUT THE FOOD.

It was enough to feed the entire floor or keep me fed for at least a week.

"Did you think I lived with a traveling circus?" I asked.

Cara shoved the leftovers in the fridge, as I held on to the cups of coffee I'd brewed.

She laughed as we migrated into the living room, settling into the sofa I'd called home for the last two days. I quickly pushed the blankets and pillows out of the way, hoping she wouldn't ask why it looked like someone had camped out here.

Her eyes shifted to the empty bottles on the table.

"Rough night," I said evasively. "Crashed on the couch."

She pursed her lips. "I'm sorry I didn't call."

Awkward silence followed.

I wanted to ask where she'd been, but then again, I wasn't sure I wanted to know the answer. If she said Tyler's, I didn't know if I could hold back the words that would inevitably fly from my mouth.

I was done being the nice guy, sitting idly by, waiting for the girl to make up her mind.

I was never that guy.

But I also didn't want to be the one who was rejected and given a consolation breakfast as an apology.

So, I sat.

In silence.

Waiting for her to say something. The ball was in her court after all.

"I know what you're thinking," she said suddenly.

I looked at her, amusement and perhaps a bit of surprise painted across my features.

"You're worried."

"How would you know that?" I asked.

Her hand lifted, and her finger extended toward my face. "Your forehead. Whenever you worry—which is practically all the time, by the way—you get this crease right down the middle, between your eyebrows. And, when it's really bad, you run your hands through your hair until you have pathways of worry etched in it."

My arms folded across my chest as the feeling of vulnerability took over. In all my life, people had always seen me in one way or another.

Rich kid.

Playboy.

Boss.

Loner.

But no one had ever really seen me.

She did though. Maybe more than I saw myself.

"And what am I worried about?" I asked, my voice betraying the heavy emotions I was carrying.

"Me. Or at least I'm hoping it's me. Otherwise, I just spent a ridiculous amount of money on bagels."

"You left. What was I supposed to think?" I said, my head falling back against the sofa in frustration.

"I know, and I'm sorry. But try and look at it from my side. I leave my cheating boyfriend, in the middle of the night, and where do I go? Who do I seek out? You. I could have gone to Lauren's. I could have gotten a hotel room, but no, I came here."

"It seemed to work out that first night."

"It did, but I wasn't thinking clearly, and if I'd returned, especially after that kiss, I would have done something I'd regret."

My head jerked back up, my eyes wide.

"Let me finish, please. I needed some time. Time to think. Time to process. And I'm not saying I'm one hundred percent okay with everything now, but I'm at least back on my feet."

"So, you're not back together with him?" I asked, feeling like a dumbass but needing to know for sure that he was out of her life. For good.

"No." She nearly laughed. "Is that where you thought I was? Back with Tyler? Oh gosh! No. My best friend from college flew in and was going to help me find an apartment, but when we went back to pack my things, I discovered Tyler had already beaten me to the punch. Plus, out of guilt, he'd paid the rent through the summer of next year. So, since I'm rent-free for the foreseeable future, we went shopping, and I've been decorating my apartment. My very own apartment. That sounds weird."

"You're babbling."

"I know, but I didn't get much sleep last night, and it only gets worse when I'm sleep-deprived… and nervous. And I happen to be both right now."

I leaned forward, my eyes following hers. "Why are you nervous, Cara?"

"Because of you. You make me nervous."

A devilish grin flashed across my face. "Why?"

"Because you're so… you. And me… well, I'm just… me, you know?" she stammered, her words not making any sense. "I was up practically all night, and you know what I was thinking about? Not my lying cheat of an ex-boyfriend. No. I was thinking of you. What you were doing, how you were. If you'd eaten without me around to remind you. And I began to wonder if that was normal, you know? To think so much about someone, especially after ending an eight-year relationship."

She was talking a mile a minute now.

"But then, as the sun started to rise, I just decided I didn't care anymore. I've spent my entire life preparing for every caveat, every detail. I research movies before I go to the theater and restaurants before I eat, and I never, ever do anything spontaneously. Hell, even moving here was planned years in advance. The only thing in my life that is spontaneous is you. And it's thrilling and exciting, and maybe it's too soon, but I don't care."

"Are you saying—"

She leaped forward, her body colliding with mine, and our mouths met once again.

Fucking hell, she still tasted like cream. Sweet fucking cream.

My mind went blank, and primal instinct took over. I pulled her closer, my hands sliding under the hem of her shirt. The soft touch of her skin drove me further, deeper. I wanted to touch her everywhere. All at once.

I wanted all of her.

But not like this.

Barely able to breathe, I pulled back, my chest heaving from the sheer restraint I was showing. For the first time, I noticed that her shirt was missing. In our frenzy, I hadn't even realized. Looking at the floor, I found it in a small heap, forgotten and crumpled.

"I can't do this."

Her eyes bled disappointment almost immediately as she tried to pull away.

"No, let me finish," I said, pulling her back into my

arms. "I can't rush this. I can't let this be like every other time."

"It won't—"

My hand flew up to her lips, still bright red and swollen from our passionate kiss. That, combined with her perky breasts saying hello to me through the flimsy bra she wore, and I was about to come unglued.

"Would you let me finish?" I smirked.

She nodded, biting the bottom of her lip, as I settled my hand back on her thigh.

"Now, it might surprise you, but I've done this a time or two."

She rolled her eyes, holding back laughter.

"And some, I'm not saying who, might consider me a bit of an expert in this particular area."

"Really? This is where you want to go with this?"

"I have a point," I said, grinning. "But none of that matters now because I don't have a fucking clue how to do this."

"What?" she asked, clearly clueless.

"Care. I don't know how to care."

Her eyes widened as she slightly pulled back. "You've never cared about any of the women you—"

"Nope." I shook my head.

"Not even—"

"This is seriously where you want to go with this?"

"Point taken."

"Listen"—I sighed—"I don't want to hurt you. I wouldn't be able to live with myself if I did. And the thought of rushing through this—I can't. I need to live and breathe every moment, in case—"

"In case what?"

"In case you change your mind," I admitted.

Her hands wrapped around my neck, and my eyes

briefly fluttered closed from the contact. I could feel the tips of her fingers as they snaked around my jawline and sank into my hair.

"I know who you are, Roman Cavenaugh. I know where I am and what I'm getting into. So, please, do your worst."

Her words terrified me. She did know me, probably more than anyone else in my life. And that was why I needed her, why I'd do anything to keep her—just to prove I was worthy of her.

I'd always told myself that I'd tell her one day—of my involvement with Tyler's infidelity. But seeing her trust and adoration beaming back at me, I knew I'd never utter those words.

Because she was finally mine.

And I was never letting go.

Her legs wrapped around me as I walked down the hallway, desperately trying not to slam into the walls. Once my mouth had found its way back to hers while we were on the couch, it hadn't left.

But I wasn't about to take her on the sofa.

At least not this time.

Right now, I needed her in my bed. I needed her to sanctify this space, so when I awoke each morning, I'd remember exactly what it was like to feel her skin against mine and her body beneath me as I made her mine, over and over again.

Thankfully, we made it without incident to the master, and as I reached the foot of the bed, I slowly let her body slide down mine until she gently fell to the bed. Still touching her while her brown eyes were gazing up at mine, I took this moment to breathe her in.

To memorize her every feature.

The sloping curves of her shoulders, the subtle freckles on her cheeks, and the way her dark hair fell around her, like tiny strands of silk.

"You're staring," she said softly.

"Admiring," I corrected her with a slight smirk. Lifting one arm over my head, I did away with my T-shirt in one swift movement.

A grin spread across my face as I watched her eyes widen in approval, like she couldn't wait to lick every damn inch of me.

"Now, who's staring?"

"What's a better word for *admiring*?" she asked, her voice slightly shaky.

"Appreciating? Applauding? Worshipping?" I suggested.

I loved the dopey look that had spread across her face as her hands reached out to touch me.

"Yes. All of those. That's exactly what I'm doing."

Leaning down so close so that she could feel my warm breath against her neck, I whispered, "Then, lie back, so I can return the favor."

She did exactly as instructed, giving me some room on the bed. Hovering above her, I felt like a king standing at the foot of a grand feast.

And I knew exactly where I wanted to start.

I inwardly groaned, loving the feel of my skin touching hers. It nearly crackled with intensity with every lingering touch. Placing featherlight kisses across her collarbone, I continued down between the valley of her breasts, still covered by the thin cotton bra. With two days of stubble on my chin, I worked my way to the button fly of her jeans, and her breath caught.

I briefly looked up, asking for permission. I wanted her

to want this as much as I did. I wanted her to need this as much as I did.

With the slightest tilt of her head, my fingers made quick work of her jeans, sliding them down her legs and adding them to the growing pile on the floor. Climbing back up the bed, I abruptly froze.

"Are those…" I paused, trying to hold back the chuckle lodged in my throat. Pointing at her bright turquoise boy shorts, I continued, "Tiny hamburgers on your panties?"

Her face quickly turned twenty different shades of red before she covered it. "Yes!" she squealed.

Laughter broke free, and as I fell on the bed next to her, I found myself pulling her rigid hands away from her embarrassed face.

"I happen to love hamburgers," I said with a devilish grin as my hand snuck down the taut planes of her stomach to the edge of her ridiculous panties. "And I happen to find these incredibly sexy."

Before she could say anything in response, I sank my hand under her panties, finding her clit almost instantly.

"Holy crap!" she cried out, her back bowing in response.

Seeing her react to me was intoxicating. I suddenly felt invincible, like I'd just stumbled upon the greatest high known to man and I was the only one who knew about it.

When I gave it a tiny flick, she inhaled sharply. As I went deeper, she let out a deep moan.

"God, you're wet." It was like dipping my fingers into hot maple syrup. And I'd bet it tasted just as sweet.

I was pacing myself, doing my absolute damnedest not to rush this, but I knew if I didn't have my mouth on her soon, I'd explode.

I felt the loss of her wet, warm body as my hand fell

away from her panties. She lifted her eyes to mine, seeking answers.

"I need to taste you," I said, my fingers curling around the hamburger hemline.

Her head lifted, hesitation in her eyes. "I've never... I mean—"

Understanding hit me like a ton of bricks, and I hated that douche of a man even more. Well, maybe not. It was one less place he'd touched her.

"Do you trust me?" I asked.

Her bewitching brown eyes peered into mine.

"Yes."

"Then lie back," I instructed, seeing her head fall back onto the mattress.

Just like the jeans, I slowly removed her panties, watching the tiny hamburgers dance their way down her legs until they fell to the floor with the rest of her clothing. I couldn't help but take a moment to enjoy my new view.

"God, you're beautiful," I breathed out.

I placed tender kisses on the inside of each of her thighs. Her legs trembled as I worked my way up, closer and closer to her core.

Anticipation mixed with her nerves, I was sure. But, soon, all that would be replaced with need.

Pure, raw need that I would give to her.

Over and over again.

I took my time, grazing my lips over the delicate skin until the tip of my nose flicked the tiny pink bud of her sex. I felt her tense, as if waiting for me to change my mind.

As if that were possible.

If anything, the smell of her, the nearness of her body, only drove me further. My arms wrapped firmly around her thighs, spreading her wide, and in an effort to calm her, I leaned down and took what I wanted.

Hungrily.

I feasted rather than nibbled. I devoured rather than showing restraint. I wanted her to know what it felt like to be me. To be so completely spellbound by another that you couldn't possibly hold back for another moment. Because that was what she did to me.

She tore me apart, in the best possible way.

Her legs squeezed around my head like a vise.

"Oh God, Roman!" she cried out.

I couldn't help the grin spreading across my face as she neared her orgasm.

I was a fucking king now.

"Come on, Cara, scream for me," I encouraged her.

Her body tightened around my tongue as she quivered and quaked, screaming out my name once again.

And it sounded like absolute fucking magic.

CHAPTER EIGHTEEN

CARA

There were a lot of assumptions about small towns. We were all inbred. We had the IQs of turnips and didn't know how to work a cell phone. The Bible was the only book we'd ever read, and good girls, like me, waited until marriage.

It was all crap.

Some of the smartest minds came from small towns. We did, in fact, have working technology and even though we lived in what was known as The Bible Belt, it didn't mean we went door to door, preaching it.

In fact, the mating patterns of my senior class could have probably been compared to some sort of zoo animal.

In heat.

While facing extinction.

By the time our tiny class had walked across that rickety stage and taken ahold of our diplomas, hardly anyone had been on speaking terms because of the drama that had unfolded outside of school.

Well, mostly outside of school...

Tyler and I had walked away, feeling like the lucky ones. We'd made it through four years together, completely intact.

Unscathed.

He'd attributed it to our extreme intellect. We hadn't let all the high school drama cloud our judgment.

I, on the other hand, had taken a different stance.

The fact that I'd made him wait four long years for sex?

Well, that could have had something to do with it.

It wasn't something I'd wanted to give away lightly.

When my mother had sat me down and had *the talk*, she hadn't muddled it by comparing my virginity to a flower, and she hadn't talked about the birds and the bees. She had been honest and real.

"I don't expect you to save yourself for marriage, like I did. I know it's an old notion and something that isn't practiced anymore, but the values behind it don't have to fade. Whether it's the first time or not, remember, making love to someone is the most sacred act two people can do together. Don't squander that gift."

That advice had stayed with me throughout my teenage years and every day since.

That was why I should have been freaking out while Roman Cavenaugh—my boss... my freaking boss— hovered above me.

Looking sexier than sin.

But, as he grinned, licking his lips after giving me the biggest damn orgasm of my life, all I could think of was, *More please?*

I'd always thought of the act of sex as pleasant, nice... maybe even a little adventurous, but that'd all changed the minute Roman's lips met mine. It was stupid to say, but in a way, he made me feel like a woman with a single kiss more than Tyler had ever done in eight years.

Roman looked at me like a man drunk on passion, like he was physically holding back the urge to screw me into submission, and damn if I didn't want him to try.

"I think I need to do a little exploring," he said, his eyes lingering across the expanse of my chest. "Right... here."

His fingers skimmed the thin fabric of my bra, and I felt my nipples harden instantly. I briefly chastised myself for not taking a moment to shuffle through my laundry in hopes of finding a cuter bra, but as soon as I felt him slowly lowering the straps, I really couldn't think anymore.

With one quick motion, he undid the clasp in the front, and that was it.

I was completely naked before him.

I should have felt embarrassed, scared.

But seeing the look of pure satisfaction sweep across his face gave me all the confidence I needed and more. I'd never felt more empowered, more womanly, or flat-out sexy before.

And it didn't require expensive clothing or shoes because I'd had it all along.

He took his time, his tongue paying particular attention to my breasts, as, I cried out, "More! I need more!"

I was so close. I could feel it—the same delicious throbbing ache deep in my belly. My thighs squeezed together as his teeth gently closed down on the tip of my nipple, and then he sucked. Hard.

"Yes!" I yelled, my body flooding with endorphins, as my orgasm finally broke free.

After two mind-blowing orgasms, I was dripping with sweat. My body was so on edge that I swore you could hear it humming from the high-frequency vibrations I was putting out.

"You're… and then… two times?" I tried to talk, tossing out random words, as I wiped off my brow.

I heard his deep laugh above me before the faint heat of his breath was next to my ear.

"And I'm hardly done yet."

The bed shifted, and the heat from his body vanished.

"You're going to want to see this," he said in a cocky tone I was learning to decipher as his bedroom voice.

I liked his bedroom voice.

I like it a lot.

Sitting up on my shaky elbows, I watched as his hands went to the fly of his jeans, and a wolfish grin spread across his face.

"Remember what I said about shoe size?" he said.

I nodded, watching him unbutton his jeans.

They hit the floor, and my eyes went wide.

He wasn't lying.

Nope, not lying by a long shot.

If making love was a gift… I was about to get the biggest, most fun gift ever.

My silent state of shock and awe was all the approval Roman needed as he slipped on a condom and crawled back onto the bed, stalking me like prey. I willingly played along, letting him hover over me like a hungry lion, as I took my time appreciating every lean line and powerful muscle. I'd always known he was built. It was something even he couldn't hide beneath those expensive suits he wore.

But seeing it up close and incredibly personal?

It was like finding yourself in the presence of perfection. I wanted to run my hands over every tan inch of him, scatter kisses along his collarbone, and feel him deep inside me.

"Yes," he said softly.

"What?" I asked, meeting his jade-green eyes.

"Whatever you're thinking of... yes. Do it. Stop thinking about it, and just do it."

He was right. I'd spent far too many hours and days dreaming of him. Of what I'd do if I had him and then feeling guilty for even considering it. Now, he was here, naked and wrapped around me like a sexy warm blanket. It was time to stop thinking and time to start living.

So, I did. My fingers dived into his hair as I placed tiny kisses along his torso and chest. My legs were tightly around him, and I felt him hard and ready against my pulsating core.

In one quick motion, he flipped onto his back, taking me with him. On my knees, I was in position just over him.

My eyes took in the sight of his rock-hard erection so close to me. All I had to do was sink down, and we'd be one.

Finally.

"It has to be your decision, remember?" he said, firmly placing his hands on my thighs. "I want you more than I've wanted anything, but like I said before... I want you to want it just as much. So, show me, Cara. Show me how much you want me."

I'd never been keen on romances. I didn't cry during movies, and I preferred a good mystery book to a smutty one. Maybe it was because I truly didn't understand romance—until now.

Tyler and I had been safe... predictable.

I remembered reading that old saying, *I need you more than air*, in a book. I'd told Tyler I thought it was cheesy and stupid. We'd laughed over it and gone out to dinner—the same place we always went when he was home. He'd even ordered the same entree.

But, staring down at Roman, seeing the mixture of tenderness, lust, and desire in his eyes, I got it all—not just the flowers and cheesy gifts on Valentine's Day, but that *feeling*.

That feeling that if you couldn't be with that one person, the air in your lungs was useless.

Because why breathe at all if you couldn't have this? If you couldn't have him?

Taking Roman's hands, I brought them up to my chest and placed each one atop my breasts, holding my hands with his.

My eyes never left his as I slowly lowered myself, savoring every sensation. The first touch, we both moaned, his fingers digging into my skin. With a gentle glide, my body stretched, making room for him, and with the smooth finish when I took him completely, the room was quiet and still.

"Don't move quite yet," he said. "I want to remember this."

Leaning forward, I gently pressed my lips to his. His hand wrapped around the back of my head, and he kissed me deeply, his tongue moving against mine. Soon, I couldn't hold back any longer. The feeling of him deep inside me was downright overwhelming, and I needed more.

I'd always need more now.

We'd barely just begun, and I thought it was safe to say, Roman Cavenaugh had ruined me for all other men.

"Fuck," he groaned as the motion of my hips grinding against his own took over.

My head fell back, and the new bout of confidence I'd

gained took over. My eyes fluttered shut, and I just let myself go. Over and over, I rode his cock until I was breathless, and he was nearly manic with hunger.

Just like before, with little effort, he flipped us. One moment, I had been above him, and the next, he was towering above me.

"You drive me insane, you know that? What I just saw? I never expected that. That my good little Midwestern girl could be so dirty. So, now… now, I'm going to fuck you, Cara, like the dirty little girl I know you are."

I didn't like the cocky bedroom voice anymore.

Nope, not at all.

I fucking loved it.

And, as his body slammed into mine and I cried out his name like a prayer, I knew.

I knew this was what I'd come to New York for.

Not the sex—although that was on the forefront of my mind at the current moment—but him.

Roman.

I'd come to New York for this brutish, arrogant, wonderful man.

He wasn't a rebound or a bad late-night decision.

He was it. The other half to my weird, complicated puzzle.

Now, to just convince him of that.

WAS THERE SOME SORT OF DIAGNOSABLE DISORDER THAT caused a person to relive amazing, mind-blowing sex over and over?

If so, I had it.

I had it in spades.

It had only been a couple of hours, and my mind was

on eternal repeat. Every touch, every lingering kiss. The way he'd moved, thrusting over and over into me without relenting.

My body had shattered into the most delicious, life-altering release, I'd thought, surely, when I opened my eyes, I'd find angels and fluffy white clouds.

Yeah, it was that good.

And now it was all I could think about.

Sex.

Sex with Roman.

Never-ending sex with Roman.

"Did you hear me?" His voice echoed through the lust haze.

"What?" I said, turning to him after realizing I'd been staring at the coffee pot as it gurgled out its last bit of coffee.

We'd decided another round of breakfast was in order, despite the bright afternoon sun shining through the windows. So, while he had been busy microwaving and toasting, I had been in charge of the coffee pot.

And my dirty thoughts.

"I asked you if you had any plans for a job?"

My eyes widened. "Are you firing me? Because I slept with you? Oh God, that's it, isn't it? You can't sleep with your assistant. I mean, how would that work? It would be awkward, right? So, of course, you have to let me go. Wait, you can't do that, can you?"

Rambling… how I hated thee.

A dazzling grin spread across his face as he sauntered across the kitchen. Since this morning, I'd seen an abrupt change in the Roman I'd thought I knew. I always thought there was more than met the eye when it came to my grumpy loner of a boss.

I couldn't have been more right.

Physical attributes aside, his entire demeanor had changed. He had a playfulness to him. He laughed and smiled, and he was downright enjoyable to be around. He was also cocky as hell—something I usually found unattractive in men. But on him? It was just plain sexy.

"I'm not firing you," he said, wrapping his arms around my waist.

Dressed in only a T-shirt, I could already feel the warmth of his fingers as they found their way to my bare skin.

"But you do remember, you're only on a three-month contract. Bethany is coming back. She confirmed with HR last week."

"Right," I said, letting out a sigh. "I guess I haven't thought about it, but you have obviously. Am I that bad of an assistant?"

He laughed. "Best damn assistant I've ever had, especially right now."

His eyes darkened as he bent down for a single kiss. I felt the familiar flutter in my belly that always happened whenever his lips touched mine.

"But, seriously, Cara, this can't be what you want to do for the rest of your life—picking up coffee and returning phone calls for arrogant jerks like me."

"You're not a jerk," I corrected with a joking smile.

"You know what I mean," he said, reaching behind me for an empty coffee cup.

I turned around, grabbing it for him. Watching him pour a fresh cup, I could see the thoughts gathering as he carefully chose his next words.

"I don't want you to waste your future because of me."

"What do you mean?"

"You moved out here because of a guy, and I know you might say it was for the adventure of it, but when it comes down to it, it was for him. Now that he's out of the picture, I don't want to be your only reason to stay. Don't get me wrong. I don't want you to go anywhere, but I need you to flourish, to create a life you love. Let me fit into your life, not the other way around."

"Why are you saying all of this?" I asked, taking the cup of coffee from his hands and placing it on the counter-top. It was my turn to wrap my arms around him.

"You were a history major, right?" he asked, placing his cheek on top of my head.

I gave a tiny nod against his chest.

"Why do we learn history? You were in all those classes, learning dates and places, facts and names. Why do we do that?"

"My professors always said it was so we wouldn't make the mistakes of our past, so we learned from it," I explained.

"Exactly. Let's just say, I don't want history to repeat itself."

I had no idea what he was talking about, but I knew he meant it.

Beyond a shadow of a doubt, he meant it.

THERE WERE INDEED A LOT OF MISCONSTRUED DETAILS ABOUT small town living. But one that was highly accurate was the gossip. It was both a comfort and a thorn in your side, depending on the situation.

The gossip train in a small town could be a huge help in a crisis.

When I was younger and my father had gotten into a car accident, my mother had known almost as quickly as the cops did. She'd met the ambulance at the scene.

How?

Gossip.

A witness had happened to be the next-door neighbor of a friend of mine, and after a game of telephone, my mother had raced down the highway toward the scene.

However, it could also do severe harm.

You shouldn't ever do anything wrong in a small town. We'd find out. We always found out.

I still remember the day my best friend in high school had discovered her mother had an affair. She had been walking down the hallway and had noticed kids talking.

Kids always talked.

But that day, the sound had been nearly deafening, and it had been all about her. I'd told her to ignore it. I'd told her to move on.

But how could she? How could she walk down the halls when everyone was calling her mama a whore?

She had run home and found her mother crying at the kitchen table, a suitcase next to her.

She never saw her mother again.

Like I said, gossip could help, and it could hurt.

I hadn't touched my phone since the moment I'd made that late-night call to Melissa. I knew it was coming. It was only a matter of time. I might have moved away, but you never really left a small town.

As Roman finished taking a shower in the master bathroom, I leaned back in the bed, letting the phone dangle between my fingers.

All I had to do was turn it on. Check my messages. Call my parents.

This wasn't my fault.

Yet…

"I've never seen anyone stare at their phone with such intensity."

Looking up, I found Roman leaning against the bathroom door, little droplets of water dripping down his chiseled chest before they disappeared into the plush hem of his dark blue towel.

He really was beautiful.

"My parents called," I said plainly.

"Right now? When I was in the shower?" he asked, turning back toward the mirror to brush the mess of hair on top of his head.

"No. But they called. Probably several times now."

His head whipped back around in confusion. "How—"

"Tyler's parents and my parents are good friends, and I'm sure he's told his parents. He talks to his mom every Sunday morning after she gets home from church. So, since it's now late afternoon, I'm assuming the news has traveled its way across town to my parents, who are now either frantically trying to get ahold of me or are booking a flight, as we speak."

"And you're just going to sit there and stare at the phone?"

I shrugged. "Maybe."

He smiled warmly, giving up on his hair and joining me on the bed.

"Listen, your parents love you. You're kind, loving, and a good daughter. The fact that you're worried about it tells me you are. So, call them and settle their fears. Otherwise, they're going to be at your doorstep in a matter of hours, and then what will you do?"

"You are a very strange man, Roman Cavenaugh," I said, taking his hand in mine. "Why aren't you like this with anyone else?"

"Like what?"

"Caring… gentle? Did your parents teach you, and you just forgot?"

He stiffened briefly, and I looked up to see a change come over him.

"The only thing my father taught me was how to be greedy."

I squeezed his hand in my own. "That can't be true."

His shoulders relaxed slightly. "You know how a parent isn't supposed to have a favorite child? How they're supposed to love each one of their offspring equally? Well, that's not how it was in my family. My father had a clear favorite… and I wasn't it. It was something I accepted at an early age. In the beginning, it was a blessing. While I was sent to soccer camp and got to stay with my mom at the country estate, playing games and going on picnics, my brother had to spend hours indoors with tutors. I couldn't fathom having to spend my entire summer learning.

"But then I got older and smarter, despite my father's best efforts, and soon, I realized he didn't see anything in me. He passed me over and trusted my younger brother to carry on the family name. That was why he was getting all the attention… the special tutors and extra training. I was a failure before I even had a chance."

"But your mom? Surely, she gave you the love you needed."

He nodded, a small smile tugging at the corner of his mouth. "She did, and she does. Or at least she tries. I'm not the easiest person to love. I know that. But she's always been there, even when I didn't want her to be. She's unrelentingly faithful."

"That's a mom's job—or so I've been told."

"It is," he agreed. "That's why you need to call yours. And then I'm taking you out. We need fresh air."

I leaned back, tossing the phone on the bed. His eyes lingered on the hemline of my shirt as it crept up my hips.

"I like the air in here," I said. "It's hot. Makes me kind of—"

I didn't get to finish talking. And we didn't make it out of that room for the rest of the night.

Returning to work on Monday was like walking back into school after a long holiday. Everything looked and smelled the same. The classrooms had been left untouched for weeks while everyone went on their own adventures. Yet stepping inside those doors felt oddly different.

Because you'd changed. Maybe not in a total world-tilting kind of way, like I had over the weekend, but still, it was a marked difference. Life had moved on while the dusty chalkboards and smelly locker rooms remained unchanged.

It was the same the day we returned to the high-rise building that held Cavenaugh Investments. The papers I'd shuffled through the afternoon I'd found Melissa standing outside my favorite deli were still stacked on my desk. The Post-it notes detailing items still left to do had been left untouched.

Nothing was out of place.

Because nothing out of the ordinary had happened here.

Except when I looked at Roman's office and felt the flutter in my belly, remembering the way each tiny droplet of water had fallen down his rock-hard abdomen, I knew.

Everything had happened between us.

Everything had changed.

And I wasn't sure how to process that, but for now, I was at work. So, that was what I'd do.

Over the past several weeks, Roman and I had

figured out how to work together like a well-oiled machine. I knew his schedule, understood his moods, could anticipate changes, and could navigate through complications.

I wonder if Bethany can do all of that, I thought to myself as I finished up a few things, my mind still revolving around our conversation yesterday regarding jobs.

Roman wasn't wrong. I didn't want to work as an assistant for the rest of my life. Working my ass off in college, studying the French Revolution and Greek culture, when everyone else had been at fraternity parties wasn't just so I could fail now.

I just didn't know where to start.

Back home, I'd had plenty of opportunities to advance. Through professor recommendations, I could have had my pick of graduate programs or summer internships.

But New York was always the plan.

I'd stuck to the plan.

Rather than intern at the Nebraska Historical Society for a few months, I had gone home and babysat for a while, saving up enough cash to pay for moving expenses and my share of the rent.

Had I blown my chances at a career already?

"You look pensive."

I glanced up from my blank computer screen to find Lauren standing in front on me. She was dressed sharply, as usual, in tight-fitting black pants and a low-cut blouse. She was the epitome of everything Tyler had wanted me to be—sophisticated, polished, and charming.

When I'd arrived, he'd wanted arm candy—someone he could bring along to functions when the occasion called for it—more than an actual girlfriend. He might not have realized that was what he was doing, but his reaching for the top had swallowed him whole.

"Just thinking, I guess." I shrugged, leaning back. I awkwardly rubbed my hands on my own black pants.

Roman had dropped me off at my place this morning. I'd had just long enough to change. Not wanting to keep him waiting, I'd grabbed the first outfit I saw.

Compared to Lauren, I deeply regretted that decision. I'd never been much of a fashionista. From the limited clothing options of coming from a small town, I'd just taken what I could find, which was why I was currently sporting a sweater I'd owned since my senior year in high school when bright colors were still in.

Lauren, keeping her eyes off my neon-green sweater, bent down a bit, leveling her gaze with mine. "I'm so sorry I didn't make it over here last week. I got your email, but I was in back-to-back meetings until the end of the day. How are you doing?"

In my misery on Friday, I'd sent her a short email detailing the misadventures I'd had the night before. I'd left out the part about spending the night at the boss's house.

I liked Lauren, but I didn't quite trust her. She was always a bit too interested when it came to our boss, which made me all the more tight-lipped when it came to Roman's business.

"I'm better, I think," I answered honestly. "My best friend, Melissa, flew in on Friday, and she helped calm me down over beer, pizza, and copious amounts of candy."

She laughed. "I'm glad to hear it. I was worried all weekend when you didn't show up at my place. I know you don't have a lot of friends yet in the city, and I didn't want you to end up alone in a hotel."

"No, well… I mean, Melissa and I did spend one night in a hotel when she got here, but actually, Tyler gave me the apartment. Can you believe that?"

"Yes, I can," she said flatly. "He should have after kicking you out in the middle of the night. You never did say where you went that night. I hope you didn't wander the streets or something equally dangerous?"

"Oh, I forgot. I was in a hotel that night as well," I lied, briefly looking away to hide the deceit in my eyes.

"Okay, well, I'm glad you're all right. Everything else going smoothly? Boss hasn't ripped your head off yet?"

"What? No. He's harmless," I said, instantly regretting the way I'd scoffed at her statement.

Everyone in this office feared Roman. If I wanted to fly under the radar—especially with Lauren, the gossip queen—I should fear him as well.

"Harmless?" she questioned.

"I mean, as long as I stay out of his way. We have a system." I shrugged, trying to seem aloof and unaffected.

"Of course. Bethany said that as well. She said the best kind of assistant for Mr. Cavenaugh was the invisible kind."

I laughed, hoping it wasn't loud and off-putting.

It kind of was.

"Exactly," I replied.

"Miss Hamilton, can I see you? Now." Roman's voice sounded over the intercom on my phone. He sounded mad and greatly put out.

My eyes met Lauren's, and all the doubt and tension in the air dissipated instantly.

"Sounds bad. You'd better hustle," she said, giving me a quick wink.

Rising from the chair, I nodded.

"Don't let him get you down. Lunch later?"

"Yes, I'll email you."

She gave me the thumbs-up before disappearing through adjacent door. Taking a deep breath as my hand wrapped around the doorknob to Roman's office, I tried to calm myself down.

It was just another day at work. I'd had plenty of talks with him like this over the last few weeks. Many of them, I'd even pictured him naked when he sat there, berating me for how I'd sent a fax or emailed a client. So, if he were about to yell at me again, it would be no different.

Except that I actually knew what he looked like naked now.

Shaking my head, I pushed open the door and walked in. At first glance, I saw him leaning back in the chair he'd huffed over for weeks but secretly fallen in love with in seconds. He seemed calm and relaxed, not at all like a man who was about to dole out a punishment or long lecture.

"You asked for me?" I said, taking a seat in front of his desk.

"Is she gone?" he asked, peeking down at me from his reclined position.

"Who? Lauren?"

He nodded.

"Yes, she's gone."

"Ah, good. Her voice was getting on my nerves. Plus, she was starting to get unnecessarily nosy."

Realization dawned. "Did you call me in here just to get rid of her?"

A wide grin appeared on his handsome face, doing all sorts of things to my body.

"No, that's not the only reason."

From the rich resonance of his voice alone, that same intense flutter returned deep inside my belly.

"What can I do for you, Roman?" I asked with a flirty smile.

Two could play this game.

His smile faltered slightly but then just grew wider. "So

many things, Cara. So many things. But, for now, I want you to do just one."

"And what's that?"

"Go on a date with me."

"Isn't that a step backward?" I asked, laughing.

He leaned forward. "Maybe, but you deserve all the steps, Cara. We deserve every single step. And this weekend we might have been a bit hasty. Don't get me wrong. I enjoyed our hasty decisions, and I plan on making a lot more of those hasty decisions with you, but I also want to make all the right ones. The first date, all the corny anniversaries, meeting the parents."

I was dumbfounded. "You want me to meet your mom?"

I knew from various conversations with Roman that his father had passed. Everyone in the company knew that.

"Don't you want to meet her? She's quite lovely," he said matter-of-factly.

"Yes!" I said, beaming. "I'd love to meet your mom and go out on a first date with you. And everything in between."

"Good. I'll pick you up at seven."

"Where are we going?" I asked, doing a mental survey of my closet, wondering what one wore on a date with a Cavenaugh.

"It's a surprise, but I can already see the wheels in your head spinning, so I'll ease your anxiety a little. Wear jeans and comfortable shoes. And prepare to get a little dirty."

My eyebrows rose in anticipation. "Am I supposed to interpret that in some other way? Because if I show up prepared for a hike and we actually go to some kinky underground sex club, there might be bodily harm. And not in a good way, Roman!"

His eyes softened. "The only place I'll allow you to get

dirty is in private where I can have you all to myself. So, no. For once, I am not being crude. Seven o'clock?"

"Can't wait."

"Oh, you have no idea."

I didn't. I really didn't. But I had a feeling, by the time the night was over, I'd be getting dirty in more ways than one.

And wasn't that something to look forward to?

CHAPTER NINETEEN

ROMAN

"Is this the first date you've ever been on?" Lailah's cheery voice asked.

I frantically ran around my room, searching for my other shoe. "No," I answered.

"I don't consider paid companionship a date, Roman," she chided.

I finally found my left sneaker peeking out from under the bed, remembering exactly how it had gotten there.

"Okay then, yes."

Her musical laughter filled my ear, and I couldn't help but smile.

Until I looked at the clock.

"Is this weekly check-in phone call going to be a regular thing?" I asked, not even bothering with the laces as I pulled the shoe on without even sitting.

"You know you ask me that every time we talk? Every single time, Roman, and what do I say?"

"I'm not going to repeat it."

"What do I say, Roman?" she asked rather heatedly.

"That you call because you love me," I answered under my breath.

"Yes," she replied.

I could hear the pride beaming in her joyful voice all the way from here.

"And when people love you, they call. Often. So, suck it up."

"Yes, ma'am."

"Good. Now, where are you taking this girl?" she asked, not even caring in the least that I was soon going to be late for this date I'd told her about twenty minutes ago.

I should have kept my mouth shut.

"Somewhere different. That's all I'm saying."

"Good. As long as *different* isn't just code for a fancy dinner. That's so cliché and predictable."

"I know her better than that," I huffed.

"I think I actually might believe you. Now, stop talking my ear off, and hurry up. You don't want to be late."

Silence fell upon me as my mouth gaped open, and then laughter followed. She knew I'd been running around for the last few minutes, trying to beat the clock.

"You are so easy to tease. But, seriously, have fun tonight, Roman. Be yourself. Don't hide the very best parts of you that I know are lurking somewhere inside all that gruff exterior."

"You really are like a happy little bucket of rainbows, aren't you?" I shook my head, grabbing the heaviest coat I could find as well as a pair of gloves, just in case.

"That's what you keep telling me." She laughed.

"Never change," I said in a rare moment of sincerity.

"Right back at you. Now, go get the girl. And do me a favor?"

"What's that?"

"When she falls in love with you—which is bound to happen—let her."

I opened my mouth, unsure of what she meant but ready to protest.

"Just let her, Roman. You and I both know that you'll try to fight it. You'll convince yourself that you're somehow unworthy, and in the end, you'll walk away from what could be the love of your life. Don't. Save both of you from a world of hurt, and just allow yourself to be loved."

I promised her, but it was a wasted promise.

Because I knew… if I were lucky enough to ever earn the love of that woman, I wouldn't run. I'd cherish it for as long as I was able.

Even if I didn't deserve it.

Because I'd taken what wasn't mine.

And like hell I was ever going to give it up.

"You know, when I pictured going on a date with Roman Cavenaugh, it never involved the subway," Cara said, giving me a sideways grin.

We were standing on a dingy platform with tons of other New Yorkers and tourists, waiting to board the next train.

"You've dreamed of going on dates with me? What else have you dreamed about doing with me?" I asked, leaning in closer so that I could whisper the last part in her ear.

I was a quick study in all things related to Cara Hamilton. One thing that drove her wild was my lips murmuring sweet nothings in her ear.

Such a simple thing. Such amazing results.

She instantly shivered.

"I said the word *pictured*, not dreamed."

"Same difference. You're stalling," I said.

Her eyes met mine, full of defiance and heat.

"Fine. Yes, I've dreamed of many things we could do together, and maybe if you tell me what we're doing on a subway platform while I'm dressed like I'm about to climb a mountain, I'll indulge you by trying a few of those fantasies. Tonight."

My grin widened.

"Wish I could, but unfortunately, that would just ruin the surprise. But good to know that you can't wait to get me back in bed."

She let out a frustrated groan and stomped her foot.

Goddamn, she was adorable.

It was something I'd always known. Anyone could look at her, dressed in those brightly colored cardigans and outdated sweater dresses, and know she oozed sweetness. But it wasn't the wide-eyed, dopey newbie-in-the-city grin that every other girl who'd moved here had.

It was just her.

She was charming and sweet, but she was also fiercely passionate when needed, especially when it involved someone she loved. She was young but not naive, well educated and even a bit adventurous—something I was looking forward to exploring fully.

The way she had taken control in the bedroom, riding me like she was made for me and me alone, was something I hadn't expected from the adorable girl who'd stolen my heart.

And damn if that wasn't just icing on the cake.

Now, I just had to convince her that she never wanted to leave. That was why we were currently standing in the grossest place in the city—the subway.

"Don't worry; I have a plan. A really awesome plan," I

said once again, taking her hand, as the train came to a stop.

"I trust you, remember?" she said, giving a quick wink in my direction before dragging us forward.

It took a few stops, but eventually, we got a seat toward the back and then gave it up to an elderly woman when no one else would.

It had been years since I'd taken the subway. If you sat around and looked long enough, you could spot the highs and lows of society as the train moved on. Families were huddled together, and tourists pointed at maps, laughing and smiling, while tired shift workers tried to stay awake. People helped one another; others ignored everyone. It was fascinating and tragic all at the same time.

Cara must have been having the same thoughts because there was very little conversation between us for a long time. Just comfortable silence as we held hands. Sometimes, her head would rest on mine, or we'd lean against each other when without a seat.

But she never asked how long or where we were going.

Because she trusted me.

Even when they called the end of the line and we didn't get off.

She turned and gave me an amused look of surprise, but then she settled her head back down and watched the doors close back into place.

"I've never been on a train by myself," she said, looking out the window as the lights flashed, one by one in succession.

"I think it's a rarity in this city. Hold on, we're almost there. Look out this side," I said, pointing toward the right.

Her head lifted, and I could see the anticipation in her eyes as she probably wondered just what could be so interesting about the subway.

The train pulled to a stop, and I heard her gasp. She eagerly turned around, pressing her nose to the window, and then looked back at me again.

"Is this an abandoned subway station?" she asked, nearly shaking with excitement.

"This is *the* abandoned subway station. Welcome to City Hall Station."

"Oh my gosh, Roman! Do you know how awesome this is?" she screamed, rushing to the door.

I had to hold her back to keep her from plunging to her death.

"Wait for our guide to attach the rail, please." I laughed, watching her eyes go wide as she looked down to find a foot-long gap between the train and the platform.

"Well, that would have been an unfortunate end to our date," she said, squeezing my hand in thanks.

Stepping to the edge, by the open doors, we were greeted by a familiar face.

"Kevin!" I said, waiting for him to push the bright yellow ramp up to the train. It provided a nice little bridge for the two of us to safely walk over, landing on the other side in one piece.

"Roman, good to see you. And this must be Cara."

She nodded, holding out her hand in greeting. She made his acquaintance, but I could tell she was itching to look around. She was twitchy, and her eyes kept darting in different directions, like a kid with a sugar high.

"How did you arrange all of this, Roman? Oh my gosh, is this illegal?" she asked,

Kevin and I both laughed.

"I happen to be a guide from the New York Transit Museum, so this is perfectly legal. We actually do tours just like this for the public several times a year. But tonight it's just the two of you."

She peered over at me, her eyes filled with questions.

"Just go with it," I suggested.

But I should have known better.

"Kevin"—she looked away from me, her focus now completely on the other man—"how do you happen to know Roman?"

"Oh, my wife works for him. Or at least she works for the company, I guess I should say. In HR."

"Gretchen?" she asked.

"Yes"—he smiled—"that's her. She's very fond of Mr. Cavenaugh. He was generous last year, giving her an extra month of maternity leave when our baby boy was born with complications. Not many companies around here will do that."

She glanced back at me as I tried to look anywhere but.

"Yes, he's a wonderful man."

"Okay! Let's get started," I said, hoping to change the subject.

All this praise was making me feel like a lab rat under a microscope, and soon, all my secrets and misdeeds would come leaking out.

Seeming to sense my embarrassment, Cara hooked her arm around mine as Kevin began leading us around the old subway station.

Unlike the graffiti-ridden dark tunnels of today, City Hall Station had been an architectural marvel back when it was constructed in the early 1900s. With its ornate tiles and beautiful chandeliers, it reminded me of times gone by when everything, from going to the post office to visiting the theater, was a grand affair.

"It's like stepping back in time," Cara said, her voice filled with wonderment.

She reached out, touching the restored tiles that marked the name of the station. Watching her filled me with a sense of pride and accomplishment.

I'd done this. I'd put that smile on her face, that look of reverence in her eyes.

I never wanted it to end.

After a brief tour of the main tunnel, Kevin allowed us to venture up to the mezzanine section where several photos and historical artifacts had been set up for viewers to enjoy.

But it was the scenery around us that stole Cara's attention.

"Can you imagine arriving here back then? I'd be dressed in fourteen different layers, probably sweating from the exhaustion of not being able to breathe properly from the strength of the corset around my waist, and you'd look so dapper in your wool suit with a ivory pipe hanging from your mouth."

"So, I'd be dying of cancer then?" I joked as we took a walk around the room.

"Well, how else would I become a wealthy heiress?" She smirked. "We'd have our adorable little children behind us along with the nanny, of course. Because what high-society family didn't employ a nanny?"

"Naturally," I agreed.

She stopped at one of the pictures and silently studied it. The scene wasn't very different from what she'd just been dreaming up in her head—a wealthy young family taking the train on a lovely spring day. The woman was just as Cara had described—over-dressed in many layers but beautiful and poised with her stylish husband nearby. A bevy of children followed behind with a tired woman holding up the rear.

"I wonder what happened to them," I found myself saying.

I'd never really cared for history. As far as my own family history went, it tended to only serve as a reminder of failure.

"Life," she simply said, still staring down at the anonymous family now long gone. "Life happened. The good, bad, and everything in between. Probably for them though, knowing the year this was taken," she said, nodding toward the date in the corner, "a lot of bad. World War I was declared not too long after this, and World War II followed shortly after. This generation suffered greatly for their freedom."

"You feel for them, don't you? Even though they're gone? Even though you never knew them?" I asked, seeing the sadness on her face as her fingers traced the lines of the grainy photo tucked behind the glass.

"I do. It was the hardest part of learning—the suffering humanity had endured over the centuries. But it makes all of this so important. The remembering. The realization that these people in this photo weren't just people riding a train one day in history. Each of them had their own stories, their own lives. And it's our job to remember them."

"Who are you?" I said in awe.

"Sorry," she said, red tingeing her cheeks. "I geek out a bit when it comes to history."

"Don't apologize, Cara. Don't ever apologize for something you're passionate about. If I had one ounce of your passion for the work I did..." I trailed off, unwilling to finish the thought.

"You don't like what you do?"

I turned away with a sigh, the sound of my shoes

sliding awkwardly against the stone tiles, as if they weren't built for the modern rubber soles I possessed.

"It doesn't matter whether I do or don't. It's mine. My name is on the damn building. It's not like I can just walk in one day and say, *You know what? I think I'm going to try out pilot school for a while. Later.*"

"Do you want to be a pilot?" she asked in confusion.

"No. I mean, hell, I don't know. I've never even been asked that question," I answered, turning back toward her.

Her mouth gaped open in shock. "No one has ever asked you what you wanted to do with your own life, Roman?"

I shook my head. "My life was already planned out for me before I was born, Cara. It was just a matter of whether I was smart enough to be in charge or not. My father needed someone to pass the company down to. That was supposed to be Jude. But, as you put it, life happened—the good, the bad—and he walked away. By the time I got him to return, his heart wasn't in it anymore, and our father was gone. So, I stepped up. I became the chosen one my father didn't trust I could be. And I've been proving him wrong every day since."

"But you hate it." She didn't bother asking. She knew.

"I like knowing I'm keeping people employed, knowing I'm putting food on their tables and helping to pay for their kids ballet lessons and soccer uniforms. But getting up every day? Going to work? It's a nightmare. I fucking hate it."

It was the first time I'd said the words out loud. They'd echoed in my head for years as the hours and days dragged on in that lonely dark office my father had once occupied. But I'd never said it. I'd never admitted it to another person. And doing so felt like a forty-ton weight had been lifted off my shoulders.

"Then, figure out how to love it," she said.

"What?"

"You said yourself that your brother tried to leave, but then he came back because this company was your legacy, your life. But it doesn't have to be a death sentence. Jude found a way to make it work for him. Find a way to make it work for you. Delegate, and switch things around. Be a boss, Roman! It's your company, not your father's. Find a way."

"Will you help me?" I asked, looking up at her in the darkened room.

She smiled a wide happy smile. "I thought you'd never ask."

ANOTHER weekend was about to arrive, which meant two days of uninterrupted time with Cara.

We'd had a bumpy few days of getting used to our new relationship and how to balance it in the workplace.

Scratch that.

I'd had a bumpy few days.

She'd seemed to handle the transition just fine.

After my little trick of publicly calling her into my office, only to ask her out on a date, she'd decided it would be best if we kept things strictly professional during business hours.

Being the boss, I'd had no choice but to agree.

Except that being strictly professional was kicking my assistant-loving ass.

I didn't know if she was purposely trying to drive me crazy or if I was doing a fine job of it all on my own, but every whiff of her fruity shampoo, every sideways glance I caught of her bending over, or hell… even when she walked, it was enough to drive me permanently insane.

By Friday, I'd sported more hard-ons than a teenage boy with a porno magazine.

When the clock hit five, I would be dragging that woman to my apartment and locking her inside for forty-eight hours straight.

I couldn't wait.

I'd been staring at the clock all day and doing my best to avoid my lovely assistant as much as possible. I was so hopped up on the idea of two days with Cara that I might just break her rule and take her right here on my damn desk.

Somehow, I'd managed to get several things done in my agitated state, and as I sat at my desk, clicking my pen like a hyped up bunny on steroids, I heard a tiny knock on my door.

"Come in," I said, not bothering to look up.

"I thought, for sure, you'd be racing out of here, throwing me over your shoulder like Tarzan the second it hit five o'clock. Imagine my surprise when I looked up and discovered it was five minutes past."

My eyes jerked up, glaring at the clock, which indeed showed it was now past the golden hour.

How had I missed that?

Turning toward Cara, I noticed she'd placed a single chocolate cupcake on my desk. I also noticed she was leaning over just enough for me to catch a peek down her shirt.

Good girl.

"What's this for?" I asked, pointing toward the confectionary delight.

"Well, you said you wanted to celebrate every anniversary. Even the cheesy ones. So, today marks a first for us."

My eyebrow rose in confusion.

"Today, one week ago, you kissed me for the first time."

"We're celebrating our first kiss?" I asked.

A giant smile spread across her face.

"But I thought we weren't allowed to do such things in the office? Professionalism and all."

"I said we had to stay professional during office hours. It's after five," she reminded me, motioning toward the clock.

Rising, I grabbed the cupcake in my hand and walked around the desk, leaning against it in front of her. She moved closer as I scooped off some of the frosting with my finger. I watched as she bent down and licked it off with her pretty pink lips.

"I'd like to see you do that with something else," I said as her mouth sucked every inch of frosting from my skin.

"I think we can arrange that, Mr. Cavenaugh."

I grinned. "Just so we're clear, you and I are no longer being professional?"

"No."

"Good. Then go lock the door," I demanded.

"Yes." Her voice was breathless.

"Yes what?"

"Yes, sir," she added, her gaze meeting mine, as she clicked the lock in place.

"I want you here." I pointed to the desk.

She did as I'd said, loving every minute of this game as much as I was.

I'd never fucked a woman at work. I'd never planned to. It was out of bounds.

But with Cara? Everything was in bounds. Everything counted.

"Hands here. Don't move them." I instructed, turning

my attention to the edge of the desk. She eagerly placed each hand flat and wide on the grainy wood. I walked around her, admiring her, loving her.

She was wearing one of her beloved sweater dresses and tights. I pushed her legs wide, running my hands up her inner thighs.

"What's this?" I asked. I'd expected to find classic tights, but I'd found lace instead. Lifting her dress, I smiled.

My innocent, sweet girl was wearing her signature cotton panties—doughnut print, this time—but today, she'd added lace thigh-highs.

"What a little conundrum you are," I said in approval, dragging the cotton panties down her silky legs until they hit the floor.

She kicked them aside as I stepped in close.

"Remember, don't move your hands," I reminded her.

I made quick work of my jacket and tie. My fingers worked the belt and fly of my pants with precision. I was already hard. Hell, I'd been hard for days, even minutes after having her.

My body craved her.

Palming her bare bottom, I heard her moan in approval as my fingers inched closer to her core. I made quick work of the condom, placing it on my shaft within seconds.

"So ready for me," I whispered.

"Only you, Roman."

Her words broke my control, shattered my focus, and within seconds, I was inside her. She cried out from the sudden intrusion and then instantly relaxed, pushing against me in longing.

The pads of my fingers dug into her hips as each thrust drove me deeper and deeper.

"You undo me, Cara," I grunted, grabbing on to her hair, as my body wrapped around hers.

Her hands were still exactly where I wanted them as my hands moved everywhere. I found her clit and slowly started rubbing it to the rhythm of my dick as I moved inside her.

"Oh, shit!" she cried out.

It didn't take long before I felt her legs start to shake, and her core tightened around me, squeezing my cock like a vise.

"I'm going to come." Her voice was barely audible. She cried out, breathing heavily, as the orgasm found her.

Knowing we might not be the only ones left in the office and being quite familiar with my little vixen, I closed my hand around her mouth at the last second, catching her cries as the first waves hit her.

Feeling her body quake around mine was the best kind of torture I'd ever found. I picked up the pace, grabbing her hip with my free hand.

The only sounds in the room were soft moans as Cara came apart and the glorious sound of my body slamming into hers.

It was rough. It was primal.

It was goddamn beautiful.

My head fell back as I found my own release. A guttural deep groan tore from my mouth as my hands reached for hers on the desk. I could feel her breathing beneath me, tired and spent from our lovemaking.

Lovemaking.

I'd never called it that before.

But that was exactly what we'd just done because, in a week, I'd fallen.

Fallen hard.

I was in love with this woman.

I was in love with Cara Hamilton, and God help me if I knew what to do about it.

CHAPTER TWENTY

CARA

"I can't believe you're doing the dirty with your boss!" Melissa shouted.

"I can hear you, you know. We might be half a country apart, but the technology of cellular devices is actually quite good."

She laughed, muffling the loud music she had on in the background—a telltale sign of stress studying. Whenever finals were near, Melissa would crank up whatever happened to be her favorite band of the month and hole herself in her room to study for hours on end. Her dedication to her studies was always my biggest annoyance in our friendship.

That, and the harm it did to my eardrums.

"So, is it good?"

"Is what good?" I asked, swishing water around with my toes, as I leaned back in the bath, letting the warmth ease the stiffness in my tired muscles.

"The sex, Cara. Is it good?" she said, like it was the most obvious question in the world.

In all the years we'd been together, she'd actually never asked me about my sex life. I'd always assumed she didn't want to know.

Hers? An open book.

I knew every position she and Jeremy had tried, every place they'd done it, including the bleachers during a home football game—which, according to her, wasn't as epic as everyone had described it to be. Lots of trash, lots of noise, and it had ended before she'd even had the chance to feel even the slightest bit daring.

But Tyler and me, she'd never asked. Maybe she'd always assumed we were already like an old married couple—boring and settled.

Looking back, it wasn't far from the truth. We'd never had those moments of passion where we couldn't hold back, ripping each other's clothes away or sneaking into hidden places just to steal a precious few moments.

I'd made him wait four years. And, by the time we'd finally taken that step, it was almost a nonevent. I'd held out, hoping it would only double the anticipation, make the moment special for the both of us. But, in doing so, I'd overanalyzed everything—the place, the clothes I'd wear, even down to how we'd do it.

It wasn't spontaneous. It wasn't passionate. It wasn't anything.

It'd turned out to be exactly what I'd feared.

Just sex.

And, from that moment on, our sex life had had its ups and downs. We had gotten better at it as a couple, but the connection never grew. I'd thought it was the distance.

Turned out, it was us.

"It's good," I answered, feeling a bit embarrassed.

The water shifted suddenly, and the phone was snatched from my hand.

"It's really, really good," Roman reiterated, grinning at me from just a few inches away.

His wet hand carefully handed the phone back to me as I took in the sight of his naked body across from me.

"I thought you said you were taking a bath?" Melissa said before adding, "Of course you're in the bath with him. I mean, who wouldn't be? With a body like that?"

His grin widened.

"He can hear every word you're saying. You're not exactly being quiet," I warned her.

She continued prattling on about Roman's finer attributes, yelling over the loud rock music in the background.

"It's not like I'm not saying anything he hasn't heard," she said matter-of-factly.

"True," I agreed.

"Well, thanks for answering my phone call. If I were you, I wouldn't have. But I appreciate the demonstration of love. Now, get back to your hottie. Glad to know you are doing well. And by well, I mean, a hell of a lot better than me."

I smiled. "Chin up, buttercup. Only three and a half more years, right?"

"Of med school, sure. And then the real hell begins."

"You could give up," I reminded her, knowing exactly what she'd say.

"No, I'm a glutton for punishment. Besides, who needs sex when you have stacks of anatomy books?"

"That's the spirit!"

"Love you, Cara-saurus.

I rolled my eyes. "Love you too."

We said our good-byes, and I carefully placed my phone on the nearby bathroom counter. Then I continued with my new favorite pastime.

Staring at Roman. Naked.

"Good?" he said as his eyebrows rose with mischief.

"What?"

"Sex with me is just… good?" He moved forward, causing a ripple effect in the water.

Iridescent bubbles sloshed around my chest and arms as his warm body met mine.

"Did I say good? I meant, extraordinary." I smiled, his lips hovering over my neck. "Phenomenal?" I continued as his large hand found my breast. "Legendary?"

"Better."

The stubble from his grin moved roughly against my neck and cheek as he kissed a path toward my mouth, pulling me into his lap at the same time.

"What are you doing?" I murmured through languid kisses.

"What does it look like?" he asked.

I could feel his smile against my lips. Pulling back slightly, I met his green eyes, dark with heat and passion.

"We were supposed to take a bath to relax from the sex we'd just had, remember?"

"Yes, and now, I'm all better," he purred, continuing his fiery path of kisses down my body.

His voice carried that cocky bedroom quality I loved. Deep, husky, and dripping with sexual overtones. It made me weak in the knees and turned me into putty in his hands.

Something he knew well.

"Come on, Cara—or should I say Cara-saurus?" His grin widened as I sent a few silent curse words to my crazy best friend. "I've never done it in a bathtub before," he murmured in my ear as his hands worked magic below the water.

Well, who was I to say no to that?

"Are you going to explain to your mother why we're two and a half hours late?" I asked, looking at the alarm clock on the nightstand as I frantically ran around the room in nothing but a towel.

"Sure. It will be the first thing I say right after I introduce you. It will go something like, *Hey, Mom. This is Cara, my girlfriend. Sorry we are late. We were fucking in the tub. Made an awful mess. Took ten towels to mop up all the water.*"

I just stood in the middle of the room and stared at him, mouth gaped open.

"You're way too easy to mess with." He laughed.

"You called me your girlfriend," I said, still immobile.

He shrugged, grabbing a pair of boxer briefs from a drawer. "Should I have asked first? I don't know how these things go. Am I supposed to ask your father? Or do I take you to the drive-in and ask you to go steady over cheese fries?"

"You want me to be your girlfriend?" My eyes softened as I took a step toward him.

My arrogant, crazy, beautiful man.

"I thought the whole speech about anniversaries and meeting my mom made that clear enough. That is what you want, right? Otherwise, this whole trip today is going to be fucking awkward. Pretty sure my mom is already naming our kids."

A couple of more steps, and my arms were around him. "Yes."

"Yes to the going steady or the naming kids? Because she picked out Jude and Roman. You don't know what she'll come up with next."

"I love you," I said softly against his chest.

He suddenly stopped breathing, like my words had

swooped the air right out of his chest, making my declaration ten times scarier.

Now, I was scared to look up. Scared to pull myself away from his chest and discover that everything had changed. One minute, we had been joking about cheese fries and kids, and the next, he'd be telling me it was all moving too fast.

"Cara," he whispered.

I shook my head, unwilling to move.

His hand grasped my chin, tilting it upward.

"Look at me," he begged.

My eyes were still shut.

"Please."

I finally willed my eyes to open, and when I did, I found him smiling down at me.

No fear, no horror, no anger in his eyes.

Just pure joy.

"I love you, too."

"But it's only been two weeks," I replied quickly.

His smile widened. "You're trying to argue me out of this? This might be my first go at this, but I'm fairly certain that's not how you do it."

"Are you sure?"

He bent down, still grasping my chin, and he placed his lips close to mine. "I've never been surer about anything," he said, taking my hand and leading me to the bed. Sitting me down next to him, both of us still in towels, he wrapped his arms around me. "I didn't have the Norman Rockwell upbringing you did. My parents… they… it's hard to explain. Let's just say, looks can be deceiving, and their relationship left me with a bitter taste in my mouth when it came to love. For a long time. Until you. You are my exception."

"I don't know what to say."

"That's the thing. You don't have to say anything. You've already said it. You're here. With me. It's the greatest gift I've ever received."

"So, what you're saying is, I don't have to buy you a single anniversary present again?" I grinned as he pulled me into a tight hug.

"I'll take sexual favors as gifts. Anytime actually. Even now," he joked. "But that does remind me…" He jumped up, still clad in a towel only, the heavy fabric hanging low on his hips.

I bit my lip and smiled, knowing exactly what was hidden beneath.

"Stop staring. Unless you really want me to tell my mom why we were late."

Giggling, I pressed my lips together and tried to look at the ceiling while he rifled through his closet. A second later, he pulled out a box and handed it to me.

"Happy two-week anniversary!" he announced proudly.

"Now who's corny?" I said, happily ripping open the box at once.

It had only been two weeks, but damn if they hadn't been the best two weeks of my entire life. Roman had opened my eyes not only to what it felt like to be a woman, but he also challenged me, as I challenged him. We worked as a team, and, nothing felt impossible.

"Is this what I think it is?"

He just smiled as I pushed aside several layers of tissue paper to discover what appeared to be a lifetime supply of panties.

But not the grown-up lacy kind. No, these were cotton and covered in puppies and candy bars. One even had characters from a popular kids movie I adored.

"These are fantastic!" I screamed, laughing like a child, as I threw panties all over the bed.

"I told you I found your hamburger underwear sexy! Now, you never have to go without your crazy juvenile, yet sexy underwear."

My hand cupped his face. I was still grinning as my eyes met his. "You're amazing."

"I am, aren't I? Now, pick a pair, and let's get out of here before my mom starts calling in a panic!"

"Good plan."

We both raced around his large bedroom, throwing on clothes and shoes. I took a few minutes to blow-dry my hair and tossed my makeup bag into my purse, so I could finish that process in the car.

Did he even own a car?

"How are we getting to your mom's? You said she'd be at the country estate today… not her apartment downtown?"

He nodded, just finishing with brushing his teeth. "For the most part, the estate is closed during the year, except for holidays when she likes to wake it back up. Since Thanksgiving and Christmas are just around the corner, she's having it aired out and decorated for the season. Jude and his family will fly out in a few weeks and get their fill of winter while the rest of us remember the good old days at the family house."

"How many years has the house been in your family?" I asked, obviously interested in the history of it.

"I honestly don't know. As far back as I can remember. You'll love it, but that's all I'm saying. I want you to be thoroughly surprised."

"You're no fun."

"That's not what you said in the tub." He winked,

smacking my butt on his way out of the bathroom. "Come on, we'd better get going."

"You never answered my question about how we're getting there!" I reminded him, snatching my purse and following close behind.

He grabbed a set of keys from the kitchen table and held them over his head, jingling them, as if they provided some sort of answer.

"Is it a rental? Is it safe? Did you look up its stats online?"

He turned around, grinning from ear to ear. "I love that you're meticulous and you can spout information quicker than Wikipedia, but sometimes, babe, you've just got to relax."

My shoulders slumped. "But do you know if it even gets good gas mileage?" I squeaked.

His laughter filled the room. "It's not a rental. It's mine. It's very safe, it gets great gas mileage, and yes, I did a shitload of research on my own before I bought it. So, see, you and I, we're not that different. Okay?"

I smiled weakly as he turned around.

My arms folded in front of me. "How much of that was bullshit?"

"Mmm… maybe half?"

"Nice try." I shook my head, following him out the door.

He waited for me, locking it behind him, and then he wrapped an arm around my waist as we took off down the hall.

"It does get good gas mileage though," he added before we stopped in front of the elevator.

"Oh, yeah?" I asked. "How good?"

"Extraordinary," he said, pushing me forward into the

tiny space of the elevator. "Phenomenal," he purred, backing me up against the wall as he expertly reached behind himself and pressed the button for lobby. "Legendary, I've heard." He grinned, and then he kissed me breathlessly until we reached the bottom floor.

"You've got to be fucking kidding me!" A familiar voice halted our frenzied make-out session.

Roman turned slowly, and I felt my breath stop as Tyler stepped into view.

"What are you doing here?" I asked.

Roman took my hand and slowly led me out of the elevator, keeping me a safe distance from Tyler, who not only looked angry, but enraged. His fists were clenched close to his sides, and he was breathing hard, like he'd just raced a marathon to get here.

"I went to our place—*your* place," he corrected quickly, "to drop off the final lease papers, showing the rent had been paid in advance in case anything happened. I wanted to check on you, to make sure you were okay, but your neighbor said you weren't home and gave me an address you'd given her for emergencies. I guess you didn't tell her."

"No. You know I hate gossip," I said fiercely.

"But I should have known," he nearly spit, shaking his head. "I should have known you'd go running to him the first second you could. Or maybe you already had. Were you fucking him before I left you? Working your way up to the top?"

Like lightning, Roman moved. One minute, Tyler was standing in front of us, and the next, he was pinned against a wall.

"Listen up, asshole," Roman sneered. "You're going to leave. You're going to leave now and forget you ever came here. Because if I see you here again? Hell, if I see you anywhere near Cara again, it will be the last thing you ever do. Got it?"

Considering Roman had him a few feet off the ground with one hand, Tyler quickly agreed to his terms before he was released, dropping to the floor like a rag doll. He stalked down the hallway and out of the lobby doorway, with nothing more than a huff.

We'd barely gotten a chance to look at each other before applause broke out. We'd been so tied up in our own business that neither of us had even noticed that others—some of Roman's neighbors, the doorman, and a few guests—were standing by, watching.

"Seems the young boy got what he deserved," the old lady who lived across the hall from Roman said in approval, patting him on the back on her way to the elevator.

I looked at him, wide-eyed, trying to hold back the laughter.

"And here I thought life with you would be dull and boring. Boy, was I wrong." Roman said, shaking his head with a grin.

Truer words had never been spoken.

───────────

"This is your car?" I asked as we approached the curb.

The bellman had already pulled the car out from the garage.

"Yep." He grinned with pride.

"It looks like something from the Indy 500."

"Exactly. I told you, she gets great mileage. That wasn't a lie."

"She? Your car is a she?" I laughed.

"Only woman in my life, besides my mom—and you."

"And does she have a name?" I asked, looking over the sleek red sports car with a bit of jealousy. I'd never been jealous of a car before.

"Lola."

"Lola, the car."

"Lola, the sports car," he corrected, bending down to open my door.

I peeked inside. All tan leather interior, expensive wood trim, not a speck of dirt.

Okay, yeah, I got it.

"Lola, it is," I mumbled under my breath.

I heard his laughter as he gently closed the door and ran over to the other side, giddy as a schoolboy in a spitball fight.

"I rarely get to drive her anymore. She was a birthday present to myself a few years ago when I was still trying to convince Jude to take over the business even though I knew it was fruitless. My last whim, I guess, before the old ball and chain were officially locked in place."

"But we're going to fix that, right?" I reminded him.

"Right," he agreed. "And then my old ball and chain can be a woman… just as God intended."

"You're horrible."

He pulled into traffic, and soon, the city was behind us.

Roman had told me very little about their country home. Just that he and Jude had fond memories of growing up there as children and always loved the opportunity to return as much as possible.

I guessed I'd always known in the back of my head that the Cavenaugh family was wealthy, that Roman himself was wealthy. But knowing and actually seeing it in person were two things entirely.

Sure, I'd been to Roman's high-rise penthouse apartment and touched his fine things, but I'd never really considered him rich. He was just Roman.

My Roman.

But as his car pulled off the main road and we entered the gated drive, I realized for the first time the level of money his family dealt with on a daily basis.

And it was a lot.

I'd never been to a mansion, but I was pretty sure the Cavenaughs country home would definitely fit the bill. With its beautiful gardens and Old World architecture, I felt like I was on an episode of *Lifestyles of the Rich and Famous*.

But I wasn't.

This was where Roman had grown up.

No, correction. This was *one* of the places where Roman had grown up.

I swallowed audibly.

"It's just a house," Roman said, obviously sensing my nerves from the other side of the car. His hand fell gently on my thigh.

"Remind me never to take you to my childhood home. It's a hovel compared to this place," I said.

He suddenly stopped the car. We were halfway down the long tree-lined drive with the house in plain view, its immaculate gardens surrounding each side.

"It's just a house," he said again, turning fully to meet my gaze. "And I would love to see where you grew up— where you took your first step and studied for all those tests that made you so smart. Maybe, if I'm lucky, you'll even take me to Dairy Queen." He smirked.

"Only really special people get to go to Dairy Queen with me." I laughed.

"Well then, I'll be on my best behavior—or worst." His grin widened. "Now, my mom is probably sitting in the foyer, waiting by the window, wondering what the hell is taking us so long. So, let's do her a favor and end the agony. She's dying to meet you. I think she was starting to believe that I'd never bring home a woman. Ever."

"Well, I'm glad I'm the first."

He leaned forward, tenderly kissing me on the lips. "You're my first for many things," he reminded me.

Visions of bubbles and multiple orgasms in bathtubs came to mind.

"Drive."

"Right." He cleared his throat, reluctantly turning forward again.

I smiled to myself, loving the effect I had on him. Knowing I could cause such a heated response in a man like him gave me a rush of power.

Something I fully intended on using later to the best of my abilities.

But, for now, I was going to meet Roman's mother. To say I was scared would be the understatement of the year. The only type of moms I knew were the apron-wearing, home-cooking soccer-mom types.

Driving up to the circular driveway of the giant house, combined with Roman's vague, disturbing comments about his parents, made me wonder exactly what I was getting myself into.

Maybe we should have waited?

Like until I was walking down the aisle.

"I'm so glad you're here!" a woman's voice called out the moment the car came to a stop.

Looking toward the front door, I saw her. Dressed understated but still sophisticated, she was in a casual pair of slacks and a thick green sweater. The older woman surprised me, coming to my side of the car first.

I was engulfed in a hug the moment I stepped out of the car, and I instantly felt all of my worries melt away.

Mrs. Cavenaugh pulled away, and I caught her brushing an errant tear from her cheek.

"Forgive me, but Roman has already told me so much about you. I feel like I already know you, dear. Please come in, out of the cold."

Her hand wrapped around me as we walked toward the door.

"Good to see you, too, Mom," Roman muttered behind us.

"I'm getting to you, son. Just wanted to meet this girl you've been gushing over first."

"I don't gush. Cara, tell her I don't gush," he grumbled.

I turned around to see him shaking his head, his hands in his pockets. He might have been complaining, but there was genuine happiness in his eyes as he watched his mother and I embracing.

"He gushes a little." I snickered.

"Of course he does. Every man who loves a woman gushes about her. Jude does, and their father did. And, now, Roman. It makes me so happy."

"Dad never gushed," Roman said, his voice suddenly changing.

His mother stopped, turning. I followed.

"Of course he did. You were just too young to notice. But your father was the king of romance, always—"

"What are we having for dinner?" he asked, clearly interrupting his mother on purpose as we entered the grand foyer. My eyes went everywhere at once.

Her eyebrows scrunched together in confusion before she gave in. "Chicken cordon bleu. That reminds me. I need to go cork the wine. Why don't you two go get settled in the living room? I'll bring a few glasses out in a minute."

We nodded as she made her way to the kitchen.

I took a few silent moments to wander around the foyer, admiring the beautiful staircase and fine tapestries and carpets. It was like walking into a museum, only there were no ropes or signs telling me where I could and couldn't go, and my little fingers were allowed to touch and investigate everything.

"I'm sorry for that," Roman said finally. "I don't like talking about my dad."

"I know," I said, looking at an old family painting.

It was quite remarkable. Our family would visit J.C. Penney every year, marking the passing of time with a ten-minute photo session. Roman's family hired a professional painter, etching the lines of their faces with oils and pastels.

"I still remember sitting for that painting."

"You sat for it? He didn't paint it from a picture?" I asked, leaning in to get a better look at the tiny version of Roman.

He couldn't have been older than four.

"No. My dad hated half-assing things, and portraits were meant to be painted from life, or some crap like that, so we sat for it while the artist sketched it out. It wasn't the entire time, but as a kid, it seemed like an eternity."

"I bet. I promise, if we get married, I will not subject our kids to hours of torture in the name of art."

"Don't worry; we won't be having any kids."

My heart stopped, and I froze, staring at the little green-eyed boy before me with his dark blond hair. He held a hint of mischief and a look of pride.

"What? But the jokes you made earlier... I just thought—"

"They were just jokes, Cara. I don't want kids," his voice said softly.

Turning away from the portrait, I looked up at him. "Why?" I breathed out.

"I don't want to pass any of this mess of a man I've become to someone else," he said. "Besides, we're good the way we are. Can't we just enjoy what we have?"

There was fear in his eyes—honest, raw fear—and all I wanted to do was take it away.

"Yes, of course," I found myself saying. "Just you and me," I whispered as my eyes roamed the empty house.

What happened to you, Roman?

Roman's lost and vacant eyes haunted me through the rest of the evening.

I couldn't stop thinking about our brief conversation.

"I don't want kids."

He didn't want them to be like him.

I didn't even know how to respond to that.

How could I agree? The man he was happened to be the person I wanted to spend the rest of my life with.

It was crazy. We'd been together for only two weeks, but I knew it to the depths of my soul. As long as I'd held out—waiting, deciding, and debating—over every single step of my relationship with Tyler, I knew none of that was necessary when it came to Roman.

He was it.

Everything I'd ever wanted and more.

How could he not see that?

"Roman tells me you were a history major?" Mrs. Cavenaugh said, interrupting my rapid thoughts.

We'd finished dinner and moved into the living room

for casual dessert and coffee. I'd been holding my cup so long that the liquid inside had gone lukewarm.

"Yes." I smiled. "I'm hoping to find a job in the field soon once my temp position at the company is over."

"I'm sure you two will miss working together." She winked. "I helped out Roman's father from time to time over the years, but we never worked together well. He liked to separate work from home, and I think me being there tended to muddle things too much for him. So, I took a hint and gracefully bowed out, letting the professionals handle his affairs."

Roman grunted. He'd obviously not meant to do so, and when he caught both of us looking at him, he coughed awkwardly and changed the subject back to me.

"Speaking of jobs, I meant to tell you, Cara. Kevin, the tour guide who showed us around the subway, really enjoyed talking with you, so much so that he asked me for your résumé. He'd like to pass it on to his supervisor. He knows you're most likely overqualified for a tour guide position, but he'd like to see what else he can do for you."

My eyes lit up like a Christmas tree.

"Are you serious?" I said, nearly knocking over my cup. "That would be fantastic. I'd gladly take a tour guide position, anything really. I'd just be happy to have a job!"

"Very serious. Polish up that résumé tonight, and I'll forward it over."

I set my coffee down and reached over to hug him.

"You know, with your interest in history, I might have something to keep you busy."

"Mom," Roman groaned, shaking his head.

"Let her continue. She said my favorite word—*history*."

"I thought *Roman* was your favorite word." He grinned.

"Second favorite word," I corrected, playfully elbowing him.

"When I moved to my apartment in the city, I had to go through almost everything in the house to decide what to take and what to leave behind. There are generations of Cavenaugh things here. I have boxes and boxes of pictures, documents, and such in the attic. I haven't had the chance to go through and catalog it, and to be honest, I don't even have a clue as to how to begin."

"Stop right there," I said, holding my hand up. "Yes, please. I'd be happy to do whatever it is you're about to ask, as long as it means I get to get my hands on those boxes."

"Really? Because it sounds like a terrible burden."

I shook my head. "To me, you basically just said, *Hey, here are a dozen boxes of Godiva chocolate. Do you want them?*"

We both laughed.

Soon, Roman was hiking up to the drafty attic with me and his mother, and we figured out which boxes could go with us that night and what would be sent by courier since Roman's car was the size of a go-kart.

"Thank you so much for this, dear. I can't wait to see what you do with all of it. And take your time."

"I'm going to dive in as soon as I get home!" I said excitedly.

"Great, Mom. Thanks for killing my sex life," Roman said behind me, making me instantly blush.

"Oh, hush, you. You're making the poor girl turn red." She said, scolding her son. Turning back to me, she winked, "I promise, I really did raise him to be a proper gentleman. It's in there somewhere."

I laughed, leaning forward. "He likes to pretend he's prickly and mean, but he's everything you raised him to be and more."

She wrapped her arms around me, giving me a long warm hug. "Thank you, Cara, and please… hold on to him."

"As tight as I'm able to," I promised, thinking back to his earlier words regarding kids.

I hoped it would be enough.

CHAPTER TWENTY-ONE

ROMAN

"You want to what?" Jude's voice boomed on the other end of the phone line.

"You heard me," I replied. Leaning back in my comfy leather chair, I quietly looked out toward the crystal-blue sky of the city, feeling light and content—two words that usually did not coincide with work.

"I did. I just never thought I'd actually hear those words springing forth from your mouth."

I let out a ghost of a laugh, bending forward to give another glance through the paperwork I'd written up for this impromptu meeting with Jude.

"Look, I know I haven't done much—"

"What are you talking about, Roman? You've done everything. When I told you Lailah and I wanted to move across the country to set up a West Coast division so that we could start a life here in California, you didn't hesitate. You just took over. And you've done an amazing job."

"I know that," I replied. "But that's not what I meant. What I meant to say is, I know I haven't done much to grow the company... to mold it into something that is truly ours. Up until now, I've basically been doing what Dad taught us to do."

"Make money," we both said in unison.

"Exactly," I said. "And it's killing me. I thought it would be enough, knowing I was prolonging the life of this company, but damn, Jude, I fucking hate it. But *this* is the one part of the job that isn't so bad. It's not much."

"It's not much?" Jude scoffed. "Roman, this is huge. If this gets out, we'll be one of the most sought-after companies in the world."

I shrugged, knowing full well he couldn't see me. "It's just a compensation plan."

"It's more than that. You're taking care of our employees. You're making them our first priority. It's brilliant really. You'll not only recruit the best and the brightest, but it makes the job of buying out companies less aggressive when we know we're going to be taking them under our wing and making them a part of the Cavenaugh family, so to speak. I'm really proud of you.

"It was Cara really who gave me the idea. She doesn't let me settle."

"A good woman never does." He laughed. "I'm glad you've found yours."

Just then, my phone beeped, telling me I had another incoming call. I quickly checked the screen, and my forehead furrowed in confusion as Jo's number appeared.

I hadn't heard from her in weeks.

Our arrangement had ended even earlier than that, and we weren't exactly the chatty sort of friends. Not wanting to talk with a former fuck buddy at work, I let it go to voice mail, figuring she'd leave a message if it were important.

Most likely a misdial.

The corner of my mouth turned upward as I remembered one specific butt dial not too long ago.

Cara, believing she was a true New Yorker now, had decided a week or so ago to purchase a brand-new phone. Hers was ancient, something that had been passed down to her in college.

She'd spent an entire afternoon on my laptop one weekend, researching phones, until she'd come to a final decision. Once she'd had that baby in her hands, she'd pulled it out of the box and fired it right up, telling me everything about it, from the high-speed camera to the storage space.

But, in all her research, she never quite figured out how to use it, and somehow, she couldn't manage to lock it.

Or unlock it.

Or use it at all.

In her frustration, she'd ended up pocket-dialing me, while she was shopping for lingerie, and I'd gotten to hear her very embarrassing conversation with the salesclerk that started out with her asking if they had anything sexy but cute.

When the salesclerk had asked for clarification, Cara had said, "You know… maybe some lace with candy hearts?"

God, I loved this woman.

"Roman?" Jude said, bringing me back to earth.

"Yep. So, I'll fax you the information once I get the final paperwork typed up. Once you go over it and suggest changes, I'll send it to HR and present it to the board."

"Sounds great, brother. I'm looking forward to hearing the announcement."

I hesitated briefly. "I want you to announce it."

There was silence on the other end.

"Don't do this, Roman," he responded, his voice low and ragged.

"Do what?"

"Sell yourself short."

"What? I'm not—"

"You are. Why do you think I kept warning you about messing up with Cara?"

"Because I'm a jackass," I joked.

"True," he agreed. "But seriously, you've got this self-destruct switch. You purposely sabotage your life, never allowing yourself to have the recognition you deserve or the happiness you need. Make the announcement, Roman. Let our employees know who has their backs. Stop hiding in that office, and show them you're working for them, not against them."

"You sound a lot like Cara," I huffed.

"Well, she seemed like an incredibly smart woman when I met her," he replied in jest.

"She is."

"I know she is, Roman. Don't screw this up. You deserve this and more. But it doesn't mean shit if you don't believe it. You've got to believe it."

We said our good-byes, and I leaned back in my chair once again, letting the cool leather melt into the curves of my back. I let my eyes close for a brief moment and thought about the words my brother had just said.

Did I sabotage everything in my life?

I was in love… something I'd sworn I'd never do.

That certainly didn't sound like a man who was about to self-destruct.

Sorry, Jude, but this time, you're wrong.

ONE MONTH.

That was how long Cara had been mine.

And, in the sprit of celebrating every cheesy anniversary, I was going all out on this one. Balloons, flowers, expensive chocolates, and dinner at one of the nicest places in town.

It was corny and extravagant, but sometimes a girl needed a little crazy.

And my girl?

My girl deserved the fucking stars.

I'd been planning this for nearly two weeks, ever since the moment we'd arrived home from my mother's house.

That house was the place where I'd spent so much of my childhood.

I remembered chasing Jude around and also hiding in the broom closet while he'd yell, "Marco!"

I'd snicker to myself, knowing I was supposed to yell, *Polo*, back, but I wouldn't.

Seeing Cara there had made everything real.

She was it.

She was mine. I knew that much.

But, now, I knew something even more important.

I was hers. Forever.

That girl—with the infectious laugh and the horrible fashion sense, with the impeccable manners and love for history—owned me.

And I planned on making sure she didn't forget it.

Every damn day for the rest of our lives.

She made me giddy.

Fucking giddy.

I was buzzing around the apartment, showering and picking out a tie, when I realized I was actually whistling.

Who does that?

It was so ridiculous. I thought I actually made myself sick.

After picking out a suit, I grabbed my phone to make sure I was still on time. When you were dating your assistant and planning an event she couldn't know anything about, the details suddenly landed squarely on your own lap.

And I wasn't good with juggling.

It was why I had a damn assistant to begin with.

But I'd managed everything up until today, and assuming the limo got here on time and I walked out of here with two shoes on my feet and the bouquet of roses I'd picked out, everything else would work itself out.

Hopefully. I didn't exactly know.

This whole dating thing was still new to me after all.

Briefly pausing to scroll through my phone, I noticed that Jo had called not just once but several times. I'd failed to call her back the first time, the phone call completely eluding me. But now, seeing her name pop up on the screen again, I couldn't help but wonder what was going on.

Looking at the clock, I knew it was a risk.

I had barely enough time to finish getting ready.

But I knew I wouldn't be in the right frame of mind if I had this looming over me.

What if she was in trouble? What if something was wrong?

She didn't often turn to me when she needed help, but if things were bad, she knew she could.

And I'd help.

We might not have ever been more than physical, but I did care for her in my own way.

"Hey, what's up?" I said after she picked up on the second ring.

"Jesus, where have you been? I've been calling all day."

She sounded edgy and stressed, the very opposite of her normal disposition.

"What's wrong? Are you okay?" I immediately thought of her and her child, all alone.

"I'm fine. We're both fine. It's you I'm calling about."

"Me? Why me?" I said, astonished.

"Do you know a woman named Lauren?" she asked.

My heart skidded to a halt in that moment, and I sank down to the soft mattress of the bed.

"Yes. Why?" I asked in hesitation.

"She was here—in the club, asking about you."

"Lauren was?" My hands started to shake for no apparent reason. But I knew the reason. My body knew it before my brain could even register the idea of it.

Lauren… Jo… Tyler…

All roads led to Cara.

"What did she ask you?" I asked, not really caring. I knew it was only a matter of time now.

"She wanted to know how I knew you. Wanted to know why I was here the night Tyler's company was here. I didn't tell her anything, Roman, I swear. But, Christ… she knows. I don't know how, but she knows."

"Thanks, Jo," I said,

"You okay, Roman?" she asked.

"No," I answered. "I think my self-destruct button just initiated."

"What?"

"I've gotta go." I hung up.

I guessed my little brother was right after all.

Turned out I could sabotage my life… even when I wasn't trying.

"YOU'VE SERIOUSLY OUTDONE YOURSELF," CARA SAID, looking around at our private dining room.

The staff had been the ones to really outshine themselves, adorning the room in tiny twinkling lights and lavish flower arrangements. It was the kind of dinner a man would arrange for a proposal or a twenty-fifth wedding anniversary.

When the manager had asked what we were celebrating, I'd laughed, saying one beautiful month together. I'd thought he might call me crazy.

Instead, he'd said, "Perfect. Don't hold back."

And I hadn't.

Looking at her now, dressed in a beautiful satin gown that was both classy and downright sexy all at the same time, it nearly made my heart ache.

Would this be the last celebration?

I'd tried to put it out of my memory, but Lauren was clearly out for blood, and I was her target. Why? I didn't know. Maybe she was still upset that I'd passed up her offer all those months ago.

She seemed like the type who got her way most of the time.

I should know.

But not everything went my way... no matter how much I wanted it to.

Somehow I'd managed to stay upbeat and involved for most of dinner, only faltering a few times, blaming it on nerves or joking that her sheer beauty was driving me crazy.

It wasn't far from the truth.

Most days, she could make me go tongue-tied with a single glance. Tonight though? I was damn near speechless. It was a memory I'd treasure forever.

No matter what happened in the days to follow.

WE RODE SIDE BY SIDE IN THE LIMO, HER HAND IN MINE, AS the sights of the city passed by in a blur. November was fading into December, which meant every corner had exploded overnight, becoming a holiday mecca for the shopping elite.

It was supposed to be the happiest time of the year.

Our first Christmas together.

But would the last remaining days of the year melt away, leaving me yearning for the one thing I needed most in this world?

Her.

As the hours faded away, my sense of urgency grew. After every glance in her direction, it became harder and harder for me to turn away. Every touch, every kiss… was a lasting imprint on my mind.

By the time I twisted the key in the lock to my apartment, I was nearly frantic.

She took my delirious advances as pent-up passion, fueling my desire in spades, and she kissed me with wild abandon. Our clothes fell to the floor, landing in a tiny trail of seduction, as I led her to the bedroom. I watched as her half-naked body tumbled to the bed, her hair fanning out beneath her, like beautiful raw silk.

"Dear God," I said, noticing the lacy lingerie for the first time.

Her cheeks reddened instantly, matching the red teddy that barely covered her. "What happened to cute candy hearts?" I asked, forgetting everything but her in that perfect moment.

"How did you—did I butt-dial you again?" She shook her head, covering her face with her hands.

"I have to say, as much as I love your particular style,

this is nice. *Very* nice," I emphasized, delicately running a single hand up the side of her thigh.

"Well, I met a nice lady at the lingerie store. And she—"

"What was her name?" I asked, smiling happily to myself.

"What?"

"Her name," I said again. "What was it? I'd like to send her a card, or flowers maybe, as a thank-you."

She laughed as my eyes continued to roam her body. "Janice. Joan? Judy? I don't remember. Anyway, I expected her to laugh at me when I mentioned the candy hearts and lace combo, but she didn't. She just smiled and said, 'Being cute definitely has its place in the bedroom, but sometimes, straight-up sexy is the way to go.'

"Now, I probably would have just walked away at that point since she didn't have what I wanted. In fact, I did. After I said thank you, I might add."

"Naturally," I said.

"But then, as I turned to leave, she commented on my necklace. Specifically, the clasp, noticing it was antique. Not many people can spot a 1920s antique clasp from across the room, so I figured this woman might know a thing or two. And, judging from the way your eyes are going all goofy and stupid right now, I'd say she definitely knew her lingerie."

"My eyes do not go goofy and stupid," I argued.

"How do you know?" She grinned.

I bent down to appreciate her lips. Slowly. Tenderly.

"Because the way you make me feel is far from stupid. It's maddening, crazy, and—"

"Roman?"

"Yeah?" I said softly against her soft lips.

"I love you."

My heart squeezed tightly inside my chest, reminding me of the hour. Of the phone call I'd had. Of the possibility that she might never say those words to me again. Because when tomorrow came and Lauren found her…

"I love you, too. Always. No matter what," I said in a blind panic.

My mouth devoured hers. There was no more time for joking. No more time for candy hearts or flowers.

There was only this, and if this was all I had left, I'd make damn sure she remembered me.

Even when she hated me.

We were a twisted, tangle mess of naked limbs and echoing moans. Lovers in motion. As much as I adored her in red lace, I loved her more naked, and the beautiful teddy she'd bravely worn for me was thrown to the floor.

I needed my hands on her.

On all of her.

All at once.

Forever.

One more night would never be enough.

As if she could sense the desperation in my touch, her movements steadied, and her touch became tender.

"We have all night," she said. "You don't have to rush. I'm yours," she pledged.

I closed my eyes, turning briefly, as I tried to push away the pain.

I could take her away.

Fire Lauren.

Do something, anything.

But I knew, none of it would matter. There would always be this burden hanging over my head, reminding me that I'd stolen something I didn't deserve.

I didn't deserve her.

It was as simple as that.

She was good. Honest and compassionate.

I was the kind of man who stole companies, slept with his assistant, and ruined lives.

We were never fated to be together.

Her gentle hand cupped my cheek, turning me toward her again.

"Make love to me, Roman," her voice purred.

It was a request I couldn't deny.

Because I'd never deny her anything.

Ever.

As our bodies joined, I never looked away. I stared into those dark brown eyes, watching them pulse with hunger and desire, as I slowly moved inside her. Every murmur, every tremor of need, was etched into my very soul as we made love that night.

I remembered it all.

The way she'd held her breath as she came, arching her back as I kissed and licked her breasts.

The way she'd wrapped her legs around my body and begged for more.

Every single moment.

I remembered.

Because, soon, that was all it would be.

Nothing but memories and dust.

CHAPTER TWENTY-TWO

CARA

Mel,

Don't stress over your finals. You know you'll do great. When have you ever not aced an exam? I know, I know… except that one spelling test in first grade that you always bring up when I ask that question… so don't bother replying with that.

But seriously, stand up. Do it. Right now. Stand up, blast that horrible music I know you have on, and dance around your dorm. It will help.

P.S. Why don't you come visit when you're done with finals? You can fly home and meet Roman and me there, and maybe your presence will help smooth over the new boyfriend introduction? Yes? Please say yes.

Love you; Cara(-saurus)

Melissa had sent me an SOS message late last night, panicking over her finals. She'd done this every semester since I'd met her. She was quite the neurotic genius.

I had a feeling her new roommate had something to do with it.

That, or it was the lack of sex.

I really wasn't sure.

But I really was serious about her coming to visit. I knew she'd come here to help smooth things over for me, but really, I thought we'd done each other a favor. By the time she'd left, her state of mind had seemed to be in a much better place.

Or at least it had been.

For a few days.

I also really loved the idea of having her with me when I introduced Roman to my parents. They had been, understandably, cautious when I told them about the new man in my life. For as long as they could remember, I was going to marry Tyler. Even when I was in high school, they'd thought it was absurd and rolled their eyes, telling me I was far too young for such things.

But now I'd done a complete one-eighty, dumping the long-term boyfriend and replacing him after what seemed like a day.

Okay, it was a few days.

But still…

For my conservative, married-for-a-thousand-years parents, seeing me basically jump in bed with a much older, incredibly rich man, who also happened to be my boss, was… well, startling.

The thought of bringing Roman home to my small town in a few weeks? I might as well be bringing home Ryan Gosling because that was what it felt like.

My mother had already Googled Roman. I hadn't even known she knew how to do that, and she'd sent his picture around to all her girlfriends. No doubt, the entire town knew about him now.

That meant Tyler's parents did as well.

The entire situation needed to be handled gently and with tact. I was going to give Roman small-town lessons soon. Possibly as quickly as this evening.

I'd planned on mentioning it to him this morning, over breakfast, but he'd slipped out early, probably for a meeting out of the office that he'd forgotten to mention. So, I tabled it for later, knowing he was busy for the remainder of the day.

And so was I.

I was now working double duty, assisting Roman and looking for a new job.

I'd already sent out my résumé to several local historical societies and museums, but I hadn't heard a thing, including from Kevin, Roman's contact at the Transit Society. I was trying to keep my hopes up. I knew Rome hadn't been built in a day, and all good things came to those who waited. But, really, I was sick of waiting!

Firing up the Internet browser, I began my daily search once more, looking at job listings on every website I could find, in hopes that something new would pop up.

Yesterday, I'd managed to find a position at the Museum of the City of New York.

It was for the janitorial staff.

I'd nearly applied—until the thought of cleaning restrooms scared me off. I was scared of my own.

The day before, I'd applied for a curator position at a small museum in Brooklyn. I'd rolled my eyes as I hit Submit, knowing full well that I was under-qualified for the position, but a girl could dream.

"Are you screwing Roman Cavenaugh?"

My heart nearly stopped as I looked up to find Lauren standing above me, her eyes wide and crazy.

How did she always sneak up on me?

"What?" I played dumb.

"Come with me," she said, reaching for my hand across the desk.

She didn't care that it was awkward. She didn't care that she'd knocked half a dozen things off my desk as she dragged me away.

As I looked back, I happened to catch one parting gift.

Roman.

Briefcase in hand, obviously coming back from his morning meeting. His eyes locked on mine and then on Lauren, and in them, I saw fear.

Empty, raw fear.

THE LAST TWENTY-FOUR HOURS FELT LIKE A BLUR.

As I sat on a plane, headed for home, I remembered sitting on a highway years earlier. Traffic wasn't something we encountered much in our rural area, but when an accident occurred, it was bound to happen.

As my mom and I'd sat in the steamy car under the hot summer sun, waiting for traffic to be diverted, that tiny mind of mine had asked, "Why is everyone driving so slow? If the accident has been pulled off to the side and all the lanes are open… why is everyone slowing down?"

My mom had simply smiled and said, "It's just human nature. It's hard to drive past something like that and not look."

I'd always been frustrated with her answer.

Yet as I'd gotten older and encountered my own accidents and traffic jams, I'd find myself following everyone else, slowing to a near halt on the road to get a good look at the wreckage, to see just what had happened.

To realize… it could have been me.

That was how I'd felt over the last twenty-four hours.

Like a passerby in an automobile accident, observing someone else's pain.

But the pain and suffering was all mine.

It was *all mine*.

He'd done this. He'd caused this pain.

And the first thing I had done when I realized this was leave.

I couldn't face Roman now.

Not yet. Maybe not ever.

Not after the conversation I'd had with Lauren. Not knowing what I knew now.

"Are you sleeping with Roman Cavenaugh?" Lauren asked again, clicking the door to the break room securely in place.

I nervously looked around, realizing we were thankfully alone.

"What is going on?" I asked, clearly diverting.

"You're not going to answer the question? Fine. I'll do the talking then," she snapped, pacing back and forth, like a furious caged tiger. "I was top of my class. I had my pick of jobs. I could have gone anywhere, but I came here. I'm smart as hell. The Cavenaughs are lucky to have me. Well, Roman might not feel that way after today." She laughed.

"Lauren? You're not making any sense," I said, taking a step forward.

Maybe the stress of work had gotten to her. Maybe she needed a break. I knew she never liked Roman much, but this? This was like watching someone go manic.

"I've been watching him."

"Who? Roman?" I asked, suddenly fearful.

"Yes. I've always known he was a shady guy, but I never knew how bad it was. This? This goes beyond what I thought he was capable of. He was there, Cara," she said, her eyes blazing. "He set the whole thing up."

"I don't understand."

"The night Tyler cheated on you. He made it happen."

My body froze.

"He was the one who brought it up to me in the first place. He never speaks to me. He never speaks to anyone really. So, when he suddenly started a conversation with me about your boyfriend at the meeting that day, I thought it was odd. Beyond odd. So, I watched him… financially speaking. I have access to pretty much everything accounting does. A few weeks later, the night Tyler kicked you out of your apartment, he was there. At the strip club. He was stupid enough to use his business credit card for the drink he bought."

I swallowed audibly.

"That doesn't mean anything," I said defensively.

"He knows the stripper, Cara."

"That still doesn't mean—"

She laughed, almost painfully. "Are you so enamored by him that you would actually stand here and defend him? Think about it—logically. If you don't believe me, go ask him yourself."

And so I had.

Turned out, Lauren was pretty damn smart.

And I was an idiot.

While Roman might not have forced the stripper on Tyler, Roman had persuaded her to hit on him, knowing that he might stumble.

Does Roman know strippers at all the local joints? Or was I just lucky that my boyfriend happened to stumble into the right one?

I really didn't want to know.

I'd stormed out of his office and never looked back.

I barely remembered the trip to the airport, handing over my luggage and ID in a daze, wanting to fly back to my roots.

Back to my safety net, where everything was easy.

My parents had no idea I was coming. In my haste, I hadn't bothered calling anyone, even Melissa.

As I exited the small airport, realizing I had no way of actually making it home, I took a left to the small rental car window and got the cheapest car I could, and then I headed west.

Nebraska had already seen its first snow of the year, and much of the ground was covered in bits of leftover snow and ice. I bundled my coat tightly together, wishing I'd packed something warmer, as I lugged my suitcase into the trunk. Knowing the way home like the back of my hand, I found a familiar radio station, silenced my phone, and focused on the road.

The stupid thing about driving alone?

The uninterrupted amount of time it gave you to think.

And thinking was the last thing I wanted to do.

After about an hour and a half, I was in desperate need of a distraction. Fully aware I was about to enter familiar territory, I decided it was time for a food break anyway. Any closer to home, and I'd run the risk of running into familiars, and I wasn't sure I was ready for that.

Still two towns away, this felt safe.

I pulled into a restaurant I remembered from high school—a dodgy little place that apparently had undergone a recent renovation. It used to be well known for a less than savory reason.

Its real name was The Caddy Shack. What we used to call it when I was young? The Shady Shack.

Although I'd never actually visited, I'd heard rumors.

For one reason or another, the restrooms had become legendary.

Not in a name-carving, oh-this-is-a-unique-restroom kind of way.

But in a oh-I-lost-my-virginity-in-that-restroom-too kind of way.

I was guessing the new frilly curtains and flowery wallpaper was a solid effort by the owners to negate that reputation for future generations to come.

I figured, in the light of day, this place and its bad reputation couldn't do much harm. Plus, I was starving, and besides the bar across the street, this was the only option for miles. I was already showing up at my parents' door, sad and pathetic because of a boy. I didn't need to be sad, pathetic, *and* hungry.

Shutting off the engine, I exited my rental and headed for the door, continuously looking over my shoulder for someone… anyone. I felt like, at any moment, I would run into an old neighbor, my high school English teacher, or the pastor. It was just a matter of time.

And then I'd be plastered with questions.

So many questions.

What are you doing?

Where are you working?

We hear you have a new boyfriend? What's he like?

What would I say? That I'd just walked out on my job, my boyfriend, and my entire life. That I'd booked the first flight home with my tail between my legs because I was hurting, and all I wanted was my mommy.

I took a deep breath, entering the restaurant and taking the first open table I could find. I did a quick glance around, checking everyone out with silent stealth.

Success!

Not a single face I recognized.

Thank you, Shady Shack.

It didn't take long for a waitress to serve me, and soon, I was back in fatty heaven, eating a huge steak and mashed potatoes with apple pie and coffee for dessert.

After my record-breaking pig-out, I headed to the restroom before getting back on the road, too blissed out on food to think about anything but getting home. I remembered why I should have waited to pee the second I walked into the ladies' restroom, hearing heated moans coming from the back stall.

"I told you to lock the door, Marty!"

Marty?

"Well, there wasn't anyone in the restaurant when we got here, sugar."

Sugar?

Oh, shit…

"Mom?" I blurted out before my mind warned me otherwise.

"Cara? Is that you?"

Why didn't I stay silent? Why couldn't I have just slowly backed away, like any other normal person?

"Surprise," I said awkwardly, desperately trying not to gag at the thought of my parents doing the nasty at The Shady Shack.

Suddenly, the food I'd just consumed didn't feel so great, sitting in the bottom of my stomach.

Welcome home, I thought.

Welcome home.

"I WISH YOU HAD CALLED, HONEY," MY MOM SAID, HANDING me a cup of coffee, as she settled onto the sofa next to me. "We would have—"

"Delayed your afternoon plans?" I said, squeezing my eyes shut in a solid attempt to erase the memory from my mind. Hadn't I endured enough in the last day or so? Hearing my parents get it on in a dirty restroom had to be added to the list?

"I'm sorry about that. It's just the craziest thing, you know." She blushed. "Ever since you left, your father and I—"

"Please. Please stop," I begged, holding my free hand up in protest.

"Okay, okay." She laughed. "I was just trying to explain."

"No need. Really, I get it. No more kids—or kid, in your case. You're shaking things up. As long as you're happy," I managed to say, feeling proud of my words.

I was still grossed out—so, so grossed out—but I could find enough maturity in me to be upbeat for my parents.

Growing up, there were times when I'd seen them fight and carry on about one thing or another, and I'd wondered what kept them going. *Was it love? Duty?*

I was glad to know it was love.

"What brings you home, Cara?" my mother finally asked.

I knew she'd been dying to know the moment she heard my voice calling out to her in that restroom, but she hadn't said a word until now.

"I needed you," I simply said.

She smiled, setting her cup of coffee down on the coffee table. "And I'll always be here. But that's not the real reason."

"How did you know Daddy was the one?" I asked, not ready to talk about Roman yet.

She looked out the window to where my father was,

laying a fresh coat of salt for the impending inch or two of snow that could fall overnight, and she smiled.

"The first time I tried to imagine life without him, I guess," she said. "We began dating in college; you know that. But there were a few weeks during our senior year when we broke up. Neither one of us could decide what we wanted to do or where, so rather than make that decision, we just determined a clean break would be best. I walked away, thinking everything would be easier without him. But, as the days went on, there were all these holes in my life where he used to exist. Holes that I'd thought would fill or mend but didn't. Holes that started to leak tears because I missed him so much."

"So, you went back to him?"

She shook her head. "He came back to me, filled with the same hollowness that we could only mend if we were together. We might not be the most successful or the most glamorous couple. We've led a simple life with plenty of ups and downs. But it's *ours*," she emphasized. "What is this about, Cara? I know you aren't just curious about your daddy and me."

I took a long sip of coffee. I smiled to myself because I realized it was the first time my mother had ever made me a cup of coffee. Usually, it was just iced tea or lemonade. Somehow, in the few months I'd been away, I'd transformed into an adult in her eyes, someone she could relax on the sofa with and confide in over coffee.

"I don't know," I confessed. "I thought I'd figured it all out, Mom. Everything with Roman… for the first time in my life, it felt so—"

"Right?"

I nodded. "I know we've only known each other for a short while, but it just felt exactly right. Not easy or comfortable, like it was with Tyler, but like I'd been waiting for him, and suddenly, there he was."

"But not anymore?" she asked, warmth in her tone.

"No, that's the problem. It would be much simpler if I didn't feel this way… if I could just walk away and never look back. Even though I'm mad and hurt, I still want to run back to him. Why is that?"

"The heart can't toss aside what it wants just because you're hurting."

I shook my head. "You don't know what he did. You don't understand."

And so I made her understand.

I told her everything. From the very beginning.

I didn't leave anything out—well, maybe the steamy bits. We'd shared enough of that for a lifetime. But the feelings I had for him, the guilt I felt for having feeling for my boss, Tyler's betrayal… the blissful month that had followed with Roman.

And the day that had ended it all.

She listened patiently, asking questions and nodding her head at the appropriate times. When I'd finished, she took her time in formulating a response. I watched her hands reach for her lukewarm coffee, tenderly wrapping her hands around the worn cup, as she found the words that would no doubt make all the pain go away.

That was why I was here. To make the pain go away.

Moms did that after all. It was their superpower.

"What are you most mad about?"

I looked at her, dumbfounded. That wasn't supposed to be her response. She was supposed to open her mouth and spout words of *wisdom and superior knowledge, making me all better in a single sentence.*

Instead, I got this?

"What am I most mad about? Everything," I answered angrily.

"No, you've got to be mad about something specific, or you wouldn't be here, asking me to figure it out for you. You'd be back in New York, fixing it all by yourself."

I opened my mouth to retaliate and found no words.

Nada.

"So, answer me. Are you mad at Roman for deceiving you? At Tyler for betraying you? Or at yourself for getting into this situation?"

"Me? Why would I be mad at myself?"

"Well, you've always praised yourself for being a level-headed person. We thought it was a little odd that you never had that normal teenage freak-out most kids have, and honestly, we were kind of looking forward to it after a while. We kept waiting for you to announce you were switching colleges and running off to New York to marry Tyler or something equally as crazy. But you never did. You were always so even-keeled. So, maybe this is your moment?"

"You're comparing this to something a teenager would do?"

"Well, not all of it. But crawling back home when things didn't go your way? That certainly is."

"Mom!" I whined. "You're supposed to fix this!"

"No, I'm not, baby. You left. You packed up your things, moved away, and declared yourself an adult, remember? Now, it's time to act like one. If you want me to talk to you like the adult I believe you are, I'm happy to do that, but stop expecting me to fix everything."

I took a deep breath, realizing she was right.

So right.

I had moved away. Declared myself an adult.

Even I knew, I was being ridiculous. Hiding myself inside my parents' house wasn't the answer.

I had made a life in New York, and sooner or later, I'd have to go back.

"I'm mad he didn't fight for me," I finally admitted.

"See? Now, we're getting somewhere. Fight for you how?"

"When I confronted him about everything. I went to him and told him everything Lauren had said to me, and he just sat there, defeated. Like he'd already known exactly what would happen. Like he'd already said good-bye to me."

My mind flashed back to the night before, how frantic he'd been one minute as we made love, only to stop and savor each second after.

Maybe he'd already said good-bye.

"You didn't want it to end then? Despite what he did?" my mother asked.

I thought about it, about everything I'd felt over the last twenty-four-plus hours. Hurt, pain, anger, and even fear. I was mad at him. I was angry that he hadn't just let me figure out my own feelings, so I could have walked away from Tyler when I was ready. Roman had caused me pain by meddling in my breakup with Tyler, this was true, but it was not as much as when I'd walked out of that office door and he hadn't followed.

He should have followed.

He should have fought for me.

He should have fought for us.

"Can you imagine your life without him? Like I did with your father all those years ago? Can you look ahead —six months from now… a year, three years—and imagine what life would be like without him? Are you happy? Or filled with holes?"

"Holes," I finally said. "So many holes."

"Then, you know what to do, sweetheart." She smiled.

"Yes, but first, I'm going to make him sweat it out for a few days," I answered with a slight smirk.

"Attagirl."

If he wouldn't fight, I would.

Because we deserved a future together. Without holes.

Without regrets.

I STUCK TO MY PROMISE—FOR THE MOST PART.

After about thirty-six hours of family time, watching my parents' rekindled love for each other… all over the house, I decided it was time to go home.

Funny… that was the first time I'd considered New York home.

I'd packed up my suitcase, kissed my parents on the cheeks, promised to return in a few weeks for Christmas, and boarded a plane for home.

Ready to reclaim my life.

And my man.

But, so far, I hadn't done either.

I'd had every intention of dropping off my things, marching back out of that apartment, and heading straight for Roman's, ready to talk some sense into him.

How dare he let me walk away!

I was a damn good catch.

But the minute I'd entered my apartment, the weight of everything that had happened sank back in. Deep into my bones. And I felt the courage and bravery my visit home had instilled in me melting into the floorboards.

The apartment felt different.

Foreign.

I'd always considered the tiny place a consolation prize I'd won fair and square after the less than amicable parting between Tyler and me. But, now, knowing the truth, it suddenly felt all wrong.

Would Tyler have cheated at all if he hadn't been pushed?

I thought back to all the nights he'd come home late at night, smelling of cheap perfume and expensive booze.

Had Roman just expedited a forgone conclusion? Or had he made Tyler a cheater?

I knew, after my few days of soul-searching in the Midwest, I would have eventually left Tyler, no matter what the reason.

We were wrong for each other.

My feelings for Roman, a man completely Tyler's opposite, had only proven that further.

Roman had brought out a side of myself that I loved exploring. He'd made me feel daring and beautiful without changing me in the process. Tyler had always been my safe, conventional boyfriend. We'd worked until we hadn't.

I wasn't brave enough to admit it.

Tyler had just tried to mold me into someone else.

It had been a disaster in the making. I knew that now. It still hurt to know Roman's part in it all.

But I hadn't blindly gone into this relationship. Although I might have fallen for my boss rather hastily, it didn't mean I was under the foolish impression of what kind of man he was.

I knew him.

All of him.

That was why, out of everything that had transpired, knowing he'd let me go hurt the worst.

Because my Roman? My Roman would have fought.

As the sun set on another day, I knew I wouldn't make

it out of that dark apartment. It was still too soon. But I couldn't help but want to be close to him.

Grabbing a glass of wine, I sat myself down on the floor in front of the small coffee table still leftover from my days with Tyler. It had been one of my flea-market finds during the first few weeks I'd arrived. Tyler had been bored out of his mind, wandering from seller to seller, bargaining over what he considered junk. To me, it was history, part of someone's life.

And, now, it was a part of mine.

I lovingly fanned my hand out over the worn wood, admiring each ding and scratch, knowing there was a story or two behind each one. It was the perfect place to discover the stories of the Cavenaugh family.

Ever since the boxes had arrived, I'd set up camp right here on this small table. Not having the space for a proper dining room table, this was the largest work area I had—besides the floor or the kitchen, and I would not allow dirt or food anywhere near these precious documents and photos.

Keeping my wine a good distance away, I took up where I'd left off—somewhere around the turn of the century.

But, for some reason, it didn't interest me the way it had.

It wasn't *him*, and tonight, I really needed Roman.

Going against my highly organized brain, I set the box aside and started searching.

Searching for Roman.

It didn't take long. Mrs. Cavenaugh had sent everything. Every photo, diploma, and document she had all the way back to Patrick Kavanaugh—the first ancestor from Ireland. I loved that it was spelled differently—the researcher in me wanted to know why.

I spent hours going through Roman's baby albums and high school yearbooks and reading every mention of him his mother had clipped from the papers. It was completely unorganized, like she'd said, with a mixture of Roman and Jude in several boxes, but I enjoyed it all.

Jude was exactly as Roman had described, studious and determined, while Roman had managed to excel in sports and various other activities.

I spent an entire hour sifting through newspaper clippings, sorting the boys.

Jude's pile was quite impressive, and I couldn't help but read a few articles. Most were from his high school paper, an elite prep school I'd never heard of. I focused on one, smiling at a young Jude looking quite bored on a stage with several of his peers. He was a stark contrast to the tattooed hottie he was today. But I could tell it was him by the eyes. He and Roman had very similar eyes.

Just as I was about to set article aside and search for more photos of a young Roman, something caught my eye. A hint of light-colored hair. The way she was looking at him.

I grabbed my magnifying glass immediately.

Every proper historian had a magnifying glass after all.

Looking deep into the old photo, I found her.

Lauren Drake.

I remembered her mentioning when we'd met that she'd briefly attended the same school as Jude. Apparently, that was actually true. Now completely interested in my little find, I read the rest of the article, noting several other pictures had been included.

Nothing about the article was particularly interesting. Just an honors ceremony. A list of awardees, including Jude and Lauren.

Bummer.

With my trusty magnifying glass in hand, I moved on to other pictures, finding nothing of interest, until I came to the last picture. It was an after shot of a parent and a student I didn't recognize, happily posing for the camera.

That wasn't the interesting part though.

The background was what had my jaw dropping.

Roman's father was grabbing the arm of another woman.

Looking closely at the photograph, I gasped.

There would be no sleep for me tonight.

CHAPTER TWENTY-THREE

ROMAN

I stood in front of the floor-to-ceiling window of the office that had been the pillar of our family for three generations, just minutes after my victory in the boardroom.

And I felt nothing.

This should have been my day to celebrate. I should have been halfway through a vintage bottle of scotch by now, reveling in my success.

My triumph.

I'd been working for months for this very moment—the moment after the meeting that either solidified my position in the company for years to come or proved that I was everything my father had believed I was.

And I'd fucking nailed it. I had owned that room and every person in it. The board had been amazed by not only my collective knowledge of the company, both past and present, but also my commitment and determination to push it steadily into the future.

I was not my father's son.

I knew that now.

And now so did everyone else.

Everyone but one person.

And that was why I was standing here, feeling nothing but emptiness.

I'd let her walk away. When I should have run after her, barricaded the door, and fought tooth and nail for every single second, I'd sat there like a man defeated and let my future bleed out all over the floor. When I'd promised myself I'd never let her go, I'd done the very opposite, choosing to believe she deserved better.

I couldn't help but wonder, *Am I too late?*

It had been four days, and I hadn't heard a single word.

But then again, I hadn't said any either. Call after call had ended the moment that familiar voice came alive on the other end, asking me to leave a voice mail. I couldn't bring myself to do it.

What could I say to the woman I'd failed?

I missed her more than I could put into words. Somehow, in the short time she'd been in my life, Cara had managed to permanently etch her name into my damn soul.

And knowing I might never see her again?

The very definition of hell.

Well, fuck that.

I might not have fought for her then, in that moment, but I would now.

And forever.

Until my last fucking breath, I'd do everything in my power to show that woman why we were fated to be together.

Turning on my heels, I took a single step, determined

to take back my life, but I found myself frozen in my footsteps by a curious intruder.

"You're the talk of the office today," Lauren said, taking a confident step into my office.

I'd been so used to leaving the door open for Cara that I hadn't even noticed the wide gap I had left when I returned after the board meeting.

I hadn't noticed much of anything since Cara left.

"Haven't you done enough lately?" I said gruffly, walking toward my desk rather than the door, still bitter over her involvement in all of this.

"Me? You're blaming this on me? Figures. You're all alike."

I raised my eyebrow at the last comment, looking up at her with a mixture of confusion and intrigue.

"Who's you all? Men? Because, if you sabotaged my relationship with Cara just because I wouldn't sleep with you, then—"

"Oh, please. Don't flatter yourself," she said, moving forward once again.

I took that moment to assess her. While I hadn't taken a general interest in Cara's friend Lauren, I wasn't blind. I had seen her around the office from time to time, and there was that one night.

The night she'd basically thrown herself at me.

I remembered how confident she'd been. How she'd seemed so sure of my willingness to participate. She'd come at me like it was already a done deal, swaying her curvy hips in my direction like she was about to cash in on a fortune.

Except I wasn't for sale.

That confidence she'd had that night in the lobby was starting to waver now, the longer she stood here. The more I looked at her, the more I started to notice the slight differences in her normal appearance. She was a little rough around the edges, her perfect hair just slightly frazzled in places, like she'd stood too close to a faulty wire.

"What's going on with you, Lauren?" I asked, trying to take her at face value.

Cara had seen something in her, something good and real behind all those phony layers she wore.

Maybe I could, too. *Maybe.*

"No!" she yelled. "You don't get to be the good guy now. Not ever. You ruined my life!"

My eyes widened as I tried to comprehend what she'd just said.

I ruined her life?

Footsteps echoed outside as a frantic Cara entered my office. She was breathless, dripping wet from the rain, and she had inky-black tracks of mascara running down her face.

I'd never seen anyone more beautiful.

"You're here," I said, nearly stunned.

"I tried to—" She held up a finger, bending over to catch her breath. "Get here sooner, but I fell asleep after my coffee this morning because I'd been awake all night, and then there was a delay in the tunnels."

Mid sentence, she looked over, noticing Lauren for what must have been the first time. Her eyes widened, much like mine had mere seconds ago.

"Has she told you?" Cara asked, looking at me.

"That I ruined her life?" I asked. "Yes, but I have no idea how."

Opening her jacket, Cara pulled out a folder and held it up. "I know why—or why she thinks that, at least."

Lauren viewed our exchange, her arms folded tightly across her chest, and then she obviously couldn't handle being silent anymore.

"No!" she roared. "This is not supposed to happen. You're supposed to leave him, and he's supposed to be miserable. Just like he deserves." Tears leaked out the corners of her eyes.

Cara made a move toward her, but Lauren deflected, stepping away from her.

"I don't understand what's going on," I said, watching the two women in my office, feeling completely useless.

"I'm only making an educated guess here, based on what I know of you and what I've discovered here," Cara said, holding out the file. "But I think the reason Lauren holds so much animosity for the Cavenaugh family is because of this."

She pulled out an old newspaper article and handed it to me. It was one of the many my mother had saved, regarding Jude's awards and accolades.

"What does this—"

"Look at the pictures," Cara explained, pointing at the picture of a bored-looking Jude sitting on a stage, about to receive his millionth award.

Next to him though… was Lauren.

My eyes flew to hers.

"You went to school with Jude?" I asked, wondering how it was me then who had ruined her life.

"For a while, yes," she answered. "Until your father made me leave."

"Why would—"

And then it all clicked into place as Cara's finger landed on the last picture in the article. A young version of my father was gripping the arm of another woman, obviously in a heated argument.

"I recognized the woman from a picture Lauren had on her desk," Cara said.

I looked up at Lauren in surprise.

"You were the daughter," I said plainly.

"You knew?" Both women said in unison.

Both women looked back at me in shock.

I nodded, sinking into the chair behind my desk. My hand went to my hair as I took a deep breath.

"I'd always had my suspicions," I said. "I remember finding a receipt for two necklaces in my dad's coat, but my mother only received one. Then, there were the phone calls and little things like that.

"Nothing was confirmed until recently though. On the day of Jude's wedding, we all headed out to get haircuts and a shave—some sort of male-bonding ritual to keep the groom from skipping town or something."

Cara grinned, shaking her head.

"When we were there, the owner recognized Jude, saying he looked familiar. When he said he used to have a regular customer who looked just like him, I knew. Jude just shook it off, but I didn't. Dad hadn't just had an affair; he'd had another life. I went back later and asked the barber for more info, and he took me in the back where he had dozens of old albums. He loved his customers dearly. He went through several until he found what he was looking for. A single picture of my father, freshly cut, standing there with his family. His *other* family. It was you and your mother. I recognize her from this," I said, holding up the newspaper article.

"He was my dad for years," she whispered.

"How old were you? When he first..." I asked, swallowing a lump in my throat.

"I was maybe six when he showed up. Old enough to remember but too young to realize that he wasn't going to stick around. I guess that same logic could have been applied to my mother as well. He'd make appearances every other week or so, bringing my mom flowers and showering her with gifts… like necklaces," she confirmed.

I nodded sadly.

"I'd never had a father—my real dad bailed on us when I was a baby, so, to me, he was the best daddy a girl could have. I mean, how was I to know any differently?"

"How did he end it?" I asked, knowing it must have been brutal if the woman was standing in my office today.

"He just stopped showing up. A month went by and then two months. My mom was beside herself with worry. I was ten by then. He'd been ours for four years. I didn't know he had anyone else, like my mom did. I watched my mom fall into a deep depression, turning on herself for letting him walk away and then turning on me."

"Jesus," I breathed. "And the private school?"

"My mom's desperate attempt to get his attention. I was fourteen by then," she said. "It had been four years, and she still couldn't let it go. She put every dime of that tuition on her credit cards, just hoping she'd be able to see him. He'd made it next to impossible otherwise.

"She got her chance—the night of that awards cere-mony. I'd worked my ass off. All I wanted to do was make her happy. But she just wanted him. She missed the entire thing because she was pining after him—her *true love*, she told me. She cried the whole way home, saying he didn't want us. He loved his own children more."

"And ever since you've been trying to get her to notice," Cara said softly, finally able to take a hesitant step forward.

"She went to his funeral," Lauren said. "Can you believe that? After all of that? After everything I'd done to take care of us since, she still only wanted him."

She burst into tears as Cara's arms went around her. I

watched the two women hold each other, and I felt hopeless.

Lauren wiped away a few tears. "I never intended to get revenge. At least not from the beginning. At first, I just wanted to be close to you," she said to me. "In a way, you and Jude are the family I never had, even though we aren't actually related, but you know, I was curious. What were you like? That sort of thing. But the more I was around you, around everything that reminded me of him, the angrier I got. You had everything, and me? I still had nothing. Nothing but a mother who still didn't see me.

"It's why I hit on you that night. I was trying to find any way to hurt you—to destroy your perfect little world."

Cara's eyes met mine, full of shock from Lauren's confession. I'd never told her about that night. I'd never told anyone.

I'd been propositioned by half a dozen employees. Some wanted the thrill of being with the boss, others just wanted money and power.

Lauren wanted even.

Sadly, I understood.

I didn't know how to offer her any comfort.

God knew the man hadn't given me any in his lifetime.

"My father was an asshole," I said as the tears quieted, and the sniffling stopped. "He wanted everything under the sun without paying for it. He took without asking. Did without thinking. And the worst part is, he got away with most of it.

"For a long time, I thought I was exactly like him. I closed myself off from the world. Hell, I was even scared to have kids, for fear they'd end up like a warped version of him."

Cara's eyes met mine, and I felt the tenderness of her gaze.

"But someone recently reminded me that we remember history so that we can learn from it, grow from it, and not repeat the same mistakes. It's time you and I stopped living in our parents' shadows, which is exactly why I think you should leave."

Lauren's eyes widened. As well as Cara's.

My hands defensively came up in front of me. "Sorry, that was worded poorly."

I really am a walking HR disaster.

"You're not fired; that's not what I meant. And I'm not asking you to leave because of anything you said or did. What I'm trying to say is, maybe it's a good time for you to cast your net and explore the world."

Cara caught on to what I was trying to say, nodding. "You said it yourself; you're a smart woman, Lauren. You could have had your pick of almost anywhere. And with a considerable severance package and an exceptional letter of recommendation that Roman will provide you with, you'll have everything you need to find your dream job."

More tears leaked out from the corners of Lauren's eyes as Cara held her tightly.

I'd gone so long without the warmth of her body wrapped around mine that I was starting to become jealous of the crying woman.

"But I don't want to leave this place," she confessed. "I know it doesn't make any sense, but you're all I have left. My mom isn't… well, we don't talk much anymore. And, growing up, it was just her and me… and your dad for that short time."

"I'm not telling you to walk away, Lauren. Quite the opposite. We'll always be here. Just go spread those wings. But I do have one favor," I said. "The affair? It stays between you and me. Jude has no idea, and I intend on keeping it that way. Dad wasn't around as much in our childhood, and Jude has this fairy-tale image of our parents. I don't want to ever ruin that for him."

Lauren nodded. "I wouldn't want that either. He deserves that."

Feeling like I was going against every instinct in my body, I walked toward the woman who, in another life, had my father been a decent man, could have been family, and I opened my arms out to her. She came willingly, and I held her like a child.

Like a sister.

After the tears had dried up and the emotions leveled, Lauren took me up on my offer in a heartbeat. Although I wasn't sure I could really consider it my offer anymore since Cara now had me writing an email to HR, explaining why we had to give one of our favorite employees a severance package.

After several hugs and a bit of help down to a waiting taxi with a box full of stuff, Lauren took her last glance at Cavenaugh Investments.

It was a happy one.

"You did a good thing here today," Cara said as the taxi pulled away from the curb.

"I'm not always a bad guy," I replied with a shrug, turning toward her.

The rain had lessened, and the sun was about to set. Cara rubbed her hands together, feeling the temperature drop with the sun.

I moved, intent on warming her, but stopped.

Would she want me to touch her?

"Why did you come today?" I asked, taking a tentative step forward.

"I wanted you to know the truth. About Lauren," she answered, the breath with each word forming white wispy vapors in the air.

"That's all?" I took another step closer.

"I don't know," she said, angling her chin forward, as her eyes darted away from me. "You hurt me, Roman. You lied and cheated, but worst of all, you didn't fight for us. You let me walk away. I needed some time to work through all of it... to decide if you were going to leave holes in my life."

"Holes?" I questioned.

"You had to be there. I'm not saying that I'm not still mad at you for what you did, but I knew the man I was falling for the minute I knocked on your door, armed with bagels and—"

I cut off her words, making her gasp, as my hands snaked behind her back, pulling her toward me. My mouth slammed against hers. For a split second, I could feel her hesitate before she surrendered.

Right there, in the middle of the street, as the sun fell on that cold night in New York City I took back my life.

No more hiding behind closed doors.

No more blaming my failures on my father and trying to be something I wasn't.

I was Roman Cavenaugh.

And that was all that mattered.

<hr>

"I'm fucking nervous," I admitted as the sound of the crowd outside the conference room began to grow.

"You'll be fine." Cara smiled, adjusting my tie for the tenth time.

"Jude should be doing this. This was a bad idea." I

turned, pacing back and forth, practicing my speech in my head for the hundredth time that morning.

Why the hell did I eat eggs for breakfast?

"Who knew big, bad Roman Cavenaugh could get so nervous over a little staff meeting?" Cara laughed.

My head whipped around, and I eyed her.

"I know what you're doing," I said. "You're trying to distract me. It's not working."

"What if I told you that I had on cute little boy shorts with Christmas trees and red lace on the hem?"

My eyebrows lifted. "That's helping. But a little visual would work better."

She rolled her eyes and laughed.

"What? It's what any good assistant would do."

"Really?" she said. "Because I'm not your assistant anymore, remember?"

"I know." I smiled. "But I still like to pretend. Maybe we can lock my office door, and I can bend you over my desk again after this?"

She bit her lip, her eyes slightly closing, like she was trying to picture it.

But I knew she was.

"Only if you make it through this speech."

My hands flew up. "You were doing such a good job, too! I was completely distracted."

She smiled, stepping forward to once again fiddle with my tie. "I know, but if you think I'm sending you out there with that..." she said, glancing down at my very prominent hard-on.

"There are other things you could do to—"

Her finger went to my lips. "You have two minutes."

"Buzzkill."

Her arms wrapped around me as her mischievous smile took on something with a bit more sincerity. "This is your moment. You worked so hard for this, and no one else deserves to share this with your employees but you."

"Thank you," I said, knowing I would never have gotten here if it wasn't for her.

Bethany popped her head into the empty conference room. "It's time!" she said with enthusiasm.

She'd been back only a few days, but I'd given her the same open-door policy I'd had with Cara, and so far, it was running smoothly.

Maybe next time she got pregnant, I'd actually notice.

I'd even buy the cake myself.

Nodding, I took one last look at Cara, the sweet girl from Nebraska who had shown me I could be so much more than an asshole, and I smiled.

Time to try my luck as the good guy for once.

EPILOGUE

ONE YEAR LATER...

CARA

"**N**o! Not *Moman*. Ro-man. Let's say it again." Roman's manly voice echoed through to the kitchen where I was helping his mother prepare the ham for dinner.

I couldn't help but smile, hearing him talk to his niece. Just a year ago, he hadn't even wanted to hold her, and now, he was sitting underneath the Christmas tree, having a serious conversation with the toddler.

Well, it was serious to him.

He didn't want to be known as Moman for the rest of his life.

"Are you sure you don't want to move to the West Coast?" Lailah joked, tossing a salad beside me. "We could use another babysitter."

The two of us laughed as we finished the fixings for dinner.

Jude and Lailah had been in New York for a week or so, making their yearly trip once more. I'd spent so much time with Lailah during last Christmas before we'd left to fly to Nebraska that I had been counting down the days until they arrived again.

She and I had grown incredibly close over the last year, calling each other to talk at least once or twice a week, and as our relationship had blossomed, I could see a marked change in Roman and Jude. Although Lailah had said there had already been some serious mending between the two of them in the last year or so before I'd arrived, it had only blossomed even more.

Before, their relationship had seemed one-sided, mostly thanks to Jude constantly reaching out, but now, Roman was making a solid effort. I'd like to think I had some credit in that change, but honestly, I thought he'd come to the realization that family was more than a name all on his own.

For so long, he'd based all his family values on what he'd observed and learned from his father. Once he'd figured out how to let go of that past, Roman was free to move on with his future, including his brother.

"When do your parents arrive in town?" Mrs. Cavenaugh asked as we all began to sit around the table for dinner.

"Tomorrow," Roman and I said in unison.

"It's their first time in the city, so they're incredibly excited," I added, feeling a flutter of anticipation in my belly. "My best friend is coming as well."

"Roman said she was transferring. NYU, is it?" she asked.

I instantly nodded. "She loved the city so much that she decided to move here. The exceptional schools and good company didn't hurt either."

"Well, they will all have one of the best tour guides around," Roman said, leaning over to kiss my cheek.

"Well, that is true." I laughed.

"Did Cara tell you she got a raise?" Roman said proudly as everyone was passing food from one person to the next.

"It's not a raise really," I said, slightly embarrassed.

"It is so. Is your check larger each week?"

I nodded.

"Well, that sounds like a raise to me."

I shook my head, lifting my napkin to my lips. "As curator, it's part of my job to bring in money for the museum. I knew that when I took the job, but I guess I didn't realize it would be such a large part. Luckily, I happen to be good at it."

"Really good," Roman added. "She brought in so much this year that the board gave her a pay increase."

"That's marvelous!" Mrs. Cavenaugh exclaimed.

Everyone clapped, making my cheeks flame.

Happy, content conversation continued around the table while everyone ate.

Cavenaugh Investments was thriving, thanks to the hard work of the brothers. The West Coast division was growing rapidly, and because of the major improvements Roman had made to employee compensation, they were now one of the most sought-after companies to work for.

And Roman was loved.

Not only for the changes he'd made for the employees, but also for the man he was.

And all he'd had to do was simply be himself.

Following the Cavenaugh family tradition, after Christmas Eve dinner, everyone gathered around the Christmas tree and exchanged gifts.

"Why Christmas Eve?" Lailah asked. "I've always wondered why we don't wait until the morning."

Mrs. Cavenaugh smiled, looking at her grown boys. "I

had a very smart boy who came to me one year and argued that it was unfair that Santa got all the attention Christmas morning while the family gifts were sometimes forgotten about. When I tried to tell him that Christmas wasn't about presents, he fired back and said, 'I know, Mommy. It's about family, which is why I want to spend as much time with you as possible.'

"So, I agreed that we could open a few presents the night before. After a year or two, it was a bit more, and by the time his younger brother caught on, it was all of them."

Turning toward Roman, she smiled. "You always were innovative."

"I just like getting what I want." He laughed as his green eyes found mine.

Everyone watched as Meara opened her pile of gifts from the family, oohing and aahing over the building blocks and cute clothes. Lailah joked that they'd have to build a second house just to fit all of Meara's stuff.

As the adults began opening gifts, my heart did a flip-flop in my chest.

Sitting back, I spied Roman fingers touch each neatly wrapped gift but mine. He politely thanked his mother for the leather laptop bag and Lailah and Jude for the gift card to get detail work on Lola.

As his hand rested on my neatly wrapped gift, he paused.

"You haven't opened any, Cara," he said as his gaze found mine.

"I was just watching for a while. You know how I love to be last," I said, my fingers shaking.

"Open one."

"Okay," I agreed, grabbing the first one I found.

"Not that one." He smiled. "Or that one."

He continued this game until I found him in front of me, holding out a tiny velvet box.

"This one."

"Roman," I whispered, seeing him drop to one knee.

"Just breathe, Cara." He smiled.

I took the box with my shaky hands and opened it. Inside, I found my hopes and dreams, a future and a family.

"There was a day when all I wanted was to be remembered for how well I ran my father's company. It was my only ambition. But then a young woman from the Midwest showed up and changed my entire life."

I laughed softly as a single tear fell down my cheek.

"Someday, someone is going to look through a dozen boxes of photos from our life and find a picture from this night. They're going to see the joy on my face because I was about to ask the love of my life the most important question a man could ask. They're going to know our lives were filled with love because of the family that surrounded us, and we will be remembered, not because of the name we had or the money we made, but because of the epic love story we created. Starting now."

There wasn't a dry eye in the house now, including the big, beautiful man kneeling before me.

"Cara, will you do me the honor of becoming my wife? Will you marry me?"

"Yes!" I cried, jumping in his arms.

Everyone cheered as he stood, twirling me in his arms.

"But wait!" I yelled. "You didn't open my present!"

"Babe, no offense, but can you really top this?"

I gave him an impish grin. "Open it."

He set me down and grabbed the large flat box, and his

skeptical eyes returned to me. Everyone else in the room was just as curious.

I hadn't even let him put my ring on yet.

Still clutching the velvet box in my hand, I watched him rip the paper away, revealing a plain shirt box. His eyebrows rose in amusement as he lifted the lid.

Inside, he found a T-shirt.

"A shirt? You paused my perfectly planned engagement for a T-shirt?"

"Just read it. And, really, you took the words right out of my mouth. 'Cause perfectly planned couldn't be any truer."

He lifted the T-shirt out of the box, and I watched as he read the words, *World's Best Dad*. His eyes scrunched together before they darted back at me.

"You mean…"

"Yep!" I lifted my shirt where, for extra effect, I'd drawn a little arrow pointing to my tiny womb along with the word, *Baby*.

His eyes welled up with tears. "Can I put this ring on your finger now?"

"I think you'd better. Otherwise, my father might shoot you tomorrow." I smiled.

Placing the dazzling diamond ring around my finger, his hand curved around my belly where our tiny child grew.

This is where our future began.

A lifetime of memories, without hollow holes, or worthless regrets.

And it all started now.

If you loved Behind Closed Doors, be sure to check out Lailah and Jude's story in Within These Walls.

And if you've enjoyed the entire Walls series, you'll love The Choices I've Made—the first book in the By the Bay series!

ACKNOWLEDGMENTS

When I sat down to write my first book, I had this panicky moment when I wondered if this one book would be my one and only good idea. I remember asking my husband, "What if I publish this and never publish anything else?" He responded, in his infinite wisdom. "Then make it a good one."

I've carried that with me through every book since.

As always, I want to thank my husband first and foremost. This last year has been especially difficult, with health issue and whatnot, and that man has been my rock.

To the rest of my family—my goofy kiddos, my wonderful parents and siblings. Thank you for all of the support of the last year. I greatly appreciate it.

A big thank you to my editors, Jovana Shirley and Ami Waters—I have no words for you two. To Jill Sava, my personal assistant.

Lastly, a big shout out to my readers! I wouldn't be here if it weren't for you. Thank you for your trust, your commitment to my words and your love.

ABOUT THE AUTHOR

J.L. Berg is the *USA Today* bestselling author of the Ready Series. She is a California native but currently lives in Virginia. When she's not writing, you will likely find her spending time with her family or watching Doctor Who. J.L. Berg is represented by Jill Marsal of Marsal Lyon Literary Agency, LLC

www.ingramcontent.com/pod-product-compliance
Lightning Source LLC
Chambersburg PA
CBHW022019310726
48972CB00006B/1715